Thirty Nights
for
Thirty Islands

John K . Smyrniotis

"I went hunting wild
  After the wildest beauty in the world."

1ˢᵗ AUGUST   LONDON

Five thirty. Nearly the end of another day at the office. Time to refocus and to laugh all the pain away, melt in with his fellow sojourners wandering through the streets as far as the eye could see. Happy hour!

He watched the crowds of Leicester Square beneath his top floor window and felt that urge in the dream - to spread his arms out, drain all sensation from his body and then float down effortlessly, like an inflated butterfly caught in a bubble of silence. He knew, of course, that, if he tried, the result might be somewhat unsatisfactory. But the dream had been so beautiful, persistent, and so real: Freedom at last! It must be wonderful to fly.

He leaned further out to look at the slabs beneath. From this high they seemed perfectly smooth, sterilized and clean, a surgical bed for him to lie on, take a cool drink of anaesthetic, and let the love of the thousands gather round him. What would a man not give for a little love and some healing.

He looked at them all and laughed out loud. Busy worker ants scurrying here and there, some in all directions at once. Most of them young, looking for a share of excitement in the bustling lights, hoping to meet someone, find a lover for the ominously looming night. Oh yes, what it is to be young!

2

He had stood there at five thirty precisely, looking through that same window every day the last few months. It gave him time and mental space to gather the pieces and get the picture, a different jigsaw puzzle each evening, after hectic hours of dealings and legal wrangles, stocks plunging and rising faster than blinking computer screens. What would he have done with all that money anyway? Throw it up in the air and watch it scatter like confetti? That's what money-making was, no more, a crazy and unruly wedding party not giving a toss who picked up the pieces afterwards. The vicar would always disapprove, the revellers would not care. This IS a wedding, for heaven's sake, eh, vicar? Let's have some fun!

And yet today it felt so different. That haunting image had drifted past him clouding the city horizon making him hold his breath back. Strange how a straightforward love-affair could get mangled up and through and back on itself and all about. Beauty turned to unnecessary ugliness. Order and clarity into heaps of carnage. So much for happy weddings and wild confetti fun.

In a few days, twenty-nine precisely, it would be his dreaded birthday and already he could feel the thirty tapers going up in flames. Hell, he could feel something that gripped him by the throat, choked him, and left him hungrier.

"Hungrier!" he yelled out madly and then stood back from the brink, astonished by his own thunder.

No one looked up. He gazed at them, two hundred feet down. They crisscrossed each other's paths, myriads of tiny figures, some paired up, ephemerally perhaps, but happy. A group of frolicking girls caught his eye, obviously shouting monosyllabic exclamations at each other in happy revelry - in party mode, as they would say, sexual-frustration-mode, more like it, by the look of things. What would a girl not give for a little love and some healing.

3

The television sound made him turn sharply. A single engine seaplane had splashed down breaking blue tranquil waters with a short backwash, came to a quick halt, then shrank to a speck of solitude on hundreds of square miles of dark blue seas. Ah, the sea! How entrancing it looked, enticing, irresistible. Ah, to be in her arms forever, bobbing up and down with each new wave, moving from one shade of blue to another, deeper and more mysterious.

His office door opened and Maxine halted just inside. "Did you shout something?" She gazed at him nonplussed.

"No." He shook his head, instantly resuming that look of authority - executive, confident, manly.

"I thought you said 'angry' or something."

"No," he repeated with perfect poise, to stamp her question out.

"You look strange," Maxine persisted, her instincts refusing to be deceived. "Do you feel all right?"

This time he averted his gaze and went to sit at his desk, switching the television off. "Come in for a moment, Maxine."

She closed the door behind her and sat down, waiting and watching guardedly.

"Did you get a call from Williams?"

"I did," she nodded.

"Nothing yet?"

"There will not be. Barclays don't want to buy them and the Revenue will not change its position. Not the right time to rescue investment sharks, and all that; and no public money."

4

"I thought so." He spoke without emotion. "Bust."

She nodded. "I wonder who's going down next."

"Everyone, perhaps, and a lot of others besides."

She waited in a brief silence. "What are you going to do?"

Yet another pause. "There will be no business for me tomorrow," he sighed at last. "I plan to vanish for some time. You will be coming in to deal with everything."

"Where are you going?"

"Don't know yet. I will call you, now and again, but you must not. Send an email if absolutely necessary; I'll take the laptop and the mobile. Tell clients I had to go abroad unexpectedly; on business." He looked straight into her eyes with warm reassurance, and it was a gaze she recognised. "I am sorry I kept you late tonight," he said standing up. "Go now, before you miss another train. I'll post the mail; leave it on your desk."

He watched her hourglass figure from head to foot as she went out. Minutes later she showed round the door again, this time with her usual cheerfulness.

"See you soon then!" she smiled.

He bowed affirmatively. "Thank you, Maxine."

When he had heard the lift go, he leaned forward against the desk and screwed his eyes up in mock pain. Images of dark blue seas rushed back in, he hovering high above them.

"Let us go then, you and I,
When the evening is spread out against the sky
Like a patient etherised upon a table;
Let us go, through certain half-deserted streets,
....
To lead you to an overwhelming question..."

He put on his jacket and went out, locking the main office door. The lift came up with its immutable whine. He stepped in. Two empty crisp-bags lay in a corner on the worn-out plastic tiles. Then the descent stopped, the doors opened and a bunch of teen-age office cleaners gushed in before he had time to get out. Deeply involved in simultaneous conversation, their vacuums and buckets clashed and rebounded wildly against each other. The exuberance of youth. If only he could be capable of grabbing a metal bucket, stopping this ancient contraption somewhere between floors and ripping its innards up - before he tucked his shirt back, and stepped off again, smart, stiff-upper-lipped, respectable, upright. And why not? Why pretend? Let's go wilding!

Walking down Shaftesbury Avenue towards Eamon's office, he noticed that ants had faces. Faces of boredom or tiredness, sparkle or idiocy, some even of grace. Very exceptionally of beauty. He could not have picked such details from two hundred feet up.

One face demanded more substantial scrutiny. She was tall and slim, with elegant limbs, her thighs in sleek designer slacks, her arms in a white silk shirt climaxing to a bow-tie. Perfectly at ease in her bearing, she looked unassuming and, as she got nearer, more attractive. Now her eyes were on him, fascinating, widening like lips, relaxed, maddening.

"Are you James Cromwell?" And she staggered past him, apparently shaken, her feet fumbling for a path through the crowds.

The moment burst forth with a peculiar sexuality. Her daring, her unexpected fragility, her bow-tie. The very incongruity of it all evoked an eroticism of rare fantasy.

He stopped when she had gone a dozen steps past him and he turned round. Later, he would wonder forever what strange power had seized him, his forethought and sensibility blown sky-high. He, of all people, running down the road after a stranger! But he was within speaking distance now and - did he dare disturb the universe?

He touched her left arm and she turned with a gasp of surprise. "Call me tonight," he smiled, recklessly handing her a card. "I will be at home from nine." And he walked away just as the perfectly shaped hand reached out tentatively and took it. Hell, he must be out of his mind!

There was a small coffee shop at street level where he sat momentarily and scribbled something, right underneath Eamon's office, his old friend and corporate lawyer. He ran up the stairs, burst through the door and sat on the chair opposite. Eamon, hardly distracted, said "Hi, James," and finished off writing. He placed both hands behind his head and stretched his shoulders. "The wine bar?"

"Do you mind if we skip it tonight, Eamon? There is something I want you to do."

"What's the matter?"

"I want to add a codicil to my will. Has to be completed tonight."

"I'll do it tomorrow. Let's have a drink."

"I won't be here tomorrow."

"The bar is open already and I want to beat the crowds. We'll come back and do it afterwards."

"No, I've got to be home at nine."

"You are going home to die at nine?"

"Stop asking questions. Here you are." He conjured an envelope out of his pocket. "I've drafted the new details."

Eamon sobered up. "All right. What's all this nonsense about? At twenty-nine you shouldn't even have a will - never mind a codicil."

"Well, I'll be thirty by the end of the month; and I'm flying tomorrow. I want to do this before I go."

"You are flying tomorrow and you want to finalise your will. Are you joining some... foreign league... Al-Qaeda camp kind of thing, are you?"

"Shut up."

"The Syrian war-zone! ISIL! In that case, your plane will definitely crash, I know that."

"You are being facetious and exasperating. Act like a lawyer. Right now, I am your client. I'm perfectly serious, understand?"

"No, I bloody well do not understand."

He breathed out in the manner of an explanation. "I've been tidying up for the last few months. Everything has to be neat and clear-cut. I want to make this last arrangement before I fly. Don't screw me up. I've got to be home at nine."

"You said that, old man. And who's going to be the lucky bastard - if your plane does crash?"

"What's left of the business goes to Maxine."

"The girl at the office?"

"My personal assistant and trusted deputy."

"You've been sleeping with her?"

He winced in distaste. "She's happily married, with two children. And she's kept me sane these last few months."

But Eamon hardly heard him this time. He had started reading the handwritten draft on the back of the envelope and looked as if something had knocked him out. "What is this, James Cromwell? This is sick. There is no way I am going to do it."

"You are my lawyer and these are my instructions. Touch wood, I am of sound mind. I don't think you have a say."

"How much of the house was collateral with Williams's?"

"All of it, if their receiver ever gets to it. We are talking several billion exposure in Greek bonds. We are talking offshore subsidiaries. We are talking years of untangling. By the time they get to claiming my house, who knows who else will be bankrupt or how much of the universe still exists. She might live there the rest of her life, she might be booted out and get nothing. That's why I am keeping Maxine out of this. I do not want her put through the fight."

"You mean you're leaving your house to someone you don't like? Who is... she?"

"I'll fax you details as soon as I have them. Overnight, or first thing tomorrow morning."

Eamon stared at his old friend and client as if he had never seen him before.

But the same face looked back at him, unchanging and unmoving.

Eamon drew up a blank sheet and picked up his pen, pretending to lift a ton of weight. "Do I get my bloody fee before you die?" Then he screamed. "You are mad! I hope you know what you are doing."

At nine precisely the phone rang and forty minutes later a *Volkswagen Golf* pulled up in his drive. James Cromwell opened the door and disappeared to the bar in the sitting room, calling her to come. She looked as desirable as she had done in the street, both sophisticated and unreal. He gazed at her, a thousand questions still buzzing him. Then he put an arm round her waist and pulled her gently, handing her a drink she had not asked.

"It's a very common thing to say, but you do really look stunning. Who did you get your looks from?"

"My looks? Oh, my parents." Her voice was chic, perfectly controlled, unassuming.

"You mean you had parents?"

She lowered her eyes. "But of course! Who did you take me for?" and subtly pretended to be slighted. "Now tell me the story of *your* life."

"Later. We've got all evening. Gin all right? I didn't ask you. Matter of habit." He sensed her eyes scrutinising his every facial muscle, so he turned aside and paced off.

"Did she leave you?" her voice pursued him gently but inescapably, like a determined bailiff, from behind.

That checked him. She had read a thought not even in his conscious mind since almost three hours ago. "I said, later. We've got all evening... You are not supposed to ask that sort of thing."

"Let's drop the 'supposes' tonight. Who dumped whom?"

He turned to scowl at her. "We just... drifted apart."

"Right, I'll shut up. You looked as if you wanted to talk. Sorry I asked."

It was that voice, not the words, that got him. "I do, I do, I want to talk, talk, yell, shout! If only the right things would come out!" And tears filled up his tired eyes.

The curious thing was he still did not know why he had picked her up off the street, and suddenly the question confronted him at this most incongruous moment. She was very beautiful, of course, one in a thousand. Ah, "of course." BEAUTY! Beauty, beauty, beauty. What exactly was it about him and beauty? An entire life so far spent sacrificing what might have been, in search of a dream, to have and to hold, instead of a homely woman with dirty linen at her feet, a couple of babies, a dishcloth, an ironing board, nappies. Or even a conversation after work, "How was your day at the office," and "What about your career, dear."

"You are strange," she whispered eventually, and he felt amazed that she could talk, this mirage appearing out of a mist in his own house, this grand illusion. "You don't add up."

"It is very late, I was up early, difficult decisions at work, and I am flying in the morning."

This took her aback but she recovered quickly. She kissed him to soothe him. "The night is young."

"Yes, I was thinking of that. I've cooked a quick little speciality I picked up from my..." he paused, almost startled by what he had been about to say. "Well, she would have been my sister-in-law," he blurted. "...And I would love you to stay for a very long, very leisurely dinner; I have the best wine in the world for you to choose from, and you can tell me what you do, and how come you are single."

11

She kissed him again, on the lips. "Tell me all about where you are going."

"You mean tomorrow? I've got a flight to catch, that's all you are going to know."

"It seems very strange to bring me here," her tone changed, "but you won't tell me anything, about your business, the end of your love affair, anything at all. You just want to have sex, do you?"

"I have invited you to dinner and nothing more. Follow me, please, to the dining room," he announced. "You are not a smoker, I hope?"

"Tonight I will be anything you want me to."

He turned round to face her square on. "I want you to be my party guest, the final guest, the only guest, at this very special farewell dinner for two, my last supper; before I leave all of this to you, as I have done in my will, the house, the cars, everything you've seen or not seen, everything within an acre or two of where we are standing."

She gave a silent laugh. "It's the best chat-up line I ever heard. How many times have you stood here and spoken those words to young impressionable girls, and they believed you?"

"I do not have chat-up lines, I do not corrupt young girls, neither do I intend to try with you now. And as to where I'm going - a place far, far from all this, to find some..., maybe..."

This time she stayed serious. "You are very tired. Don't know what you are saying. We'll eat, and chat, and then cuddle up and... go to sleep. And you'll feel better in the morning. I am inviting myself to stay the night."

Ravishing in a certain light, some other time he would have consumed her in an inferno of lust. Mentally now, he pushed her onto a pile of cushions. Her top peeled off, her limbs unfolded and opened. The path from her breasts was brief, her warm incision intoxicating. He could see, smell, feel and even taste but it was pure fantasy. "We will eat, that's for sure, have a drink, and when you are ready, I will see you to your car and kiss you good night."

She looked chastised. "What made you say all that stuff? About dying, and your will and all that. It's weird. Are you not afraid that a total stranger might talk to someone? It could ruin you."

The situation as to ruin was not something he could go into with her. He almost looked guilty that he did not, but she did not pick that up. "I will not be here to be ruined, not any more," he said at last. "Don't even know where I will be. A mountain monastery maybe, a tiny room by the sea, perhaps on a desert island. I'm going looking."

"And what will you do with your life on a desert island?"

"I will think about it."

"What if you met somebody and wanted to marry her?"

That question had always troubled him when coming from a single woman. It felt like an important junction. If he did not know where he was, did he turn right or left? Was she proposing to him? Was it an opportunity, like those instant decisions he was so good at making at his desk, always closing the right deal? When it came to money, he had an instinct which rarely failed him, and that had made him rich. But it seemed that marriage was a harder decision to make than mega-deals. What if, indeed! She was waiting for an answer: "That's already happened," he said. "And it un-happened. It's in the past."

"So you broke up once, and made a vow of chastity," she stared at him. "It's the sort of thing old maids do."

13

"You are being rude, young lady. Don't push it or you won't get pudding."

"You love women, I can tell that."

"Maybe a little too much."

"For someone who likes women that much, your whole life seems bewildering."

"To you, maybe."

"You look for perfection in women, like in your cars." Her hard stare pinned him reprovingly. "What sort of woman are you looking for?"

A couple of seconds passed. "*Had* been looking for. Past. Past perfect."

"Past *perfect*. Ah! Told you. You'll never get that."

"Not any more, I won't."

She brought her voice down. "I'm just afraid you might do something stupid."

"I've figured it out, rationally. My mind is made up."

"Rationally? That's where you may be going wrong. What are you searching for, rationally?"

He smiled. "I do not know. That's the whole point. I think I know I don't want all this to continue. But then again, *'I only know one thing for sure, that I know nothing for sure.'* Someone called Socrates said that," he patronised her.

"The Greeks said a lot of things," she hit back. "They also said we should have fun and be merry."

"...For tomorrow we die?" he mocked her, and led towards the wine cellar.

Her porcelain hand suddenly shivered in his, as he pulled forward. "How did you know that?" she choked, trembling.

****

2nd AUGUST   ATHENS

Free! The morning tasted wonderful out of a paper cup ahead of a great flight. Already he soared above the departure lounge, surveying the world beneath, without prejudice, from higher ground. Travel does broaden the mind.

A sea of dull grey light streamed into Heathrow, upon the dull grey crowds. They queued, robot-fashion, for their daily caffeine, revelling in mediocrity, blase', happy.

Further   down   still,   more   of   them   scuttled inconsequentially from one corner to another, while the great clock ticked off each step against a pre-allocated count.

> *"And there were circles even beyond these - people who wore nothing but a loincloth, people who wore not even that, and spent their lives in knocking two sticks together before a scarlet doll - humanity grading and drifting beyond the educated vision, until no earthly invitation can embrace it."*

"Excuse me." The voice came from behind. "Lobb is my name, from Scotland Yard. This is my colleague." A second man nodded much more self-consciously. "Do you mind coming with us for a moment?"

"I have a flight to catch. What is it?"

"We have asked your flight to be delayed. Perhaps I can explain somewhere a bit more private." Lobb had this mannerism of pressing his nostril shut with a finger, while taking a quick sharp breath through the other.

He followed them into an office and eyed them both impatiently.

Lobb produced a printout of a photograph. "Did you know this person at all, please, Sir?"

"I took that picture last night. The lady was with me."

Lobb nodded. "Yes, she had your private card with her. If I may be indiscreet, Sir, what was your... knowledge of the lady?"

"I had the pleasure of her company for dinner. How did you get hold of that?"

"She sent a copy to your solicitor overnight. With a message for you - rather distressing I am afraid." He paused. "A suicide note, Sir."

"Suicide?"

Lobb scowled. "We found her body, Sir, in a Soho bedsit, early this morning. I wondered whether you could give us any assistance. We think she died of an overdose. The pathologist will be telling us shortly."

"I am shocked. How can I help exactly?"

"Did the lady try to supply you with a substance of any kind?"

"Of course not. I had trouble getting her to drink wine. She was always going to drive."

"And just what state of mind would you say she was in at the time?"

"Normal. Very normal."

"For someone who was about to inherit a fortune from a total stranger, what exactly do you call normal?"

"What on earth..." He checked himself. "Normal. Both feet on the ground. A medical-student normal. Good-looking normal."

"Good looking... But not perhaps very happy."

"Obviously not. But it's strange. She seemed to have everything. Certainly, could have."

"Might have had, if yourself died, Sir. Strange position to be in, don't you think?" He pushed his nostril again. "Nevertheless. Not a police matter."

"What does she say in her note?"

"I believe your solicitor is on his way to the airport with some news about your personal safety. But apparently, she did not wish to be in your will while you went about travelling." It did not come naturally to Lobb, such sentimentality. "Sadly, it seems, being left behind had been the story of her life." He paused. "We see this sort of thing all the time. It takes very little to push such people over the edge, when in this state of mind."

"I feel terribly responsible, but there was no indication at all. I would have done something."

"Well, you did. Don't you think it - how can I put it - a rather eccentric thing to do? A rich stranger leaving his fortune to her after a chance meeting?"

"I got the impression she was used... she had come from a wealthy family."

Lobb nodded. "I understand." He squeezed his nostril again. "At what stage did you realise she was a working girl, Mr Cromwell?"

"What did she do?"

18

Lobb coughed at his apparent naivety, while his deputy glanced aside. "She was a prostitute, Sir. In her spare time."

His mouth froze. "I refuse to believe it." He pondered the floor, with all three of them lost for words momentarily. "There was no money involved, if this is relevant." His mind raced over their first encounter way back in Shaftesbury Avenue. "We spoke because she recognised me."

Lobb nodded concurringly. "We did not mean to intrude any more than absolutely necessary. My deputy will take a formal statement from you, briefly. I have to leave. Thank you."

James Cromwell looked at her photograph again. Suddenly she haunted him, her face strangely veiled with a quality he had not noticed, an inexplicable sadness.

He dismissed the vision from his mind.

The moment he stepped out of the interview room, Eamon materialized before him. "Are you all right? I told you it was a mad thing to do."

"Hullo Eamon. Always the best legal advice."

"They think she had been trying to phone you. Did you have your mobile off?"

"I had been sleeping."

"You did not tell me she was a prostitute."

"Leave it, Eamon. I don't want to believe this."

"You might have to. There is something important."

"I know already. She faxed you a suicide note. I do not want to see it."

Eamon dropped his voice a little closer to that of a professional advisor. "Her father threatens to kill you. Lobb does not take it seriously but I thought you had to know."

A stewardess came to escort him. "We have had clearance from the police, Mr Cromwell. Please, come to the aircraft with me."

"Thank you Eamon. Don't contact me while travelling. Leave messages with Maxine."

"Won't you be on the same phone?"

"It will be switched off - permanently."

"I'd leave it on, if I were you."

"Good bye Eamon."

He waited until after takeoff and pulled the mobile out of his pocket. He viewed that photo he took last night of her. In colour, she came to life again, and all the tragedy of this morning's news seemed unreal. "Seemed" was the only word to use about her, for nothing turned out as it had appeared.

'Delete,' Click.

'Are you sure you want to delete ADDIE.JPG?'

'Y.' Click.

The woman who sat next to him on board the *Airbus* looked through the vacancies in the *Guardian* and then gently probed the possibility of conversation. A charming, delicate person in her early fifties.

"There is never anything in Cambridge," she pronounced without taking her eyes off the page.

"What are you looking for?" He had felt obliged to say something.

"Oh, it's for my son. He'll do anything, but anything is hard to find."

"Especially in a university town."

"I don't think he will ever leave Cambridge. He loves his libraries, the lectures, the student life. Hardly does anything but read and write."

"There is always hope for an inquiring mind."

She turned sharply. "I think the opposite. What else can such minds do except inquire? He wants to read everything, know everything, and I mean *everything*. He doesn't want the world to run away with itself out of his sight. Keeps his tabs on it. All things have to pass his judgement."

"In that case Cambridge is the best place for him. He will probably get a teaching job and die happy."

"You are so right. My late husband taught all his life. He never wanted to do anything else. He died last year and I still mourn him. I didn't think such precious men ever died. He was gentle, sensitive, a true lover of the human being. But I wish he had lived a bit more sometimes. Lived! Do you understand me? And now his son follows behind." She lost herself in reflection. "'Let yourself go,' I tell him, show a bit of emotion, be spontaneous, take a wrong step once in a while. I've never heard him comment on the taste of strawberries, good weather, the perfume of a good brandy." She shook her head in desolate desperation. "He's got his head sterilized."

"Ah! A genius. Like his father." He was struggling.

She had run out of breath but seemed comforted. "Do you think he'll ever manage to earn some money? He's got nothing but a pair of jeans and an old bicycle from his father.

And what he gets from me will be out of fashion and the wrong size."

They eyed each other mischievously and burst out laughing. Had she made this whole thing up for his benefit, conjuring husbands and sons out of the clouds? As a matter of fact, they *had* been eating strawberries at the time.

They cruised in clear sunlight, the soft underbelly toeing and heaving silently to the sky. And this older woman just wallowed delightedly in tales about Greece, where exactly she had been and how to check in advance whether hotels stocked gin and tonic. She became effervescent, enchanting, infusing the plane with extra buoyancy and making the air skip a little more lightly in the duty-free bubbles.

But the bubbles burst after they landed at Athens airport, she joining the man from the agency, he taking a suddenly forlorn taxi. "Omonia, please." It was supposed to be the heart of Athens.

The driver looked at him in his mirror, nodded vigorously and shouted "Yes," twice. "No problem! My name is Christos, and I am captain of this ship! This is a good ship! And I am the best captain. You like it?"

In truth it was a very aged taxi. But he was about to sail in it, so he might as well bless it. "It seems very nice," he said, instantly regretting his own lack of enthusiasm. But, hell, he was new to this land of exclamatory superlatives and this was the start of his Odyssey; give him time.

They swept out of the airport, gun-totting traffic policemen waving them by. The vessel soon reached speed-boat velocity along the clearway.

"New road," the driver said.

"That's good."

"Everything different in Athens now. Built roads, new airport, and stadiums for the Olympics; not new any more the stadiums. But they were new then. We used once, so they are still new I think - maybe." He turned his head an incredible hundred and eighty degrees to look at him directly, on the back seat. "Now we have to pay for all this, but how?"

This was supposed to be a sore point for James Cromwell and his junk bonds, but how was a poor Greek taxi driver to know? 'Well, I paid a chunk of it with everything I had,' seemed an inappropriate reply, so he said nothing.

"You have business here?" the driver came back at him.

Business, indeed. How unfamiliar this sounded. "No. I will not stay in Athens long. Passing by."

"Where to?"

This did require some genuine thought. "Perhaps one of the islands."

"Ah! The islands. Very nice."

"Why all these policemen?" James Cromwell changed the subject. He had felt uneasy after seeing guns at the airport.

"Mh!" He shrugged his broad Greek shoulders. "Not many. You should see much more in the Parliament. Fights, fights!"

"We are not passing through that, I hope."

"Why not!" Then he let on this was a joke. "You afraid? Students throw some stones at you, you throw them back. Easy." He laughed but a little late. "Get used to it. This is Athens now."

He was more concerned about his road safety as they sped onwards with no regard for the traffic. Almost any encounter with other drivers induced a long hoot, a vigorous shake of the head and some sort of comment, with both hands off the wheel and raised in invocation heavenwards. All was obligingly translated for him by the driver himself when they got stuck behind some tarmac-laying machinery.

"No *respossible* people." The head shook alarmingly. "No *respossible*."

He looked at the miniature photograph of the driver with his family, a proud wife and three olive-eyed children specially marshalled for the camera. And next to it a fading football team cut out from a newspaper and glued directly to the dashboard.

They had left the barren hills of the rural outskirts and were entering the suburbs. Large banners flapped in the *meltemi* wind, getting more numerous towards the heart of the city.

"What do the banners say?"

"Ah! Of course! They say WELCOME!," the driver lied loudly to reinforce the delusion. But there was genuine sincerity in his heartiness, which anywhere else would have been deemed artificial.

"That's a lot of banners to welcome even an Englishman. What are they saying about me?"

The driver shook his head in a deliberate display of sadness. "People suffering, my friend. They say 'We cannot take much more of this.' They say 'Let the rich pay.' They say to Germany, 'Don't rescue us any more,' it's too much pain."

"How many are like that? Most people?"

"Don't know. Many, too many. You don't see the rich in the streets. You see people like me. I work, I drive from morning and night, then take all money to pay electric bill. Same day. They put taxes on the bill. If you not pay, no more electric. And now no food for children, so I stand in line and get a... what you call - gift from foreign."

"Charity."

"Charity, that's right. French charity. Then take the charity home and back to the streets in taxi."

"That's hard."

"Too hard. Pain, pain. You wake pain, you sleep pain, your children pain. And then some thugs throw stones and give more pain. I cannot go Syntagma any more. Don't ask me. Omonia, you said, right?"

"That's right."

"Yes, thank you. I cannot go Syntagma any more. Stones in the windows, stones on roads. They steal museums to throw at the police. Thousands of years of history. This is worse than Afghanistan."

"People must be desperate."

"Desperate? I am desperate, but I not steal museums. We pay taxes, now also pay for the breakings. Who you think is going to pay for it all? Me and my children."

"...Just when it was shiny and new," James echoed in sympathy.

"Nothing stays new. Everything gets old in the end. This city is very old. Three thousand years. The Parthenon was new once. And our new Metro will be as old as yours one day. Did you see what they dig up to make it?"

"No; archaeological stuff?"

"Yes, archaeological. Greek word. Statues, jew- what do you call - gold and silver."

"Jewellery."

"Bravo. *Jewlery* and vases by the ton." He waved both arms to indicate both quantity and magnitude. "You take the Metro now and you are in ancient Athens. You travel through people's houses, shops, everything; they found so much stuff. When you come to a station you see a tomb, with the man still inside. They left him there and put glass. All that was new once. Now...," he waved his arms again, "thousands of years." He dropped his voice to a whisper for more profundity and pointed a firm finger downwards. "Three thousand years from now they will dig again for another Metro, and you can see MY bones in a train station." Shrug of shoulders. "Why!"

James Cromwell laughed. "You are very philosophical about life."

"Of course. I am Greek. All we do is *philosophia*. That's why we cannot pay the bills."

But they had reached Omonia somehow, despite philosophy, and jointly opted for a hotel of the driver's recommendation.   The driver insisted on carrying his suitcase in and upstairs to any unspecified level. And the traffic police protested savagely.

Inside the first-floor room, the decor looked strikingly obsolete, the sparse furniture tragically bankrupt. Freshly painted but probably the oldest hotel in Athens. It was as if antiquity had ended yesterday and there had been no time to change the sheets, let alone reflect on the difference between nostalgia and redundance. He walked round once, taking the details in - the motif wallpaper, the ornate basin, the Aphrodite lamp-stands.   Plato or Homer would have approved. He looked out of the window at the fountains in the middle of the enormous roundabout. All Greek roads met there.   Some pre-war buildings stood sandwiched between modern office blocks, the latter four times as high. In the evening, the banners and neon lights could turn this into some semblance of harmony.   For now it looked a shambles.

A telephone over a lace-cloth, on a small walnut table: He picked it up and dialled a number.

The voice at the other end was instantly recognizable: "Yes."

"Sonia, it's James; I'm here in Athens. How are you?"

"All right. This is a surprise."

He had expected some caution; now he adjusted his voice. "I want to see you, and maybe you can help me book one or two internal flights.   How about we go out this afternoon?"

"You are asking me to take you out?   Always a gentleman, you. Where do you want me to take you?"

"I don't know Athens at all.   Plaka?   Glyfada? Marina?"

"You think these are girls' names, don't you. I know your mind."

He did not like to hear such a crude reference to his former self. "It's all the same to me," he said softly, letting go. "I want to see the real Greece, small intimate places. I want to meet real people. The hidden, shady side."

She laughed. "Real people are not shady. Be careful what you say. OK, I'll take you to Glyfada - we'll promenade along the seafront. Tell me where I can pick you up."

"Omonia Square. By the two yellow kiosks. Will you still recognize me?"

"Six o'clock sharp."

This was early afternoon and the hottest part of the day in the hottest month in this country. Cacophony and pollution brought it much closer to Hades. He now decided that his taxi driver had been positively restrained with his horn, by Athens standards.

So Omonia was a mistake. The heart of Athens was not exactly Kensington even if quaint and romantic. Sonia would tell him where he should have gone. Sonia would tell him what he should have done. Sonia would restructure his whole life.

Two years had passed since they had celebrated the multi-million deal she had seduced him into. The first memory of her voice on the telephone was still vivid - it was a voice with power. She had cold-called him, a stranger then, out of the blue, to ask if he had wanted to make an investment. Simple, but turned out to be very complicated, including him nearly marrying her half-sister, Julia, and all three of their lives changing from fairly normal to totally outlandish.

Sonia, it turned out later, had always felt secure enough to take big risks. She had been the product of a normal and stable marriage. Even her father's well-known flings never had threatened divorce during her childhood. And Sonia had grown to be a real woman. Big woman. You got your money's worth with Sonia; well, metaphorically, if not literally - she was not as astute with her financial investments.

Her half-sister, Julia, on the other hand, had been the product of a casual affair, one of her father's regular. Unlike Sonia's mother - a no-nonsense business-woman in her own right, Julia's had been a lowly young school-teacher.

The one thing the two girls had in common was that both had grown up to be like their mothers. Sonia had left home at sixteen to make her own money, whereas Julia never had a proper home, as such, but liked to read and practice her cello, always wearing specs over her petite features.

When the two girls had met as adults for the first time, it was Sonia who had pursued a closer relationship. Solid and sure-footed as her home-life had been, the one thing it had lacked was any kind of parental warmth, either from her ever-busy and frequently absent father, or from her dragon of a mother, a real vampire in her world, buying stagnant businesses and stripping the assets. In the midst of all that, this newly found half-sister, Julia, had offered some family closeness.

When she had phoned him first, Sonia had said she did not want her parents to get involved, and needed him for his business acumen. A blatant lie; she had wanted him for his money. So James had told that voice on the telephone that he might want to hear more, and Sonia's investment had turned out to be diamonds from Liberia. Then came the *Fowler Report,* the criminal trials had started, a lot of *blood diamonds* were confiscated before they could leave Africa and *Certification* made the rest of them impossible to sell at any reasonable profit. And by that time James had fallen for soft, sensitive, bespectacled sister Julia, and they had got engaged.

He should have suspected trouble with those diamonds but he was dazzled by the glamour, the danger, and the rock-bottom price. So he had not used his business brain. The deal had appealed to his other side, his wild self, which always simmered beneath the surface. For James Cromwell had two personalities: Monday to Friday, he was the most respectable gentleman you could trust your money with. Then, on Saturday nights, he would dress right down and play with a rock band as a different outlet to his testosterone. He was on rhythm guitar with *Ithaca,* neglected rather than disbanded now, and even screamed a couple of choruses into the mike, which made some girls scream back with excitement.

This diamond deal had been the start of the slippery slope. And the world financial crisis, which came later, had not made things any better. One bad thing had led to another. Sonia's mother got killed flying her own helicopter in South Africa. Then the girls' father died leaving behind enough debt to bury him with, several times over. Julia's mother, previously kept in the cold, was left the sole triumphant, surviving parent in the equation, and a source of comfort to both girls, but she was still a poor school-teacher. So each half-sister was practically on her own.

Waiting for the clock to move now, this sordid hotel room in Athens took his mind back to their infamous celebration when good times had seemed unstoppable. They had worked to exhaustion the whole day in the conference room of *The Mayfair* hotel, and when the deal was done, they had moved into a bedroom suite and opened enough champagne to sail their imaginary yacht across the Sahara. Next morning they had woken, all three of them in the bed, Julia as always shy and unsure but Sonia not caring in the least, her assets, always conspicuous, now exposed to the four winds without a hint of modesty from their redoubtable owner. She, of course, had done this sort of thing before and James was accustomed to girls flaunting their physical attributes at him while waiting for autographs and offers of sexual adventure. But here the presence of sensitive, decent Julia had changed the tenor.

Later on, it had been Julia who made him hate his former self as a pretend rock-star, and he had started to look for something less carnal.

Just before six he stepped out to take a closer look at the Athens streets. He then spotted Sonia in a *Ford Fiesta,* circling the roundabout interminably, trying to tell one yellow kiosk from another, and he remembered her cursing her car's hot weather temperament. She had called it her Ford Siesta.

The first thing that struck him when he joined her was how unlike Julia she was in appearance. Not the first time he noticed that, but he might have hoped for similarities, subconsciously. In a way, Sonia was a painful reminder of what he no longer had: her eccentricities were bringing Julia's beloved simplicity back to mind. Wacky as ever, Sonia now lived in Athens because she had married a Greek airline pilot. She had gone on to learn the language and become obsessed with everything Greek, and that was that: might as well stay.

They did not kiss because it hardly crossed their minds.

"How is Kostas?"

"All right, I think." This was a very reticent Sonia.

"I take it he's away flying."

"Johannesburg." Her driving would have left stunt-men in tears. It looked certain to leave him with a heart condition and a few limbs in plaster.

"He gets around," he blurted nervously.

"You could say that again."

"Something wrong?"

"On the contrary. We are getting divorced."

"Divorced! I'm sorry. What happened?"

"I don't know. Something in our family doesn't agree with marriage." She looked at him. "*You* should know."

"Well, it wasn't entirely your sister's fault that we split up, and I know it isn't yours, whatever happened with Kostas."

She choked back a sarcastic moan. "Change the talk, please. I don't care what he does. He's entitled to live his life."

He gazed at her. "You are taking it all very coolly."

"Of course I take it coolly," she exploded. "What did you expect? Screams, red eyes and tears just because he's a fucking bastard?"

There she was, wonderful indomitable Sonia spelling it out as nobody else could.

"Does Julia know?" he ventured tentatively.

"I told you to drop the subject. Yes, she does know but I don't suppose she would have rung to tell you, would she?"

"No."

She smiled. "Sorry. You still love her, don't you?"

"No. I don't. Sad to say."

"It was a mistake from the start, you know. Julia's idea of a man is a father-figure cum Romeo. She doesn't know what she wants. You are not her type." She grimaced. "How has life been since?"

"Rather empty. One comes to discover the pointlessness of certain things. Thankfully you Greeks went bust, took down a few good banks, my own business reduced to a telephone and a desk-lamp... all of which took my mind off Julia."

"I am not Greek, but I suppose you should be grateful. How would you like to pay me back?"

"I'll thump you and tell you to shut up when appropriate to do so."

"Ah! A violent man. No wonder my sister split up."

"Is she happier now?"

"Between you and me she felt exactly the same."

He looked away indifferently. "I'm only sorry I lost some friends. People felt they had to take sides. Either that or I became a threat and a rival."

"The lone male is always a threat and a rival. But, James, women love them. Which is rather suicidal of them, I suppose, but there it is."

His eyes darkened as if a transient ghost had haunted the road. It crossed slowly like a stray dog, long ago driven from the pack, tongue desperate for water in the dazzle of the low sun simmering on the burning asphalt.

The next thing he registered was the ice-cream shop. Steel tables and benches in the open air, a parasol. Noise, scooters, the screech of trams, and chaos sprouting everywhere. Sonia sat down and pulled out a cigarette. Formidable but adorable, she faced him from across the table, larger than Julia, almost ample, but solid and real, like land to a shipwrecked mariner.

Tonight, she said, she would take him to the *bouzoukia* in Plaka, keep him entertained during the vacant hours before his head-hunting expedition to the islands. That was what she said. But deep under her mask of self-assurance and control, he could feel the hidden torrents of loneliness. What could James Cromwell do for this great woman, an island in her own right, himself on a passage across the seas, and did he dare presume it?

Tomorrow, probably. Must try to think of something.

****

3ʳᵈ AUGUST   ATHENS

He woke up, sat up and found himself in enemy territory. Upon closer examination it proved to be Sonia's bedroom. He swore and his headache swelled and pulsated. Bloody Greek gods: *"This woman which you gave me..."* Besides, Greek dancing makes your whole body ache.

One of his hands fumbled for the side-lamp switch, and by this time the light had come on by itself and a magnificent Sonia towered above him wearing nothing but nipples and pubic foliage.

This could not possibly be Omonia Square, and it seemed ages since they had sat drinking at the taverna in Plaka, right by the dance-floor.

"Get up, James, it's almost noon and we are going swimming. I don't want to get stuck behind some dim-wit all the way to the coast."

"Where am I, and why am I being tortured? I refuse to talk."

"Turn over and fall under that shower."

"You bloody Russians are all the same."

"You'll recognize me with my clothes on."

"And where exactly have I left mine?"

"They are right here and so is all your luggage and stuff. You didn't think I was going to let you sleep in that brothel with some fifty year old virgin?"

"Who the hell are you to deprive me of the privilege?"

"Till you sober up, I am your legal guardian."

"More like the Spanish Grand Inquisitor."

"You are in Greece, not in Spain. They are Orthodox here. And I am your host, remember?"

"Where did *you* sleep, exactly?"

"Don't flatter yourself. I slept in the other room and locked myself up, to be sure." She stared at him with a reproving glare. "Get up!"

They drove off to the sea, down Syngrou Avenue at top speed, with a torrent of traffic chasing them like angry waters. Now the coastal road, past the old disused airport, car-windows wound down to beat the heat off. The beach to the right was seething with bodies. This was the sea of *Saronicos* which, Sonia told him, had been de-contaminated. They swarmed in their thousands, devoutly worshipping their sun-god at the nearest available holy Ganges. Children and babies, old men and women in nothing but their underwear, people playing and shouting, celebrating - humanity shifting and grading and drifting.

> *"The sun was returning to his kingdom with power but without beauty - that was the sinister feature. If only there had been beauty!"*

Then past Glyfada again, with its veneer of sophistication carelessly scratched and bruised, prettiness missed by a mere fraction, cleanness and order failed by a whisker. Two piers with hundreds of private yachts on one side of the road, streets lined with fashion shops on the other - open air cafe's, bars and restaurants strewn everywhere, a huge modern church in the middle of the square. Most shops stayed closed, graffiti the main feature on shutters that would not open again until the next generation of Greek babies had paid the government debt off.

Beyond Glyfada, if you dared sail, you fell off the edge of the universe. They drove on to the sound of cassette music, saying little except to indicate dislike for one spot of beach after another. The road took them beyond the last outpost of the Greek capital and began to wind its path towards Sounion, eating its way out of solid rock, leaving a sharp cliff rising to the left and a sheer drop to the sea on the right.

Here the waters revealed the full splendour of their dark blue, stretching out to the horizon. They had an enthralling mystery which the rocks had failed to decipher and so had remained hot, arid, and bare.

"About last night," he said unexpectedly.

"Hmmm."

"I cannot remember anything."

"James, it was beautiful. You danced like a satyr."

"Are you speaking metaphorically? What happened?"

"How dare you suggest I would do such a thing. Get out of the car," she shouted without stopping.

"Calm down, it is important to me."

"It's just as important to me, and to every woman you sleep with, Mr Casanova."

"Sonia, you don't understand. I've put all of that behind me."

Her eyes popped as she looked at him. "You've turned gay?"

36

"No!" he laughed. "Oh, forget it."

"You think I'd get you drunk and then rape you?"

"That's not what I meant. You know what I meant."

She grimaced and pretended to be slighted.

They were running out of beaches as they got closer to Sounion, so new ones received more lenient study. Finally a place was spotted, a stretch of sand at the edge of a small bay shielded by a rockfall, down which they would have to descend.

The sand was too hot to touch and there was nothing to shadow them from the relentlessly scorching sky. But the place was unfrequented, and the sea cool, clear and tranquil. They spread bath towels and let their raw flesh receive the full ferocity of the heat, with occasional dips in the water. And so the hours rolled and their skin turned more and more sanguine and their tongues more and more dry.

"I used to do this with Kostas," she murmured almost to herself, "find a deserted beach and then spend the whole day lying under the sun, making love, talking, laughing." Her voice, so like Julia's, mixed with the sound of waves lapping the beach, as if the sea spoke. "It seems like a dream now. It wasn't real. It wasn't us doing it. I know it wasn't him, for sure."

"What do you mean, it wasn't him?"

"Not the man I thought I had married. Kostas was a man of the world, you know. He had done just about everything before we met and by the time I came along there was nothing left. He didn't want to go through it all from the beginning with me again. So I was simply ... neglected."

He sensed the pain edging to the surface at last. "You'll get over it, Sonia. We all do, eventually. You'll move on to something better."

"Not me. I'd never been one for marriage in the first place. Suspicion verified."

"I did not mean to another marriage. You'll move on to something new. I felt the same," he said, "but in a different way. I turned against anything conventional. Because people do, they go looking to fall in love, or simply to like someone, not necessarily their ideal partner, just for getting married. And then they say to themselves, I've seen enough, this will do, it's about time I settled with someone. And life becomes a business partnership, with all the fringe benefits, the sharing and the status... Life becomes easy."

"I think it's difficult one way or the other." She hung on his every word while pretending indifference.

"You don't want life to be hard, but it should not be mundane or repetitive, either. And that's what marriage does to most people: it makes them settle into a pattern. I could not see reason behind this daily routine of getting up, working to make money, going home to eat and to sleep, same thing year in - year out, until you stop caring. What is the point?"

"Yes, what is the point?"

"I thought of you living in Greece and what an experience it must be. It's an assault on the senses. I almost feel I have a new body here. Don't you think? Or have you got used to it?"

She laughed. "James! I don't believe all this. I've always thought of you as a practical man; you are English, for heavens' sake. Pragmatic, not philosophical. Rational, maybe, intelligent certainly, but not intellectual."

"Tell me what an Englishman should be saying then, because I've lost it already."

"Forget logic. That makes things simple. We just decide what to do. Or we follow a gut-instinct."

"You mean Greece is the wrong country for me? Or do you mean something here has changed me, from day one, already? Do tell, what do you see in me that's Greek?"

"They twist logic because they are good at it, so skilfully, they turn anything into sense, if they want to. A whole country go bankrupt? Yes! It can make sense. Bring all the banks down and the whole world with us. They make it sound so logical. And when you talk about life you sound just like them."

"Then Greece is what I need!"

She smiled. "You need a woman, not a country. And if I'm honest, no matter what I said, I'd love to have my own man, almost any man, as long as he is truly mine. You are talking poetry, but poetry is hard. Just give me something prosaic. You talk of beauty, perfection in a sense; I just need someone to live with. Sod reason, philosophy and ideas."

"Who said, 'The reflected life is the only one worth living?' Was he Greek?"

"Sod him as well. I'm fed up hearing it."

He chuckled. Years ago he would have supported Sonia's argument. Not any more. Not even worth considering. But he decided to shut up and let her be. The day was an unexpected relief for her. She would have been at work, or stayed in absently leafing through magazines, bored with her *Facebook* "friends," wondering what to do next, hour after hour.

She would ask him to go to another party tonight, without doubt. But no. He had come here to break that pattern: No trivial talk, cliche' pleasantries, worn-out jokes diluted in French wine. Those vain hopes of meeting someone interesting, exciting, divine... This second day of freedom was decreed to be spent entirely in shorts, with comfy trainers on his feet. He was left with just one evening to see more of this great city. The day after, he would get a ticket to somewhere and leave all suburbia for good.

Sunburn. Sonia screamed at the touch of water under the shower and cried for him to go and dry her back gently and cover it with *Nivea*. The apartment had escaped the pervading heat and the curtains remained drawn to make the mind forget that the sun still reigned supreme outside. In the silence of the afternoon, the waves echoing in his head were the only sound.

He watched her dress, fast and methodically as if dealing with some business matter. She had shrugged off his refusal to escort her, with classy superiority. Her black summer dress, very short, very low cut, sleeveless, paid little complement to his shorts and trainers as they sat having a cold drink before parting. "Let's go!"

She drove him to the commercial centre of the city, placed him under orders not to get lost and made him promise to be back in the flat by midnight.

Having established his position in the general area of Syntagma Square, he decided on a quick sight-seeing tour and also to buy some trousers. All his own clothes were useless in this sort of heat. For a short while he followed one of what they called 'The seven routes,' no more than suggested walkabouts.

Even to someone who could not read Greek, this was obviously a city in turmoil. Large banners hang over burnt-out buildings. A giant video screen - smashed, street gatherings everywhere in groups of ten or a dozen talking or arguing on the pavements. Weaving a path around them, municipal workers planted, watered and cleaned up debris, the modern ruins of a Greece with disintegrating finances, which hit the rocks and was hit by rocks thrown by its own people. The bills had come in and stones rained down as if the glorious antiquities of the past unravelled above their heads, and their wiser ancestors reproved them. Plus numerous one-man protests: People who camped on the pavement, put up some home-made slogans around them, and had occupied prime public real estate. Once or twice even the occupant was missing, but nobody touched their stuff, each little enclave a shrine to a dysfunctional Athens.

There was a queue outside the bank even at this late hour, all locked up but its cash machine working overtime. Next door, shutters down and multiple layers of graffiti on top of them. A different queue tailed out of a modest, unmarked building and stretched along the pavement. He poked his head through the door and smelled the cooking before he could see the pots, some colourful steaming stuff that looked like a pea soup being put in take-away food containers, one ladle at a time. Some mild protests were shouted at him, pointing to the end of the line. These did not look like homeless vagrants, their faces and clothes not a world away from the people at the taverna last night.

"Can I have some?" He signalled with hand to mouth to the first man coming out past him.

"*Ne*," but the plastic spoon was offered to him generously.

So '*Ne*' must have meant 'yes' in Greek. He sampled the stuff warily. This 'pea soup' was anything but a soup. Scrumptious and instantly satisfying. It was more solid than watery, the peas unmashed, with onions, olive oil, tomatoes, herbs and meagre bits of potatoes.

"Nice!" he nodded with a full mouth.

"*Arakas*" the Greek man said, whatever that meant.

"Thank you," and he walked on, suddenly hungry. It was striking how different and unexpected the behaviour of these folk seemed, their every small gesture a surprise.

And then there were scores of younger people prowling the streets, smoking furiously. Those with the advantage of a private scooter flaunted their cigarettes with greater abandon, flinging the glowing stubs away with practised gusto and spitting manfully after them.

At long last, a pair of white cotton trousers in a window, light enough for this heat. An inch too long. The shop assistant knew somebody who would perform the alteration, if only one ventured the two-minute walk, nearby. He wrote the address down, politely stressed the superior quality of the cloth and rang up a higher price than on the tag.

He picked up the carrier-bag, paid and strolled out.

The two minute estimate turned out wildly optimistic. He was being funnelled into an obscure part of the city, with cobbled lanes winding crookedly right and left, going up-hill then plunging steeply. He could not be far from the taverna of last night.

Plaka, the old quarters of Athens, had a peculiar fascination. One turn revealed a glittering jewellery shop, the next an eleventh century Byzantine basilica. Trying to find an address in such a labyrinth was mesmerizing. There were houses stacked like cards, up every alley, each propping the other. People sat in their front yards, unconcerned, accustomed to prying tourists. In places there was poverty, next door spotlessly kept pot-plant gardens.

The search continued up a steep, narrow passageway lined with pre-war houses, each individually improvised. And at the prescribed number, a large imperious woman opened the flaking door, took one look at the plastic bag and beckoned him in.

The house enshrined him like a tomb. Stifling browns subdued what little light there was; the air was musty. Rows and rows of faded photographs and a plethora of inconsequential ornaments competed for his attention, without form, order or pattern. The staircase groaned under his feet. He followed her large shape into a tiny room and there his eyes rested on the delicate figure of a girl bent over a bare bulb, a sewing machine and a mountain of cut fabrics.

She looked up, the most extraordinary face under her dark hair, her skin white like it had never seen the sun, the sweetest, tranquil expression. She smiled at him cheerfully. "Come in. My name is Katia. I speak English a little."

There was hardly room enough for him to accept the invitation. "I'm James. Sorry to trouble you."

"It's all right," she said while threading a needle. "There is always someone in the evening." She hurried to clear some working space. "I hope my mother didn't put you off."

He laughed. "Not at all. Why should she?"

"She's in a serious mood. Most people get used to it. Could you go next door and put the trousers on?"

He came back and found the mother talking earnestly, but she went out to make room for him.

"Where are you from?" Katia asked bending to the floor with her pin-cushion.

"London." He was more concerned where her pins probed.

"I'd like to visit London sometime."

"You speak the best English I've heard from anyone here."

"Could be better. I learned from a friend who went to the institute. She used to come here every evening and do her homework."

She stood up and faced him, her eyes six inches away from his, her lips scarlet. He looked at her in long silence, mesmerized. There was that feeling of something hidden beyond, far beyond her dainty figure and sympathetic look; the gleam of a strange power.

She read his mind and pulled back. "I think that's about right. Mustn't cover the shoes too much. If you can call them that."

"What *do* you call them?"

"You'll need a proper white shoe for this trouser. Should be smart." She raised her chin and fixed him with a mock reprimand. "I'll need them off again now."

Katia was silent on his return. She seemed conscious of him watching her. She pulled her naked feet out of the slippers to work the sewing machine, and somehow this got to him and drove him almost wild. It seemed an erotic thing to do, sexy, sensual. How could this woman live here in such a catacomb, caged and entrapped when in fact her wings spread far, her spirit large, her every movement pulsating life, freedom, defiance. Why did she not smash the shackles, revolt, break through the prison walls, and fly?

"How long have you been doing this?" he asked.

"Three years." She smiled again. "I wanted to study but we needed the money." Each phrase was accompanied by a small gesture and an instinctive clenching of the knees - a habit from working the sewing machine all her life.

"Why not both? Time goes quickly when you study."

She laughed. "My parents are getting old. You know what you call Victorian in England? No one's more Victorian than their generation of Greeks. Very strict, reserved, puritanical." She laughed again. "Mother thinks the worst thing that could happen to me would be to meet strangers. Me talking to you makes her writhe."

He looked through the door but the mother had disappeared. "Have you ever tried to shock her and bring a man home?"

She feigned extreme horror. "It is they who brought the man here for me. That's how I got engaged."

It took a long moment for that to sink in. He could not imagine her standing for that sort of thing. "So you worked for three years and then got engaged. Will you still study, with a husband to look after?"

"It all depends. With music it's easy. You can do a lot on your own. If he can put up with a piano - if there is room for a piano. If there *is* a piano." She carried on sewing as if none of this touched her, flying unaffected above it all.

"If you want it badly."

It pained her being patronized. "You look at things differently," she said calmly. "Always do what you like. I'm not sure I'd be much happier."

He watched her work, unperturbed, as if nothing mattered. Her choice had been for destiny and permanence, rather than experiment and transience. "Tell me more about him," he asked tentatively. "What's he like?"

"My father knew him before we met. He's much older than me. Younger than father." She glanced at him mischievously. "That doesn't bother me. He says he's got money but I've seen very little of it. I didn't really want him at first, but I can't stay here and work all my life."

"That's very cruel on you."

"What is?" She looked up, her eyes on fire.

"Having to marry someone you don't like."

"I didn't say I don't like him. I don't know him yet. When we live together, I'll get to like him."

"Don't you want to fall in love first?"

Her monumental mother came through the door pretending to look for something.

"It's all right, she doesn't understand," Katia reassured him. And again that smile.

"Have you been in love, Katia? Ever?"

She looked at him candidly. The mother had gone again, too proud to seem ignorant of her daughter's foreign talk. "I'll be told off when you go, but I don't mind." She said it without sadness. There was no hint of discontentment. Just as a matter of fact. She knew her own place in the universe, God's grand plan.

"You must tell me more about life here," he said casually. "It's very confusing being a foreigner."

"Are you alone?" Her train of thought startled him. And then he saw her lightning eyes read deeply into his mind with a split-second glance. "There are some things you need to know before you should visit Athens."

"What did you have in mind?"

"Oh, little things." She glanced up briefly. "How to see beyond the surface; how people think." Her casual delivery was devastating.

"What if we met somewhere tonight? Then you can tell me." The words had come out before he had meant them to.

There was silence. "Where?" She viewed him guardedly.

"Anywhere. Out."

She shook her head. "It's impossible. I have a Greek mother, as you know. And a Greek fiance!"

He stretched out a hand and touched hers. "Trust me."

She shrugged her shoulders vaguely. "All right."

He waited until dusk in the cafe' at the bottom of her street until she emerged, sort of dressed up, all flesh covered up except her face and hands, legs in dark stockings. But he was falling for her and this only made her look more exquisite - a face unique, his perfect iconic face.

"I normally go to church this time, will you come with me?"

He would have gone any place. "Let's."

"I told my mother you wanted to see a church. And there will be people there who know me. It sort of stops evil tongues talking."

"You describe her like a dragon."

"I would not use that word. Anyway, I put my foot down; she had no choice. I couldn't do this regularly, but it seems easier with you. You look like I can trust you."

"Ah! Beware Englishmen bearing gifts. There is a sting in the tail."

"Don't make me laugh; I might giggle in church and they would never forgive me. What is it about you that gives me a sense of daring?"

"I could say the same about you; you breathe freedom."

"No, no. I would never have come out like this in a million years. Just for you. I may be wrong and stupid, of course..."

"Of course!" He laughed. "This is very embarrassing for an Englishman. We don't give compliments like that in England."

"Forget I said it, then. You are bad and evil. And a hopeless sinner. Come to church and let God forgive you."

He let her take him by the hand and pull forward, almost running like a pair of children, as she must have done in this street many times growing up, her close little world limited perhaps but secure.

She pushed the door gingerly, stepped inside, and an echo enshrined them like in a cave. Then she let go of his hand, crossed herself, made a little curtsey, and walked on tip-toe.

"We'll sit here under the cupola, so we can hear the voices bouncing back," she whispered. "Listen... Do you like it?"

"Awe inspiring," he tried to whisper too, but the congregation, mostly old women in black, turned in unison with a look of reproval. No more than fifteen or twenty of them, either kneeling or sat with heads half bowed, a deeply devout world of richness and passion. And he felt a thief in a holy shrine among them. "What is the chanter saying?"

"The vespers."

"Oh, thanks."

"Told you not to laugh. Just listen and feel. Stop thinking."

This was his second reprimand, and so he looked upwards for redemption. It could be overwhelming here. There was that sense of seclusion to start with, a sense that the whole world did not exist once you set foot inside. Then the incense smell, constantly replenished, an excess of crosses big and small, the burning candles, and a pageant of images. This was the richest art gallery, more colours than any artist could conjure up in an earthly studio, with every sense catered for, not just vision. There were a thousand years of tradition plastered into every tiny space, on every square inch, colour, colour, colour, and gold and silver and precious stones a-whirlwind. Opulence those poor widows could not afford, Christ crucified over and over. And at the top of the dome, God, surrounded by all the myriads of saints heaven could hold, with more arriving by the minute through the stained glass windows.

He gazed at every fresco, lingered on each icon - this was assault on more senses than man could dream of. And when eventually he remembered who sat next to him, he turned and he saw the most overpowering vision. For she seemed an angel too, transformed from the slave girl in her room, and raised up to a divine apocalypse.

She left him to go and light her candle, dropped a few coins into a box, crossed herself again and walked back to him like a floating apparition. So God must be cruel, if this sacred creature could never be truly his, with or without her thousand years of history and tradition.

But he knew he was unworthy, despite his oath of abstinence and the disavowment of materialism. His vow, of course, had not been religious, just a crude reaction to a trauma. Rash at best, brainless and meaningless probably. There was no room for comparison. Stop thinking, Katia had said, and just feel, yet it seemed appropriate to question just where James Cromwell stood on all this, not the Greek church but the whole business of religion.

"Let's go now," Katia said. "Are you ready? Converted or are you bored?"

He followed her outside. A different universe re-emerged once out of that magic door, and it took awhile to regain his disoriented coordinates. "No I'm not converted as yet," he answered.

"There's another church I want you to see some other time; I want you to meet Papa-Viron, my favourite priest. He will convert anybody over a coffee and a cake."

"Not me, I don't think."

"James, don't be so bloody stubborn. That's an English phrase, isn't it?"

"Sort of a swear word."

She brought her hand to her mouth and blurted something in Greek. "Sorry."

"Not a bad word. Very common."

"You made me sin with bad words, you are a bad influence. How would you like the priest to forgive you and make a good man out of you?"

"I would never consider it, but... never say never, et cetera. And that is another phrase."

"Well, don't consider it with brain only."

"How does all this square with your school education? I mean, no room for Plato and philosophy in that place, no rational thinking. You have to accept the dogma, or little old ladies cast a spell on you and you get kicked out from the community. Where is your Greek reason?"

"Me personally?"

"Yes. Have you ever questioned what you believe in, or don't you believe it really?"

She crossed herself. "Holy Mary! How long have you got? I'll take you to the Acropolis one day. The Parthenon. Have you been?"

"Not yet. And the list of sights-to-see is growing."

"We'll stand on the Areopagus, a great big rock now, the supreme court then, and I will read you the speech of Saint Paul at the very place he gave it. The glory of Athens was so much ignorance to him. He called statues idols, and said that God does not live in temples, He lives in truth. *The God you worship in ignorance, this God I preach to you.'*

Everyone had told him this was a different world. Now, this particular young Greek epitomised the problem. "Katia, what is the truth? Was there no superstition in that church? Were those icons not idols, and does God need churches instead of Parthenons?"

"We need the churches, not God. There is a place and a time for everything. And right now I want to show you another side of Greece which you seem to have missed. We'll go for dinner to Piraeus."

"Are you taking me or am I taking you?"

"Well, if you have a better suggestion..." She fixed him with raised brows. "Mr James, please, let me hear it."

"I know a place where I'd love to take you, but it is far away, and difficult right now."

"Ah!" She screamed. "*'Let me rescue you from all this.'* I knew you would say it soon. Just wait till you get lost, with this *Baedeker* you hold. And see who needs rescuing."

He took her by the hand and she followed him to a taxi. She sat close to him, matter-of-factly, but the driver chuckled and grumbled knowingly. "Where?" he demanded aggressively.

"Piraeus," James shouted back, and double-checked his *Baedeker*.

The doors opened half an hour later and they emerged, jetlagged from the driving, but little caring.

He leaned back against an iron rail and pulled her closer. Underneath, a sheer drop, and at the bottom the sea glittering with froth, a gentle swash, the promise of later calmness. He studied her face but she looked beyond, dithering between retreat and abandon. And so he took her hand and led on, along the narrow footpath by the precipice, to the tip of the promontory.

Now the lamplight shone down through eucalyptuses, sweeping the pavement before them. In the near distance, cruise liners loomed out of the dark, floating somewhere between water and air, like chunks of a strange city suddenly cut off and cast adrift downstream, tall, silent, haunting.

They heard the sound of an accordion from the water below. Some fishing boats tottered in the dying backwash, tethered to the rocks at the cliff-foot. And there a handful of people sat, feet submerged, their skirts or trousers rolled knee-high. They took turns to fish beer cans out of the sea, drink and re-join the chorus.

Somebody shouted at them.

"Shall we come down for a beer?" Katia translated.

A rowing boat came to pick them up from the nearest accessible point. The water had never looked so dark, the passing ships never taller. They scurried from rock to rock like scampering crabs, while the singing continued uninterrupted. From this close, the sound took on a different dimension, each breath the struggle of a hidden sore, dressed as joy.

Then everyone stopped and laughed and the accordion man opened his eyes and smiled.

"Sing, sing!" a woman shook James by the arm. And a new ballad struck up, much faster, merrier, and all their feet marked the beat in the swirling water.

When the moon rose, Katia decided the two of them should stroll their way back, the lone accordion following them fainter and fainter in the distance. It was still echoing as they reached Tourkolimano, where the bustle of the fish tavernas took over. A table was put up in the far end and a waiter lit the candle and leaned over them for an order.

Then nothing but holding hands, saying little, as if they had been childhood sweethearts.

They crossed the neck of the peninsula in the early hours and took a boat to Salamis. Night-shift waiters sat around them, commuting home, hardly capable of a prying glance, exhausted. They watched them scatter tiredly into the dark on arrival and paid the fare for the trip back to a weary boatman. Now on the top deck, they sat alone under the stars, wide awake, watching the island fade fast into a mist and a zephyr.

They would have done the same crossing over again, but there were no more passengers and the ship moored against the quay, its lights off, helm deserted. They found a bench and sat by the promenade, not far from the fish taverna, hardly talking.

And then she said she got tired, so he led along this narrow back street to a decrepit hotel, not much wider than its open doors, abandoned by its proprietors long ago, and to a balcony upstairs. Behind the balcony, in this diminutive chamber, there was a bed to sit on and stare out over the slope of other red-tiled roof-tops. They did not speak any more, just held each other, then lay back on the bare mattress staring at the ceiling. The sea, far away, could still be heard whispering around those frothing rocks. And the sprung bed just creaked and rattled with every breath she took.

Lovable in the faint light, a month ago he would have consumed her in an inferno of love. Mentally now, he pushed her down to the floor onto a pile of cushions. Her top peeled off, her limbs unfolded and opened. The path from her breasts was brief, her warm incision intoxicating. He could see, smell, feel and even taste but it was pure fantasy. "I know now this will be my best loved memory. Ever." He kissed her. "Talk to me more."

"About what?"

"Anything. I like to hear you talk. I wish this night would last forever."

"You keep saying things that you shouldn't. 'Best loved memory,' 'This night to last forever.' What are you going to say to your wife on your wedding night, if you've said these things to others before?"

"Wedding night? I'm not getting married."

"What, never ever?"

"Just broke an engagement. Marriage hardly features in my head right now."

"My wedding is looming; I have to think about it."

"Big fat wedding, is it? Typical Greek?"

"Are you crazy? There isn't the money for the bus-fare to the church - for some people."

He had put his foot in it. "Sorry, it's just a film title..."

"I had always dreamt of a big long dress, but not these days. We can't afford the cloth for a ribbon." She laughed. "I'm making something myself from offcuts - like from your trousers." Her laugh was like striking a match in a gloomy cave - bright, unexpected and short-lived. "The top will be a slightly darker shade from the skirt part. I've made a belt kind-of-thing for over the joint, and I'll hold flowers over it. What else can I do? We have to have a few guests and relatives, and they need food - my mother and aunt are cooking - what else...?"

"And what of the groom, can he contribute?"

"Ah! That would be an insult to my father. I am worried about him as it is. His heart is no good, he cannot breathe much when he gets nasty letters, I can see it."

"Letters about what?"

"They've cut his money twice now, his pension - very small, but it's all he's got to give him some dignity and his pills. He lives on pills, some very expensive. An insult like that would finish him off completely."

"He can do it secretly, your fiance, I mean. He does not have to flash money to your father's face. Give some cash to you to buy... the necessary."

"No, no, no! Not for the wedding. That's down to father, he is strict. To tell you the truth, I do not know he has much money, my fiance. Maybe he had and he lost it. So many people lost money. Or lost their houses when salaries got cut, or they were fired. It's not the sort of thing you can ask. Maybe he never had anything and was just trying to impress me."

"Where are you going to live? With your parents?"

"We'll rent a flat, like most couples at the start. We haven't looked yet because you need a deposit. And then one day my parents' house will be ours, handed down as was before, five generations in a row. That's how it's done in Greece."

So she was probably richer than he was, if his London house was repossessed eventually. But she was not to know how close to him all this was, and the question did not seem to cross her thoughts. She probably took him for a vagrant tourist, like thousands criss-crossing Greece every year with only a rucksack as their worldly possession. It just did not seem to matter to her, money itself; she only got on and tackled each problem the lack of it had created, trying to get by.

For one crazy moment he thought of opening his wallet and giving her all his cash, but he was rescued by an even crazier thought: maybe that wedding of hers would never be, that somehow she might be his instead, and all this discussion would only prove ironic.

In the brief silence that followed, a great calm came over him, as if he suddenly knew everything a man ever needs about God and the universe. This was light years away from his world of deals and money making, from networking and social climbing, from balance sheets, bailouts, pursuing creditors. This was a different planet from chatting up girls in bars and dinners for two in restaurants, or pizza on the sofa in front of the television, and from so-called 'relationships.' His past life seemed more and more like a dark cave without a match to strike the gloom away. A whole world away, so very, very far away...

And so he cupped her cheeks with both hands and kissed her again and she just yielded and shivered between his arms, breathless, excited, apprehensive. Ah, to be in her arms forever, rolling up and down with each new wave, moving from a shade of blue to another, deeper and more mysterious. She curled up close to him like a child, and he explored every curve of her face with his finger-tips. Her eyes serene, her lips the sweetest thing, this was the moment for him to question just about everything he had ever contemplated.

"...To lead you to an overwhelming question."

For the moment all he could do was wait, becalmed, in some back street, in a downtown, faraway harbour.

****

4th AUGUST   SALADI

Her house looked different at first light, much smaller, lopsided, with hollow eye-sockets and a crooked balcony. He was taking her back to be purged, expiated and re-admitted into the tribe, back to the stability of eleventh century basilicas and Byzantine holy rites.

They crossed a desolate front yard, up the steps and into the house. He waited downstairs while she went from room to room, turning lights on, double-checking. There was nobody.

Then a hand touched him hesitantly. "Katia?" There was devastation on the woman's face.

He pointed up but Katia had heard and came down to meet her mother, in silence. The two women looked at each other then she whispered something and a brief conversation followed.

"My father is in hospital," Katia turned to him. "He fell in the street last night. His heart, they say."

"How is your mother?"

"She was there all night."

"I wish you would let me stay."

She shook her head. "It's best if you kept away."

He looked at this new, adult woman, suddenly grown in the hold of his own arms.

"Go," Katia said, putting a hand on her mother's shoulder, and the two women sobbed quietly, embracing each other, on level terms for the first time.

He turned round, speechless, closed the door behind him and strolled down the cobbled street, benumbed, humbled.

"How to keep - is there any any, is there none such nowhere known some, bow or brooch or braid or brace, lace, latch or catch or key to keep
Back beauty, keep it, beauty, beauty, beauty,.. from vanishing away?"

Sonia's flat was unoccupied. He packed his suitcase and walked in circles around the room drinking coffee.

Sunlight, and the first sounds of the city filtered through the French shutters. He would not wait for Sonia. Better leave now and call her later. He stuck a brief note inside the door and slipped out.

A shoeshine boy, twelve or thirteen, was busy already, touting for customers.

"Hey! Mister! Polish?"

He declined with an acknowledgement.

"Do you like the Greece?" There was a roguish smile on the boy's face.

He stopped and looked at him. "Parts of it. Do you understand? Some parts only."

The boy nodded gravely, hanging on to what he could of his wounded pride.

"Don't you want to go to school?"

"School?" He laughed. "No books. And is holiday. And also... faint; I faint. No bread, nothing." He made a gesture of hand to mouth. "Teacher said 'you faint, you go home.' So I work now, school maybe later."

He walked ten paces then turned back and gave him the first large note that came out of his wallet. But now his path was cut by agitated passers-by and by the sound of commotion. As crowds scattered, he saw the front row of an approaching procession, in marching step, a forest of banners and flags, swastika-like emblems. It felt unreal, and he just froze on the spot. Had they been blonde and young, he might have thought he was in Nazi Germany. But there were grey-haired men and old women among them, all in black, some in paramilitary uniform. And he was lost, for a moment, in time, in place, and in his head. They passed in front of him almost grazing him in the kerfuffle and disappeared as suddenly as they had come.

A flock of pigeons erupted into simultaneous take-off and he came to. The shoeshine boy had been watching him silent from behind, so he went back to him yet again, and bent down. "What were they shouting?"

"Jobs for Greeks only!" the boy smiled with a much brighter voice.

And James Cromwell nodded and strolled off.

At the station he took the coach for Ermioni, a small village on the Peloponese opposite the island of Hydra, his destination. They moved ponderously through the outskirts of Athens, along the Corinthian route, his fellow passengers looking out of windows with bored familiarity. Half-derelict, prefabricated factories lined up both sides of the road, each with its own display of industrial junk, their borders vaguely defined by wire-mesh, torn, flattened, trodden. Junk, junk, junk for mile after mile, an occasional figure here and there, and a torrent of lorries, buses and scooters gushing by.

Further on they skirted the shipyards. It seemed that all the world's ships had come here to die. They dotted the straights of Salamis in countless numbers, defeated, covered in rust, decomposing. Large cranes, abandoned, hang in gruesome postures over the quay. Monumental chunks of dismantled machinery littered the grounds, ruins from a modern Greece of much lesser glory. And at the gate, a forlorn group of protesters, mostly silent, hanging around with droopy banners.

The woman next to him said something in Greek.

He resented being disturbed. "Sorry, I don't understand."

"You're English!"

"What did you take me for?"

"I wasn't sure, but I thought I'd try Greek." A cosmopolitan woman in her middle forties.

"You are French, of course."

"No. I used to live in Paris but not any more. I travel."

"All the year round?"

"Most of it," she nodded. He looked again and it was all written there, the years of wanderings, strange places, and one-night lovers. "I've just spent a month in Greece and I'm going to Cuba next. Best country in the world."

"Really?"

"Beautiful place!"

"You speak Spanish as well as Greek?"

"Just a bit of each. Enough to get by."

"What did you say to me just then, in Greek?"

"Oh, the shipyards. That was the wreckage we saw just then."

"You thought the wreckage a landmark for sight-seeing?"

She checked back her irritation. "Well, yes. It is a shrine these days. Thousands are laid off work. Wonderful people, when you meet them, but broken. Their wives are begging in the streets. Their old folk are rummaging dustbins. They have no food. They have no medical care because, losing your job, you lose insurance also. And there is no chance of work for years to come, nothing."

"Worse than Cuba," he muttered.

She pretended trying not to sound dogmatic. "At least with Communism you have a guaranteed minimum. Nobody starves."

"Not even political prisoners in jail."

This got to her. "But they have prisoners in all countries."

"Do you think the Greeks should do an armed revolution?" He was insulting her now but subtly, and it gave him a smug superiority, for this was what the English knew how to do best, especially in an unwanted conversation.

"That would be terrible," she exclaimed, refusing to be snookered, "but they have done it before. After the Nazis left Greece, there was a civil war, and the left in Greece is as strong as ever."

"Secret Bolsheviks waiting in the barracks..."

She knew she was really being goaded now, but it was too late to turn back. "There is a revolution in the streets already. Against the government, against the Germans, against capitalism. They are burning swastikas in Athens.

And petrol bombs and all that. That's how revolutions start. A few burned buildings, then Molotovs and Kalashnikovs."

It was the sort of discussion that would have made him angry in the past, but she had her Gallic charm, and a curl of hair tumbled down each time she raised her little red flag, and the French accent topped all of that, and he smiled.

"The Corinth canal is coming up," she nudged him pointing out of the window. "Have you seen it?"

"No, I've seen it on television but this will be my first crossing."

She nodded. "There is a new bridge I am told. A first for me too."

The coach braked dramatically and joined a line. They would be crossing from mainland Greece to the Peloponese any second now. Suddenly he peered at the abysmal depths under them, and there was his first island - well, sort of.

"I am Nicole."

"James."

"Are you going to Saladi beach?" She accompanied each question with an animated expression of grown-up girliness.

"I don't know the place. Where is it?"

"I'll show you when we get closer. You can't actually see it, it's over a mountain. Very remote. My favourite spot in Greece."

"I'm going to Hydra," he said absently. "Have you been?"

"Oh, you should have taken the boat. They have hydrofoils for Hydra. It only takes an hour and a half from Piraeus."

"It doesn't matter. I wanted to see the mainland; tick it off. Although there wasn't much to admire."

"This part isn't pretty but it's interesting. Did you see Salamis - the straights - where history was decided, Western civilization rescued?"

So he had passed the straights of Salamis. Did that mean there was no going back? Salamis to Saladi beach... Half of his brain was on other things - mostly to do with last night. What did 'sala-' mean in Greek, he wondered. Very incoherent. Route words for 'salad' and 'salami', perhaps? This woman, Nicole, was leading him headlong into a muddle. Was there no escape?

"There," she pointed. "That's where Saladi is. Over that mountain."

"How on earth did you find out?"

"A Greek friend told me. Former boyfriend."

"It looks impossible to reach."

"There is a road of sorts. You climb all the way up to the summit and then you see it on the other side. Breathtaking. Literally."

"We'll take a taxi, shall we? From the coach terminal."

She laughed, presumably at his sudden conversion on the road to Saladi. "If you like."

"I hope you've got this right."

"Trust me. You'll love it."

And so the hour-long taxi ride began, through small villages, the driver stopping frequently to shout at somebody or something. It was exactly as she had described it, a rough ride up the mountain until Saladi bay spread into view. Pines covered the slopes to the very edge of the sea, and there a multistorey square monolith, dropped massively from the sky.

"What do you think?" She was ecstatic.

"I haven't seen much yet."

"Oh, come on. A step at a time. Do you like it this very minute - here and now?"

"Will they have any empty rooms, here and now?"

She feigned exasperation. "You can always spread a blanket on the floor. Stop fretting. Enjoy the moment."

There was a double bed on *her* floor. Room 409.

The path from hotel to beach wound through the forest, past the obligatory tennis courts, swimming pool and an open air disco with a few chairs scattered untidily. They roamed away from the crowds to a place where trees waded into the sea, and there she took her bikini off and dived in, jubilant. He watched her from safe ground as she swam and played and splashed about like a child. That's what he loved about women. She came out, her body glistening, hair washed back, breasts hanging over his head, ominously.

"Aren't you coming in? It's wonderful."

"Don't splash water on me. Sit over there and dry."

She sat on the sand facing him, legs parted provocatively. "What's the matter?"

He hardly knew what had got to him suddenly. There was something about her he resented. Her vivaciousness, her sexuality; he hated being there. "Nothing."

"Pathetic, you are."

"Maybe."

"And what were you doing last night, may I ask?"

The question lingered in the air for some time. He searched for something to say, as much to himself, but he could find no set of words to sum up last night.

A cloud drifted over her face momentarily, and then she smiled again and brushed it aside. "You were seducing some innocent Greek girl for the first time."

He glared at her. "Nothing of the kind."

"You could have ruined her marriage chances." She watched him shake his head dismissively. "I see. More serious than I'd imagined."

And now he cracked under her interrogation. "I should have taken her away."

"You can't be serious. This is a different world, James. She has lived here all her life. Her front yards, her balconies, her blue seas and skies."

"Please, don't."

"Once I came in the spring," she persisted. "Ten years ago. You've got to come in the spring to understand Greece. Easter-time. Every inch of earth was covered in poppies, and colours... wild flowers; you could smell every imaginable herb, every pine-tree, the barbecues and bakeries, in every town. Now think of taking a creature out of this earth and putting her through London winter nights."

"She wasn't exactly strewn in a field where I found her."

She took a deep breath. "The world is too big to regret anyone overnight. There's too much to do, too many lovers. I want to have them all before I die." She came closer and passed a wet finger through his hair, then rolled down the sand until the waves washed over her.

He knew now what he resented about this woman, her sheer enjoyment of all this and all the other Greek things, while his Katia had stayed behind, bent in her room over a sewing machine, like in a prison.

He dived in as if to drown himself and floated motionless, afraid to wake up, embraced by this blue sea, the greatest lover. Cocooned and weightless, he swam out farther from the coast, to deeper waters. This must be the closest to tasting death before the moment of dying. He heard distant shouts from the shore but they meant nothing - only the cries of sea-birds, the faraway diesel boats, and a sweet voice from last night.

Nicole then dragged him by the hair, ripping the dream up, pulling him angrily to his senses. "I thought you drowned, you bastard." She was crying.

"You should have let me."

"I care for you, swine."

"Isn't the world too big to care for somebody?"

"I'm doing it for your sake."

"For my sake? Why?"

"You look like a lost child." Her logic took sidesteps from time to time.

"Will you remember this day ten years from now?"

"Will you remember an old crazy woman who saved your life?"

She was not that old and he not a child. And the last thing he needed now was a matron to save his life.

In the late afternoon he decided to phone Athens but could not find his mobile. There was no place for it to have gone and nobody to have taken it, despite retracing in his head every step all the way since unpacking. He looked again, the suitcase, the wardrobe drawers, the beach-bag - nothing. There was a land-line at the hotel, but only one, since it would have had to come miles over mountains. They told him the place was lucky to have a phone in the first place and he should be satisfied.

This minor hitch loomed disproportionately in his mind. Somehow it got to his very core, and sapped him. Cut off from the mainland, these mountains and this sea became overbearing, claustrophobic. What if Katia should need him, he thought, then scolded himself as childish.

Having to queue for the phone, he decided to call London instead, and got through on first attempt. Maxine sounded happy, businesslike and well on top. Not much had happened, she said. Would he be back soon? Office doing well. Should she bank the pile of cheques? Burn them? An obscene caller had rung a couple of times. Much better compliment than he ever paid her. The photocopier needed servicing and the lift had been vandalized. No bad news as such, really. His desk missed him. She certainly did not. Where was he now? Where? Bloody hell! What country was that in, then? Anyway, love and kisses.

Nicole proceeded to announce a candle-lit dinner for two on her fourth floor balcony overlooking the bay. She spoke to the waiter in fluent Greek, ordered everything exactly as she wanted it, and bribed him just as eloquently.

"Did you get through to her?" she asked James.

"My secretary? Yes."

"No! Your lover."

"Stop prying."

"You can't hide the fever of a great passion, James."

"I'd rather we talked about something else."

"Eat this. I'll tell you what it is afterwards."

"Kalamari. We had it last night."

"Wish *I* could remember last night."

"More wine, madam?"

"Yes, please, Sir. Is everything to *your* satisfaction?"

"You are a very good hostess."

"I know what's missing. Music. Can you find something a little Greek? Do we get any music in this bloody monastery?"

He looked around. "Piped music."

"No piped music," she protested. "Please. It's like *dolmades* from a can."

"I'll ask the band to strike up, then."

"Ha, ha, very funny. You are insulting your hostess." She was becoming more ebullient by the glass, her eyes watering. "You are not filling me up," and a swift glance let him know she was not talking of wine.

He feigned naivety to discourage her. She was offering but he held back. Likeable in a certain light, a month ago he would have consumed her in an inferno of sex. Mentally now, he pushed her onto a pile of cushions. Her top peeled off, her limbs unfolded and opened... But he switched off. "You drink too fast," he replied.

"Not fast enough. Let me do it. *Retsina* all right?"

He held out an indifferent glass and breathed in loudly the smell of the sea and the pines.

"This is wonderful," she enthused. "To wander endlessly along, and then to pause, breathe, find somebody to cosset you, care and tend to your every desire."

"Shame it never happens."

Her face hardened. "It has happened, fool. What do you think we are doing? Answer me."

"If you were sober, maybe I would answer you. It is a difficult subject." He took a sip and shook his head to rebut her.

More exasperation. "Enough of this talk. Raise your glass. To us, to this magic night, to the good life!" The blood was rising to her cheeks. "And all our past lovers!"

Soon the sky darkened. Minute by minute, mainland Greece seemed more and more distant and unreal. Perhaps it had never been, he had imagined it. Did he like the here-and-now? Half-liked. It might do. Better in a port of some sort than roaming rudderless on the oceans. He looked around and wondered why not stay here overnight.

But the feeble promise of refuge failed to bear fruit and it withered and died. Along with the *retsina*, the conversation dried up.

"Talk to me," she murmured.

"Mmmmm..." He shrugged his shoulders.

She pulled out a cigarette. "Help me to forget, please, James. Cheer me up."

He looked startled. "Forget what?"

"Everything. Everyone. I want to forget them all but they keep coming back."

He looked again in the candlelight and saw a different woman, worn and weary, storm-beaten, alone at the end of a distant table, bankrupt.

Her drunken hand slithered towards him. "Hold me, James."

He took it reluctantly, and it was cold and pale under the tan, and shaking.

The waiter materialized. "Coffee madam?"

"Just leave the pot, please," James cut him.

"Will you be joining the dancing, Sir? We have a band tonight, in the restaurant."

"I think so, but later."

"You hear that James?" Nicole mumbled. "I had a band for you after all. Do I get gratitude? Do I get anything from you? Nothing." She tried to turn to the waiter, droopy-eyed. "*Champagnia!*" She was on the verge of collapsing.

"Certainly, madam." The waiter went discreetly, never to return.

James poured the coffee and they sipped slowly, in silence.

"Did you enjoy it?" She was sensing his disapproval and her head sagged.

"Yes. Let me clear the table."

"Sit down. It doesn't matter."

"I don't like talking over dirty dishes. It's ugly."

"You have a weird sense of ugliness. Things don't have to be detergent-clean to be nice. Let's go dancing." She was making a remarkable recovery.

"One more coffee and then." He lifted the last few plates.

She stood up and embraced him, with the dishes, sending the crockery crashing to the floor and treading over the pieces. "I want to dance. Now!"

"Sit down!" he shouted, and instantly regretted losing his temper. "In Greece it is customary for the gentleman to ask."

"I suppose you learned that last night also." She curtsied and took his arm, as if about to make a grand entry. Then she strode alongside him to the lift, fanning a royal hand magnificently.

Ground floor. The doors opened and he let go of her.

Most of the dance-floor had been taken over by a pack of young males, prowling rather than dancing, cigarettes precariously dangling from their mouths. One shaggy stray took centre-stage and posed motionless, eyes inwards, puffing macho style. And all around him dust and smoke rose to some vulgar god in sacrifice.

"It's great!" Nicole screamed plunging into the party, and it was the last he ever saw her.

At three in the morning a porter found him by the pool and offered a tray. "This must be yours, Sir."

There was his mobile phone, with the panel lit-up, a text message showing, but otherwise soaked in water and none of the functions responding. "EAMON SAYS THREAT IMMINENT. CONTACT HIM."

"Ah, this isn't mine," he said and handed it back. "Where did you find it?"

"Someone had thrown it in the pool. From a balcony."

He hurried to gather his luggage from Nicole's room. Moments later he asked for a lift from a departing supply lorry and hit the lone dusty road.

****

5th AUGUST   HYDRA

This was a sea so perfectly still, he could have walked to Hydra. It mirrored the local universe, with its fishing boats, the port, the modest landscape along the shore, the village. And in the distance, the mirage of a welcoming island upside down.

He studied the red-rimmed sky. Not a bad crossing - please, gods; grant safe passage. But the sun peered back ferociously, turning to burning white. He stood up as two local fishermen pushed off a caique, sending the first ripples to the horizon. Within minutes the peace had disintegrated. Donkeys and dogs were joined in a chorus by sojourners dragging rucksacks. They would be sharing his brief journey on the *Flying Dolphin*. He joined the stampede and told himself he must love them.

On closer examination the dream-sea turned into a lake of litter and engine oil and ghastliness, and the shores of Hydra hardly looked like an oasis. The hydrofoil skirted the most precipitous rockfalls in order to make port. This place was too barren to be real. Every inch was bare, every stone dry, each blade withered and yellowed and shrivelled up.

He disembarked and gazed at the cascading houses, all dazzling white. The town fanned out like a symmetrical embrace, an amphitheatre. Each house had climbed a little higher and jostled to glimpse the sea and the new arrivals. And at the front, a sprawl of inert, stolid cafes.

He took the nearest chair and surveyed the passers-by.

To ring or not to ring Eamon in London? There was no reason why he should. The thought of a murderer tracking him here – unlikely. Only the office had known his last stopover. The decision crystallized over a coffee. Here, if anywhere, was real safety. He sank a little deeper into his chair and watched a small boat approaching.

There was a woman passenger on board, her wide-brimmed hat flopping to one side. He judged her movements youthful and callow. She hopped off and carried her shopping basket into a grocery shop, then re-emerged, sun-glasses in place, heels clicking on the unfamiliar cobble-stones.

He checked an indulgent smile. It would be unfair to judge by mere mannerisms. She might be out of place here but showed a sense for colour and style. No sense of occasion or circumstance - pity - yet she did have a shot at beauty.

She burrowed into the newspaper shop and came out with her weekly *Annabel*. The basket weighed heavily. Two *Annabels* would have been an overload. But no. He rebuked his own preconceptions. Who gave a damn on an island which had not changed for two hundred years?

"Can I get you a coke?" he called out and pushed a chair towards her.

After the initial misgiving, a childlike openness and trust. "Thank you." The chair was taken up. "Have you just come?"

He pointed to his luggage. "Yes, on the hydrofoil. What is it like here?"

"It's different. A bit quiet sometimes." She said it with sadness. "How is London?"

"Very drab. I'm still drying out from all the rain." His rain had been metaphorical, but he thought it best not to complicate the conversation.

"Won't take you long in this sun."

It seemed impossible that she was English. She had absorbed too much of the Mediterranean browns. "Did you live in London yourself?"

"Once," she moved one finger slightly. "I come from Torquay." She pushed back the long black hair and two plastic earrings swung vigorously around. They were quite pretty, with little triangles in more colours than the rainbow, like Calder's sculptures, just smaller. "I've been here a long time."

"What do you do?"

"I teach aerobics in various places. I'm off to Athens tomorrow for classes. Then here again." She pulled a face to suggest boredom and shook her head. "It's difficult living here; without all the small things you take for granted: washing machine, telly; the luxuries. You've got to be rich to run a little old car."

"You must like it to have stayed."

"Mmm; I miss London, but there is no work in England. I miss my friends, the clubs and pubs..."

"Same here. I've been away three whole days. Too much."

She had an impulsive, exuberant laugh.

"Is there a good hotel on a beach somewhere?"

"'Little England'. It's a yachting club. Got to have your own boat." She eyed him studiously. "But I could help you cheat."

"It's good to have friends in high places. How big is *your* boat?"

"This dinghy here," she pointed jokingly sticking up her nose. "Why do you ask?"

"I want to take advantage of you."

She stifled a smile and pulled the brim of her hat.

They sat on opposite sides to balance the boat, much like two children on a seesaw, and the rightful owner instantly turned up.

"Kamini?" he said, obviously knowing her destination in advance.

Then he saluted and disappeared again. They heard his voice shouting in the distance, a popular alternative to the telephone here, quicker and more reliable. He came back, pushed off and switched the engine, all at once, and before they knew it, the vessel was bobbing over the backwater of a manoeuvring cruise-ship. They were thrust forward by two big waves, then slowed down to maximum speed.

"What's your name?" she shouted over the engine. "Or are you supposed to be in disguise?"

"No, no disguise. You can call me James." He leaned back and sliced the sea with his hand. "I *am* a fugitive though. Your name?"

"I'm Jenny." They must have made a wonderful spectacle from a distance, the boat, three travellers and the hat. She held on to it demurely, more as moral support than for shade. The breeze kept teasing it out of her hand.

"Hurricane, eh?" The skipper laughed. "Not worry, not worry." He slapped his chest in a display of fortitude. "Hold on tight."

If she were slighted, it stayed a secret under the brim and the sun-glasses. There had been hints of self-consciousness she had been trying to hide, which made her vulnerable and attractive.

The half-mile journey ended in the most isolated village cove. This humble spot was not remote, it was unearthly. The very smell of its dust breathed mustiness. Nothing that moved could be seen, and not a soul to greet them but a few dogs, sleeping. The boatman abandoned them to each other.

She took the sun-glasses off to wipe the sea-spray. A young face, nineteen or twenty, with eyes that found this a simple world to read. Pretty. She strode over the rocks as if on a cat-walk, poised and unconcerned, unworldly. Kamini stood back in sharp contrast, a cluster of houses, no more, old and magnificently authentic, a forgotten place of dusty browns, a dry river, a bridge.

And then she raised a wand and conjured an artificial oasis of lawns and sprinklers, a private harbour, bungalows, a pool. The 'Little England' hotel.

There was no trace of romance in this green and concrete desert. Every blade of grass imported, the pebble-beach polished up. A few tons of sand had been deposited between two rockfalls. This could have been any old vulgar commercial resort, the sort they sell you at Gatwick without you ever knowing where you are going, or have been to. Much better to have camped out in the bustle of the real harbour, with the mule-drivers and the fishermen laughing coarsely.

Jenny went straight to her rehearsals while a boy explained the intricacies of his room. He ran a bath and tried innumerable switches before turning the light on. Too much luxury. Everything a traveller needed to forget life and home. Fine sheets awaited the unwary, soft to both flesh and soul. The air-conditioning threatened to turn him into a pillar of frost.

He found her later, practising a double act on the disco stage, with a young brawny male.

"Do you like it?" she cried between breaths.

"It's great!"

"We wrote it in two hours," she exulted. "New routine."

The two of them carried on dancing, counting reminders to each other against the rhythm. She looked fragile and sad under the smile, a lonely girl but endearing. Hers was a different earthiness from Katia's, with both feet firmly planted down, the spirit unflown yet.

She ran up to him at the break. "How does it look?"

"It's beautiful. What happens right at the end?"

"He chases me like a savage and catches me on the final beat."

"I think you should kiss after the conquest. That's what the music suggests to me."

The thought found a gaping hole in her. "All right. You must meet Andonis." She called her partner over and he shuffled up to shake his hand, reluctantly.

Andonis was the last vestige of Greekness in this counterfeited haven, with curly black hair, non-designer stubble, and cannibalized shorts.

"Doesn't he look scruffy?" she played her two men against each other. "He's always like that."

"The man is an artist!"

Andonis laughed. "True enough. How did you know that?"

"Don't encourage him. Why do artists have to look so bad?"

"You mean you actually paint?" James asked.

"I paint better than I dance."

"He does everything." She flourished a grandiose hand.

"I'm a student - Fine Art," Andonis tried to show some modesty. "I can't afford make-up."

"That doesn't mean you can't shave," Jenny pounced, "and put a decent shirt on, once."

Her argument floated high above Andonis's tangled hair.

She turned sharply and left in a feigned huff.

"Nice girl but she talks nonsense," Andonis declared his own philosophy. "*'Malakies'*; you know what it means?"

"I don't speak Greek."

"Let me explain. You know *'malakas'*? It means wanker. It's not an insult. We call each other *'malakas'* in Greece. It's like saying 'Don't be silly'."

"All right, I understand."

"No. Let me finish. Because we use it all the time, one friend to another, it means we all act silly at times. It's human. It's an expression of fellowship."

"Would you call your father *'malakas'*?"

He burst into hearty laughter. "Good, good! Personally I wouldn't, but my father called me *'malakas'* when I was little. Therefore, I had to philosophise it."

"And did you like it?"

"You don't understand. Let me explain. What do people mean when they use it to describe themselves? Because they do! Men and women. It means," he pointed to his brain, "There I go, I've done something useless again. Get it? It's all futile. The ultimate of futility. Either screw or do nothing. No middle solution. That's what it means: don't be stupid. Don't do something that has no meaning. You see?"

"Surely you can't call a girl 'wanker' and mean it as a compliment?"

"We don't take it like this!" he pleaded. "When Jenny talks about prettiness - pretty shirts and a pretty shave, I say to her, 'Don't be *malakas*.' What difference does it make? I still have what it takes. And the same to her. I don't care about her nice hats and everything." He shook his head gravely under the burden of accumulated erudition. "Not part of the necessary." Jenny reappeared and he brought his voice down. "To tell you the truth, she won't do it. Got nothing against the girl but she's funny. No easy lay, I tell you that."

"Coming down the beach?" she asked matter-of-factly.

"I'm going to town." Andonis stood up and lit a cigarette. "Will you come?"

"No, I want to sit in the sun."

"You can't get any more tan. Come to Spiros's for lunch."

"I don't want to."

"I'll see you at the show tonight." And he ran off, the fag dangling from his mouth as a gesture of nonchalance.

They joined the sun worshippers, tribal bronzed bodies under a forest of parasols.

Jenny preened herself constantly, brushing every hair, checking toe-nails, packing her spare bikinis with great concentration and profundity. "I've never seen him so edgy. He doesn't like you being around," she said.

"He has a point. It's his male territory."

"We just work together. He's so possessive and stubborn; throws his cock about as if there's no other man."

"Don't you like his fire, his rawness and spontaneity?"

"Only when we are dancing. I'm more used to English blokes." So there she was, take her or leave her, an uncomplicated Torquay lass.

"What show was that he mentioned?"

"The beauty contest," she blurted and continued juggling sun-oils, hand creams, her hair-brush. "We do it in the disco once a month."

"It's difficult to imagine Andonis organizing a beauty contest."

"He doesn't. Nobody organizes anything here. Things happen by themselves."

In the evening the sun deferred judgement upon them. They parted, exhausted, to soak the tortured flesh in a bath and met again an hour later high on a cliff-face, at the restaurant. Candle-lit tables lay perched, finely balanced on the sheer precipice, with hidden floodlights searching the waters below. The sky was changing from red to dark.

Infected by the mood, Jenny became subdued. She gazed at the foaming rocks beneath, beaten and then washed in white lather. "I sit here every evening," she said, "and I wonder why I am doing this. One day after another. It's like a tunnel with no end to it."

"Perhaps being here is the reason itself."

"Look at the rocks down there. They've sat, being beaten, one wave after another, time after time, day and night. Thousands of years. Can you imagine?"

He had not expected such profundity. Perhaps this land had impelled her, as it had impelled its own inhabitants once. Unknowingly, she was paying him back for denying what intellect she did have. It seemed inappropriate to reply; he bowed to her instead.

At eight o'clock she phoned to find where Andonis was. They said he had not been there and sod her dance and her beauty contest. James proposed that nobody could get lost on this tiny island. But they could see crowds gathering at the discotheque and she was anxious.

They went backstage to wait for him and sent warning of the delay, but nobody cared much. Then someone called it time to start. They watched the Greek hostess take the dais, raising a tumult of wolf-whistles and admiring cries from the audience. It was several minutes before she spoke a word. In the rollicking, someone tripped over a table and a fight started - and finished.

Jenny went frantic. Her dressing-room became a clutter of shoes, stockings, costumes, clothes. James went out to check the scene from behind the bar. The hostess was in full flight in three languages. She saw him and asked whether Andonis was back, and the crowd whistled and echoed, "Andonis! Antonia!" and every possible variant.

Back inside, Jenny was boiling in her outfit, more furious than Cleopatra. "I'm not doing it," she cried. "He's done this too many times and now he's gone too far."

They heard catcalls and slow-clapping and knew that time was up. The contest started, the dance was put back. More clamouring for the local beauties. More messengers scoured the vast empire for Antony.

"Can you dance?" she asked him, shaking violently.

"We will afterwards."

"I mean on stage. Is there a dance you can do?"

He stared in disbelief. "I don't want to be lynched."

"You won't. Listen."

The lions outside roared at the arena, thirsty for blood. "I'm not listening."

"Yes, you are. Now; you have to be bad for this. We'll turn to comedy. I'll do a few steps first and then you'll try to copy. Like a fitness class. At first it will be easy. I'll get the audience to clap. Then more difficult. The harder you try the funnier."

"Many thanks."

"In the end I'll put on the fancy stuff. And when you think you've reached the point, just stand there and do nothing. Get stubborn, something like that. The more I try to get you going, the more stubborn. Until the finale when I get hold of you and lead into left-side, cross-over, step-twirly, bend, jump, freeze. You freeze on five. Can you remember that?"

"How can I forget!"

"They'll love it. I promise you that."

"Let me see if I can get Andonis one last time."

She seized his arm. "Are you ready?"

The noise had reached a crescendo. They stepped out of the dressing room and saw the amateur beauties take a bow. Orders came that she should dance on her own. She slammed the door and, before he knew it, a curtain opened and they advanced to cheers from bloodthirsty hooligans.

She leaned over the very edge, taunting them with her cleavage. And then her figure began to move like no human body ever, bending like a puppet but full of dazzling carnality. She stopped and coaxed him to follow. Nothing; he shook his head. Big roar of laughter from the crowd. She flaunted herself again, more passionately, the music possessing her like a female satyr, some men advancing to touch her before she pulled back.

She smiled at him encouragingly, then launched another attack. It was impossible to tell what was happening in the audience amidst the frenzy, the shouts, his own attempts to not dance.

And then he looked at a group of men sitting motionlessly in the chaos, and saw Andonis among them, staring back. "Come on, James," she shouted, and the crowd echoed her, "Come James!" She circled him touching sensually, then rocking from side to side. And by then it was impossible to hear the music, and something rent the audience apart.

In a flash, Andonis climbed the platform and pushed himself between them with a spectacular jump. But then the music just stopped and the crowds followed him, flooding the stage. They carried her shoulder-high before he could get to her. Someone produced an olive wreath, probably intended for the freshly crowned Miss Hydra, and put it over her head. Andonis had disappeared in the stampede. And she was savouring her triumph, blowing kisses, then begging them to let her go again.

Backstage, James found the other girls clubbed together trying to glimpse at the scene. Suddenly Jenny was thrust towards him. He seized her hand and run to the dressing-room.

They locked the door and paused, panting. He picked her up and span round once. "You gave it everything."

"Let me down. I'm so hot."

"Shall I undo the zip for you?"

"Do it slowly." She turned her back. "It's so sticky. I've never sweated so much."

He looked at her perfect features, the perfect hair, the master-crafted feet and hands.

"Let's go down the pool," she said undressing. "No one will see us."

"No, stay awhile, yet."

"I'm leaving tomorrow. Did I tell you? I have classes in the afternoon."

"Don't talk. Listen." The sound of crowds dispersing heaved like a river rush. "How do you feel when you dance like you just did?"

"I get a pain in this knee, here."

"Do you forget where you are, who you are, what you are doing?"

"I don't know what you mean. I'm not philosophical like that. It feels magical."

He half-heard a voice repeating that sentence with a different meaning. "Stop thinking and feel," that voice said. And it was here he knew that Katia would haunt him forever. No woman could take her place, ever. For she had meant something more. But Katia was unattainable and Jenny was right here, and so he brushed Jenny's cheek instead.

Jenny sensed the tenderness in him but thankfully not the meaning. She offered her lips but he held back. Lovable in a certain light, a month ago he would have consumed her in an inferno of lust. Mentally now, he pushed her onto the pile of rags behind her. Her top peeled off, her limbs unfolded and opened. The path from her breasts was brief, her warm incision intoxicating. He could see, smell, feel and even taste but it was pure fantasy.

What was his problem? Jenny was as pretty as living flesh could be. He just had to reach to find a haven from his shipwrecks, to find warmth and a little earthiness in her sacred crypt. Surely this was not a question of a stupid vow, not any more. What was it? A strange belief had surged in him that he should be faithful. He could not conceive who this fidelity should be to. It was as if he were trying, but could not fathom it. His brain would not work. He had stopped thinking. And could only feel instead.

When he recovered, Jenny re-materialised and knotted her shirt at the front. At last, he leaned forward and kissed her, and she just melted. It lasted ten seconds, if he was thinking, an hour was what he felt. Slowly, the chaos and the frenzy vanished and they both floated, free-falling into the void. And when the ten seconds finished, she just pushed him back, very gently, for it seemed that she also would not 'do it,' just as Andonis had told him. And he was grateful to her.

They floated in the pool until the sky began to brighten. In the early hours, they sat at a table sipping *Martini*. Suddenly he could see no prettiness, only the naked soul of a single girl, sunbathing, browsing, dancing, preening

- a lone female, fleeting from one ephemeral moment to the next, drifting.

"Do you believe in God, James?"

The question fell out of nowhere, as if the good angel had prompted her from under the guise of an approaching waiter.

Which god did she mean? This was a land of so many: some made of marble, some of gold, some who danced and drunk all night long, some crucified in rich spectacular catacombs.

"I do," he said absently, for the angel had arrived with an almighty tray, threatening to serve up next day's travails imminently.

****

6th AUGUST   HYDRA

With Jenny gone, Hydra's aridity became complete, the heat devastating. It was mid-afternoon and a blistering day. In the distance, white sails zigzagged to and fro, frantic to escape this monster. They sought refuge in the port, then pushed off again into the simmering zephyr. He watched them evaporate, up, like phantoms into thin air.

There was an oppressive mood in the marina today, a sense of foreboding and apprehension. After an hour's sleep, he had woken with a vision of Katia calling his name and it tormented him. Now, well past midday, Hydra ensnared him for another day.

"You dance well." An American voice.

"I did not dance. But thank you."

"Step on for a drink." An amiable man, in his sixties, with a Texas hat and a *Boss* T-shirt.

James went up the gangway, more interested in the yacht than out of courtesy.

Two women emerged out of a hatch. "This is my wife, Mary, and this is Elena, our Greek friend. She's our neighbour on that side."

"We fight it out for water and gas," Mary said, while Elena concurred politely with a reserved nod.

"I'm not taking sides yet," James said and Mary roared.

Elena scrutinised him curiously for a moment. "Thank you, Mary," she said at last and went over to her own boat.

"She's a wonderful woman. She travels alone, apparently."

"Tom, she doesn't travel. Have you ever seen that boat move? She spends the whole day locked in. I can't understand it."

"Why don't you ask if she's O.K., honey?"

"I have, Tom. She says she's O.K.."

"Ask her to come over for dinner tomorrow. Get her to talk. There might be something on her mind."

"She probably doesn't want to talk. You can't pry."

"Mary, try!"

They hardly noticed when James Cromwell left them to argue it out.

Shortly afterwards, he was surprised to find Elena at the beach-bar, writing. He had been hoping to see her again, but now held back from making an approach. There was something puzzling about her, a strange reticence, the Americans had been right. He judged her to be in her early forties but looking younger, an assertive woman, reserved, authoritative.

She put her documents in a briefcase, then gazed vaguely towards him but gave no sign of recognition. He sensed something wrong when her head tilted back and she was facing the sun, unflinching. Then she keeled over. Alarmed he stood up and by then two waiters had jumped to her aid, picked her up and carried her.

"Money problems," one of them muttered grimly. "She's got too much." He laughed. "Know who this is? Diamandithou."

They reached her yacht with James in toe and one went for the doctor. A small crowd gathered. "That's the second time," Tom and Mary told him. "It's the heat; the heat. She can't take the heat." They put ice to her head and Elena half-opened her eyes. "I'm sorry," she mumbled.

James nodded and withdrew before the doctor arrived. Outside, the white armada burned, its glory tarnished. A whole arsenal of masts tore restlessly at the sky. Their mariners had hid to escape the fire and he no longer imagined Odesseuses inside.

At about six, a message arrived at his room from Elena Diamandithou: "Mr Cromwell, many thanks for being considerate. I will be sitting on the deck this evening. Do come for a drink."

And so, just before dinner, he went to visit her, carrying a bottle of gin, his digital camera and his laptop.

She seemed cheerful but kept the same distance reflected in the brief letter. "You are not a journalist, are you?"

The truth was he had felt awkward about bringing his gadgets, but he had dreamed of his own yacht, before the crash, and this was a chance to gather some knowledge, and perhaps dream a little longer. He hoped that she would be flattered. "I am a businessman, like you," he dropped his voice, apologetic. "Your secrets are safe on my laptop."

"Don't use the headline 'OLD SCHOONER SINKS UNDER BAR' whatever you write about me."

"You look far too slender and sophisticated for that."

She feigned mistrust. "Say what you like. Must have been the heat. I can't take it very well."

"I'm not sure I can stand it much longer either."

"August can be dreadful but I think today has been a record." She spoke with warm elegance, unpretentiously.

"What is it like to be out in the open sea under such heat? Where do you escape?"

"You don't. You can stand in the breeze, or splash water over yourself. But, you see, its's so beautiful out there, in the middle of all that blue, that you don't think of your creature comforts." She raised a brow. "Besides there's the air-conditioning."

"And a good supply of refreshments," he second-guessed.

"Oh, thanks for the gift!" She poured straight gin over the ice. "Iced gin! It's the most important thing in life."

"After money and what else?"

"I haven't found what comes first. Your guess is as good as mine." She looked at him expecting some self-revelation, almost demanding it.

"Are you at all hungry?" he asked. "Will you come to the restaurant for dinner?"

She smiled, unexcitable, dignified. "We could stay here, and I can cook something Greek."

"No, I insist. We'll taste your *haute cuisine* another time. Can I leave all these gadgets here? Must apologise, I've almost married them."

"Absolutely. I would have insisted you came back afterwards."

They reached the edge of the rock and looked down. The sea had turned black in the twilight. It hardly seemed twenty-four hours since he had dined at the same spot with Jenny. Tonight it looked as deep as Elena's mystery, calling him to venture closer, lose himself in its darkness. He had the sense of entering something new, with Elena presiding over the rock, her black dress evocative of pagan rites.

"I want you to tell me what makes this place what it is," he echoed Jenny's profundity. "Why does it feel like another planet?"

She shrugged her shoulders. "I don't know. It's where the elements come to meet." She looked like a high priestess in charge of all earthly powers. "Land, sea and sky."

He gazed out to the east, watching the end of another sunset. "Does it make a change for you to be in Hydra alone, away from the city life?"

"I've always lived alone, except for my son. And he's at university now. I keep moving from one boat to another."

"You can't run your business from the boats."

"Boats *are* my business. One to Egypt, another cruises the Mediterranean, a third the Greek islands. That's my favourite. But I love them all. They are my life and my daily agony. If Greece or the Euro goes bust, I will die with them."

"It must have been hell the last few months." He was extrapolating from his own parallel experience in financial suffering.

"I have had to follow every number from zero to infinity and back again. I cannot miss one minute, I eat and drink television. Is Greece bankrupt or is it not? Default? No default? Will it, won't it? Opinions, politicians - one has had to learn seven languages in a year. So far, I have not laid anyone off. No worker of mine has lost his job. But they have to pay new taxes. Plus, business is down; if I give raises, we all go bust together and everyone is out of work."

"Is there a lot of hostility, you know, personal, against the so-called 'rich' in Greece?"

"There is the odd incident, no more than the usual. They cannot do any worse to you than the hedge funds and the politicians already have. What, break something that costs two thousand? We're losing millions here."

"No personal threats, I hope."

"Not as yet. It is all the stress that sends you to hospital. One minute Europe says yes, then no, talks, rescues and bailouts, a referendum is called and back to the start again - the suspense is killing us. Literally. Suicides are up, equally among the rich and the poor."

He was shaking his head. "I have been through it, believe it or not, even in London. You are still afloat, but I am not."

She chose to deflect his personal revelation. "You learn to swim, my boy. If I survive this - best swimming lesson for generations."

"Your son is too young to help much, I would imagine."

"Sakis has other interests at the moment. He likes fast cars and motor-bikes. I've tried to interest him in girls but he's very shy. I blame myself for that. He grew up without a father and I tried to be both his parents. I never had a husband, you see. Never had a father myself, for that matter." She checked herself, on the brink of opening up completely. "I think I was too tough on Sakis."

"The first man you could lay a claim to in your life."

She bowed agreement and lowered her gaze to the bottom of the cliff, stooped under some burden.

"Does he talk to you about it?"

"About what?" she gathered her thoughts again.

"About girls. I would have thought you have the means to throw a party or two. There must be plenty of girls for a rich young man at university."

"More difficult than you think."

"Why do Greek women make themselves invisible?" The question originated from his constant thinking of Katia, which then matched his short experience including Elena now.

"No - well, to a tourist maybe - they are not invisible to Sakis. He can't find - I'll sound snobbish - the current fashion is to be rough and aggressive, more loud and - difficult for me to put into words - uncivilised. They don't think anything of insulting you to your face for no reason. They don't have social skills, *agriokatsika,* like wild goats from the mountains, as we say in Greek. They lack basic politeness, let alone finesse." She made a grimace of hopelessness. "It's in to be rude, crude, irrational, adversarial; to smoke your head off, to be up-front and uncaring."

This put his back up. "You *are* snobbish. The ones I've met were anything but."

"Then get hold of one quickly; and introduce some to me. There aren't many; you just struck lucky."

He put his hand on top of hers. "Elena," he gently disparaged her. "You know what you sound like? Like you are looking to marry one of these girls yourself. She is for Sakis, remember? He belongs to this generation, not to yours."

"It's what he says. I disagree with him, then blame myself for his shyness."

"Sounds like you've made his mind up for him. If he keeps hearing such things - no wonder he is not interested."

"On the other hand, I keep telling him, a Greek girl will always stick to him and be faithful. And it's true. They do devote themselves to one man, totally. Again, we are talking generalities. There are many notable exceptions."

"Is there a class thing here," he said at last, "as there is in England?"

"Not as you would recognise it. There are only differences in money and education, but no class barriers, no cultural features to section you for life."

"Who is the typical Greek, then?"

"That's as difficult to say - as it is an Englishman: The working class labourer swearing his head off at football thinks he's very English, but so does the chair-lady of the Women's Institution. But they don't share much. I know England - am I right?"

"They are different aspects of Englishness."

"Exactly; same with Greeks. One will tell you, 'I'm very Greek, I like *bouzoukia* music, out every night, *glendi* - a kind of party with folk dancing and excessive food...' Another will say he's very Greek because he read philosophy and always talks philosophy. Yet someone else, 'I'd fight wars and die for my religion and my country.' He'll wave the flag and all the saints at you. When the Greeks won the football in Europe, archbishops were the first to be invited. Priests bless the arts, culture, government... Nothing ever happens without the clergy. Some think this is what it means to be Greek. Others still, mean to be fanatical at sports. You follow me? Each unto himself, and each of them thinks they are typical."

"Like invisible girls who insult you and live with goats on the mountains."

"You've got it! End of interview, OK?"

"Do my questions tire you?"

"There are moments you seem a bit psycho-analytic."

"Do I?"

"Mmm. You touch from a distance, by remote control. I'm like that too, sometimes."

"So I remind you of yourself... There's a surprise!"

She hesitated before going on. "You like everything in glass-jars and sterilized."

"It's true, I hate ugliness."

"I like beauty, but I think people who are happy expect very little of it. They find happiness in what you and I call dirty and rough; in blood and sweat, things earthy and elemental."

Everything in glass-jars, and sterilized... Perhaps he had sought the beauty of the operating theatre, smooth, spotlessly clean, demanding surgical gloves, forbidding. People like him and Elena had had their fingers amputated and they could only experience by dissecting and analysing.

"Maybe," he said finally. "I hope you're wrong. About us, I mean. I can get down and dirty."

"...and very deep. How did we get on to this?"

"We were talking about Sakis and Greek girls."

"Oh, yes. Sakis was born in Italy," she continued. "I loved Italy then and I still do. I thought it would be a marvellous place to be born in, so I went there to have him." She paused. "His father was Italian. A sculptor. I don't know what attracted me. We both were twenty-two and he danced well. I thought he was a god at the time."

"Does Sakis see him?"

"They've never met. We split up before Sakis was born and I haven't seen him since. Sakis is very against, although it must be agony for him. He says it makes him feel independent not to have a father. But often I'll see him in deep thought and I know what's going through his mind."

"I'd probably bring them together somehow."

"You think that's the right thing to do? Who knows what kind of man has become of Pedro? I'm afraid of him for some reason."

She looked so fragile just then, her tough exterior crumbling. He knew she held something back, something that threatened to open up and devour her into the blackness.

They went back to the yacht for coffee and brandy and she showed him photographs of Sakis and of her cruise-liners. Her whole life had been one long sea-crossing. Endless pictures of dining on one ship after another. She showed them with childlike pride, almost embarrassment, and he found it difficult to reconcile such power with this lone woman talking to him now. "Not half as exciting as sitting behind a desk, nine to five," he commented in self-irony.

She smiled. "It's not all glamour. Nobody photographs the dull moments."

"Another dull moment like this and I'm never going back to London." He stood up with pent up tension. "Shall we do something crazy?"

"Crazy? Why?"

"Let's go round the island. Just once. I've always wanted to circumnavigate something."

She laughed. "You won't see much. It's dark."

"Better still. It will be fun."

She took a hard look at him. "It's a very small island," she stressed. "We'll be back in half an hour."

"We'll do it slowly. Stretch it."

"All right," she agreed decisively and jumped to the cockpit. "A one hour special for one passenger. I should be charging you the earth for this." But the engines roared over his answer.

She steered out of the harbour as if leading the Achaean navy against Troy, then increased speed, quickly losing 'Little England' behind. Soon there was nothing but the galaxy and fragments of moon floating by.

"I've never wanted to circumnavigate anything," she said. "Do you know what my dream is? To buy an old Edwardian house in England and, when Sakis is old enough to look after the ships, to go and live there with an Edwardian gentleman who likes to go to the theatre and for walks in the country. Someone who can dance and talk intelligently about paintings."

"You don't know what you are saying. The species has been extinct for some time."

"I disagree with you. I bet there is one somewhere."

"Well, I've never seen one."

"They only move in a certain class of society," she taunted him.

"Ah, that explains it. I don't mix with certain classes."

"Oh, be quiet or I'll throw you over."

He gestured to throw her overboard instead, but the joke went unacknowledged.

More bright dots shone on Hydra. In the distance, the main town and its waterfall of houses tumbled to the sea like gleaming jewels. Two days ago he had sat there, in the centre, loving the bustle of the port, but it looked much prettier from afar, in the night.

She stopped the engines and let everything drift out of view. In the darkest part of Erebus, at the darkest moment, a group of different lights glowed.

"Watch," she said. "We are surrounded by gods and goddesses. Look at them one at a time. Over there, in the mountains of Arcadia, sleeps Artemis, the huntress goddess. But don't make eyes at her for she will set her hounds on you.
"In the sky, the brightest deity is the Moon, Selene. She bathed her body in the Ocean just before rising in her glorious robes through the night. Should you desire her beauty, Zeus will grow jealous and sentence you to eternal slumber.
"In the waters below us lurks Poseidon, the brother of Zeus. He formed the Greek islands by splitting mountains with his trident and rolling them to the water. He is the most terrible of all, for if you neglect your sacrifices, he'll pierce your ship with his trident and raise it and scatter it all to pieces."

"I wish you'd given me some warning."

She went over and sat next to him. "I had the forethought to pour what was left of your gin overboard. He loves gin. I've never been bothered by him."

"Oh, that's all right then." He put an arm round her but she withdrew gently.

"I've only displeased one. Hera, the goddess of marriage."

"Ha! What can she do to you? I shouldn't worry!"

She stood in front of him gravely. "A forty-two year old Italian has arrived in Athens, dressed in tatters and carrying only a sculptor's tool-bag. He is half-mad with alcoholism, and spends his nights brawling and picking up prostitutes. He has discovered he has a son and is determined to meet him. He also wants to find the mother, make up to her for lost time. He wants to look after me. Protect me. Sakis refuses to see him. And on his advice, I have set sail and vanished until he goes back to Italy. I am torn with pity and guilt and anguish. I don't know what to do." She wept silently, standing still like a rebuked child begging for mercy.

He held her tightly. "I have the perfect solution," he soothed her. "Pour some more brandy for the gods, and I will tell you all about it." She let him finger her hair for the first time. "Are you listening?"

She nodded.

"Maxine will send him a formal letter from London: 'My husband and I hear that you are trying to find me. Please, send your address to this office. We will be visiting Italy soon.' Signed, Mr and Mrs James and Elena Cromwell, London."

Her tears convulsed into laughter. "You idiot," she cried breathlessly, the brandy glazing her eyes. "Elena Cromwell, indeed! I am supposed to be Greek! The whole country will disown me. And all the wrath of the gods will be upon me."

"Bloody gods." He kissed her. "We'll come up with something else, I promise."

"I take it Maxine is some sort of secretary."

"Personal assistant. That's what we call them to make them feel important. I'll show you a picture of her." He opened his laptop and Maxine appeared on the screen after a few clicks, sitting behind her desk, almost smiling. "I do not normally try to impress a lady with pictures of another woman, but you asked for it..."

"She seems a worthy rival."

"Hardly that at all. But she is a wonderful girl and I trust her with the business. In fact, just before I left, I put a note in my will that, should anything happen to me, the business should go to her."

Diamandithou sobered immediately. "That's a very strange thing to do."

"It's not such a big thing. If anything's left of it, she would deserve it."

"You have no wife or children? ...but... There must be family, or..."

"No, no family." He knew that would sound strange and tried to stare her into silence.

But Elena was a business-dragon he could not escape from. "You must tell me more sometime. Next slide, please."

He mimicked the tone of an old bore: "And this is me at the office," click, "and here you see the house," click, "my old E-Type which needs restoring, and," click, "If I hold this up here..."

"I can't see anything. What is it?"

"It needs to be dark," he took some steps backwards to the stern, "Can you see? It's just a video clip, look, if I hold it up here, you can come closer, can you see? There's me, the Queen - here comes..."

"Looks like the premier of a film. All lined up..."

"Exactly that, I had put in some money - here she is now, but she did not speak to me; those other guys had put more in; and if you wait you'll see... Oh, no!" he screamed as he stumbled, nearly fell over, and the laptop splashed into the sea while both of them scrambled to the rail, but far too late to reach, and so watched in horror as the image looped to re-start and the Queen entered all over again, drowning this time, the swirling water waving her hand for her.

James Cromwell and Elena Diamandithou stared silent into the abyss, until the screen disappeared.

This was the second gadget Greece had stolen from him, again through submersion in water. "I don't think your gods will like what is on that computer."

She laughed, both of them still gazing overboard in case Atlantis lit up on battery power from his laptop. "They'll steal all your business plans," she mocked him.

"No, it's not that. They'll find an Englishman they can't stomach; reserved, undemonstrative, a bit aloof, who knows what he likes and is not partial to logic; who lived for the sake of Englishness and felt awkward with all things foreign; and spent all his life to better his place is society. Real Englishman. Not too clever, decent, a little preoccupied with class, understated... What am I talking about?"

"Your lost hard disk."

He nodded agreement vehemently. "Let your gods have it. I sacrifice it willingly."

She snuggled up to him. "Hold me closer. I fear them dreadfully." And then she slept in his arms, and all the furious gods were appeased, for one moment.

****

7th AUGUST   PIRAEUS

Sakis materialized on the deck out of thin air the next morning. A handsome man, looking like a classical Roman, with a nose good enough for an emperor. He was tall, athletic and had an aristocratic bearing, but the unexpected presence of Mr Cromwell threw him. He stood off James, more out of shyness than pride.

For Elena too the moment was uncomfortable. She could sense that something important must have brought Sakis to Hydra, but she had had no time to prepare for introducing a stranger to her son. They had made port, slept properly a couple of hours before dawn, then her son woke them.

Sakis did not seem to fully grasp the position, or otherwise he covered his puzzlement under an inscrutable face of discretion. He looked younger than twenty, a romantic beau, better placed in the forest of Arden than here. It was clear he had news for his mother but James appeared to affect the urgency and even the news itself. For a moment at least, Sakis looked as if he wondered whether he stood in his father's presence. The whole thing stayed up in the air as they sat at the beach-bar for a coffee of introductions.

In the scramble of the breakfast rush, 'Little England' was a very different place. It had lost its veil of luxury and seemed mundane. The green lawn out of place, the tea and toast predictable, the table manners too tedious - a life of trivia, ugliness of another kind.

"Now that Sakis is here we can tour Hydra again, in the daylight." Elena had a natural bend to being mother.

"I'll be leaving you shortly," James replied and watched her bosom sink. This had been her second torpedoing this morning.

"Wait," she exclaimed confused. "You can sail with us on *Helena* the day after."

"I've got to be in Athens this evening. I'll see you there when you get back."

The news demolished her. She stared at him unable to understand it. "James, you are being naive and irrational," she threw the glove to his face. "Sakis doesn't mind you staying."

Sakis maintained characteristic silence.

"I've got to meet somebody," James insisted.

She shook her head incredulously and lowered her gaze. "I can't hold you."

Last night there had been a possibility of making this a longer sojourn. She had looked lovable in the moon-light. And a month ago, perhaps... Mentally, while she slept, he had pushed her onto the deck; her top had peeled off, her limbs had opened, unfolded... But in the morning he had come up for air and found her gods had fled, leaving an emptiness behind. The vision had returned of Katia with him in a back-street in some downtown harbour; she had yielded, breathless and still, while a Greek band heralded the *Dionysia* nearby. And he re-ran the sequence in his mind.

Sakis wandered away, hardly having spoken. "I think he wants to talk to you alone," James told her.

"Sakis can talk to me privately, if he wants. You don't have to be a hundred miles out of hearing."

"Have you asked him why he came?"

"I dare not."

He suspected he was the subject himself and so averted his eyes. "I'll get in touch with you, I promise."

They stood up. Sakis waved from the yacht as they approached. "I'm off to Hydra harbour, anybody ready?"

It had been the longest sentence to escape his lips that morning. "You don't mince words, Sakis."

"I'll bring you back," he said guiltily.

"No, leave him there," Elena cut in. "Take all his luggage."

"Your mother is right. I can't afford the return fare." He went to clear his room and pay the 'Little England' reception.

An impatient Sakis piloted *Helena* from Kamini to Hydra town in seconds. It was a fair assumption he was relieved to get rid of James. Difficult to know what to do in this case, but James had the sense of being a traitor, abandoning Elena at a critical moment. She had exposed her secrets to him and he had given her nothing back - not even his own.

She held on to him until the very last moment. Finally they parted when a port official hurried him on the boat to Piraeus, unceremoniously. The vessel drifted and reversed outwards. Elena's stature diminished from high priestess to a diminutive figurine, waving. The engines accelerated and she vanished.

This time he knew exactly where the journey would take him. He was completing a circle. A dreadful longing took hold of him to find the place where he had walked with Katia along that cliff, the bench they had sat on and talked all night. A mere two hours away. Hydra quickly became a vague mass greying on the horizon.

They skirted the easternmost tip of the Peloponese. The land rolled, devoid of human traces, bare, dry. And coming away from the shore, a single solitary sail. They passed it at great speed and it shrunk into a dot with no destination in sight.

An hour later he stepped ashore into the chaos, dwarfed by cranes, juggernauts, railway carriages. Gigantic steel containers passed overhead, hooked to chains. The place was hostile. Stark, monolithic warehouses along the waterfront, a concrete wilderness behind. He stood and watched from a low rise. Innumerable ships unloaded simultaneously, travellers scampered the port for taxis. This was a place for functionality, not aesthetics - Katia's fish restaurant, cliff and bench a world away.

He took what seemed like the High Street of Piraeus. The road went up, then downhill past cafes and shops, to a different harbour. Packs of stray dogs roamed from one pavement to another. And at the bottom, a forest of cargo ships, their empty crab-shells idle in death, upside down.

The scene was soul-destroying. What looked like homeless people and foreign migrants had camped in abandoned doorways. Green spaces were full of mattresses in the open air, their night occupants now begging in nearby corners. There was no place for him to pause - a mocking sun, at its peak, had burned every spot of shade.

Suddenly a cafe' of sorts, consisting of yet another doorway with three tables in front of it, on the pavement. He sat at the roadside and looked at a map of Piraeus. The waiter got up, chased after a dog for a hundred yards, then asked to take his order. Would he like a *Pepsi*, some fast food, perhaps? Could not stomach food. No, thanks. Better leave, perhaps. The waiter kicked his tray.

He took the short trip to Athens and found *Olympic Airways* on the Syngrou Avenue previously traversed with Sonia. This was a ground-floor shop with office desks. Inside, the atmosphere was more explosive. Work had come to a halt while the queues waited, swelling by the minute. Weary Athenians, reduced to a flock, shoved and shouted inquiries over each other.

"Can you tell me what is happening?" he asked a girl behind the counter.

"The computer is down, Sir. Wait."

"Nothing works," someone intervened from behind. "When Greece works, *Olympic* will work." This one-man political liberation cry had been in English, so obviously for his benefit.

"Now," the girl addressed him, ignoring priorities. "Where?"

"Rhodes. Two tickets."

"First seat to Rhodes, twenty September."

"Try Santorini."

"Let me check. Santorini's a bit earlier. Fifteenth."

"August?"

She winced disgustedly. "September!" she shouted with an exasperated gesture.

"What about Skiathos?"

"I don't think there is anything." She played with the keyboard. "No."

"What we need is Onasis," the mysterious voice rose again from behind, invoking the founder of the airline like a patron saint. "He should be Prime Minister."

"He's dead isn't he?" James played the unflappable Englishman to hot-headed foreigners.

"Better him dead, than anyone alive. Better government. We have the Germans again now."

"They are efficient, at least," James was risking his life.

"Not here in Greece. We pay German money, we get Greek ticket line."

"If you don't like it, go by boat," the girl shouted the rehearsed reply. James made to push his way out. "Here, mister!" she stopped him. "Skiathos. Two seats. Tomorrow. Just cancelled. Do you want them?"

The political rally spilled over into the street. He tried to escape on a bus but the driver started off while he boarded, bumper butting into the crowd. The crowd snarled at the driver in retaliation and James jumped on regardless, squeezing through closing doors. "Can't you wait for people to get on?" he yelled, furious, the unflappable Englishman gone native after all.

"You sleep on your feet," came the ferocious reply. It had been established that all Greek drivers could give as good English as they got.

"You have to wait."

"Move into the back."

"I prefer to stand here."

"Nobody has beaten you up, that's why you talk like that."

"I usually do the beating."

"Hm!" he snorted and drove off furiously. Some innocent passengers were heaped on each other.

When daylight began to wane, a different mood spread over the capital. Along with the heat, the city's workers went, and casual crowds ventured out. James Cromwell retraced his steps along the only route he knew to Katia's part of Athens.

Plaka had a much deeper redolence that evening. Tin-pots had sprouted new geraniums, perfuming and punctuating each crooked lane. Swarms of tourists explored every corner of the bewitching chaos. It was like the film-set of a mid-thirties romantic movie.

What he had hoped was to meet Katia at the bottom of her street, if she did happen to pass that evening. There was no question of visiting. The plan had run through his head like a reel of film, all morning. Each time it ended differently, then started again from the beginning. Never before had he felt there was so much at stake. His every fibre tingled, every sensation was amplified and exaggerated.

When he did see her, she seemed to move on a cinema screen, real but untouchable, performing for him alone but oblivious to his existence. How could he walk up to an illusion and speak to it?

"Katia!"

She turned round sharply and stared at him.

He took a step towards her. There was a long silence.

"What are you doing here?"

"I've come to see you."

"But people know me."

"Come with me for just a few minutes."

She shook her head. "I can't. My fiance is home waiting."

"Come. Just ten minutes."

"No. I will see you in an hour. Go to the tailor-shop. Where you bought the trousers. Wait exactly opposite. And don't look so stiff. You make people suspicious."

"Opposite the clothes shop."

She nodded and run off, agitated.

It took him the hour to find that fateful shop. The streets were unrecognizable in the dark, spellbinding under neon lights. They had the bitter-sweet excitement of a great liner's moment of arrival. Each flicker turned this into Hong Kong, Seoul, Manhattan.

He watched her come and flagged the first taxi down. "Tell him to take us to that same street in Piraeus."

She gave instructions to the driver. "I told them I was going to the shop to pick work up. Look, the keys. I said I would be back in half an hour."

"We'll drive to the port and back."

"I can't believe you are here. Why did you come?"

He kissed her.

"This will have to be the last time. I'm almost married."

"When is the wedding?"

"Three weeks' time."

"Do you love him?"

"I do." She trembled. "We learn to love our husbands when we belong to them."

"You belong to no one but yourself," he said knowing he sounded stupid. He held her with both arms. "Katia, I am blind with jealousy. I don't know what I'm doing."

She raised her face and he devoured her savagely.

"We should never have met," she said. "I think I was happy in my unhappy mind. Now you threaten me. You could ruin everything. I don't know what to do because you've taken something important from me, I should not have given." She looked down again. "Do you think I can live happily, with you inside me all my life? Tell me. You know everything."

He could not speak.

"When I have children, when I look at them, will I feel like a liar? Will I manage to love them as much as I should, when I can't stop thinking of another man, not their father?"

"I think you will. You'll love them." They hugged hungrily together and fell to silence.

Then she pulled herself a little apart and dropped her voice. "You've got so much. What can a poor girl give to you?"

"I own a worthless pile of bricks and an old office. And that condemns me forever to stay away from you, I suppose."

She lowered her gaze even more, under some invisible burden almost too heavy to bear. "I haven't told anybody."

"What is there to tell? Two strangers met and liked each other. One of them fell in love. No crime has been committed."

The taxi driver hummed cheerfully to himself through the journey. He changed musical key with poetic licence each time the gear shifted. There was a hint of irony in his virtuosity, as in the wailing of an incompetent fiddler. He gave them a puzzled look at the end of the journey and shook his head mournfully. "Merry Christmas," he shouted scraping imaginary sweat from his brow.

"Happy new year," James retaliated.

Katia led the way to that footpath of four nights before, that bench on the promenade. Over to the left and behind them, some cheap hotels of dubious character, the back streets of a downtown harbour. And to the right, a string of fish restaurants circled the waterfront, each with a band of its own. The clamour of revelry was infectious. It filled the air seductively for those not yet partaking, calling them to leave their cares and join. This could be a real night under the stars, the potion that drowned all anguish and every evil.

"I've come to ask you," he said searching for words to conquer this pandemonium.

"Ask me what?"

"To come with me."

"Are you crazy?"

"I have two tickets. First flight tomorrow."

"On the plane?"

"Of course."

She shook her head. "Impossible."

"There's nothing to stop you, Katia. We could choose one of these boats, right now, to any place on earth. You name it, we'll go."

She looked at him, unbelieving. "You mean it, don't you?"

And he just looked straight back, eyes burning.

"James, what are you saying? I can't do this. We'll have to start getting back. This is crazy."

"Just a small jump from the quay to that ship there. Any ship;" he read their names at random to force the argument. "We'll take the *Patmos*, the *Kerkyra*, the *Cefallonia*. Step onto the *Ithaca* and a complete new world, freedom! It will never be easier."

She trembled visibly in his arms, breathless with incredulity. "Please, stop it."

He sensed that the battle was not resolved inside her. "Do you love me?"

She shook violently. "Please, James. You are torturing me. My father made me promise before he died."

The news of his death checked him and she took the chance to snatch herself away. "We have to go."

He held her again. "Do you love me?"

She struggled. "Please, James. I don't think we should see each other again. If you love me you'll let me go."

He let her hands fall from his, and they stood facing each other. Then she leaned forward and kissed him passionately and tears sprung up like a torrent.

****

8ᵗʰ AUGUST SKIATHOS

"Wish that the road is long,
That the summer mornings are many
When, with such pleasure and joy,
You enter new-found harbours...
But do not ever, ever rush the journey..."

"Good morning." The piped music had stopped and the celestial voice of a siren set out to bewitch him. "On behalf of *Olympic Airways,* the captain and crew welcome you on board flight seven eight four to Skiathos." He could see the heralding angel speaking into a microphone at the front of the cabin. "Our flying time will be twenty minutes, and flying conditions are excellent. We wish you a pleasant journey."

She must have said something wrong for the engines roared menacingly and she sat down. With order at last restored, ship and voyagers prepared for this new frontier. Every single seat on the *Boeing* had been taken up.

He gazed out of the window as the aircraft gained altitude and Athens shrunk down to a street-plan. There was an affirmation in that moment of power, of how trivial the things left behind. Last night he had convinced himself the plane would never reach Skiathos. He had wished it would stop, switch the ignition off and stay up there, forever floating in the middle of the oceanic sky. But in the morning, at the airport, he had seen the faces who would be travelling with him and had decided differently. People who belonged to this earth, with all its faults and inadequacies, who almost endowed it with beauty.

He tucked his own shirt in and tried to smooth the creases. This time, please, God, let this ship come to a magic place of happiness, without evil. He had always known that paradise would be disguised like this, away from prying pilgrims. Now, from this altitude, he could see exactly where the gods had hidden it. And after touch down, he would probe its every corner and crag, and never leave it.

But twenty minutes were not enough for such a prayer and it stopped unfinished. No sooner had the plane gone up than it dipped forward, changed course and climbed down. It rolled sharply from side to side, then dropped lower still, and Skiathos Town sparkled below him like an object of extraordinary beauty. It rose out of the Aegean sea, a low hill covered with bright white houses and scarlet rooftops.

Then a bump, reverse thrust, and a good landing.

So this was it. Heaven's baggage reclaim door and bus terminal. People just stood in the dusty heat, waiting, relishing the prospect of a good scramble. Oh, let them be. Minutes later everyone squeezed in, the bus set off and war was over. He stuck his neck between two rucksacks so he could breathe, and viewed the scenery.

Skiathos was for her beaches. They had an exotic beauty, unlike anything he had ever seen. The fine white sand, wide and plenteous, stretched like a ribbon, strewn with clusters of pine trees. Next, the sea, ubiquitous and prolific, in numerous hues of indigo. It was a combination of colours for him unseen, unimaginable. As for the town itself, it welcomed strangers with more acceptance than enthusiasm. Places had always felt different according to his means of arrival. Skiathos town just let him be, without scrutiny or drama.

A hundred yards from the bus station the port lingered leisurely, its sprawling expanse lined up with cafes. This was a place for breaking one's journey, for taking stock, not for departures or arrivals.

He dumped his belongings in a hotel and went to explore the labyrinth of back alleys glimpsed from the sky. But the essence of Skiathos's charm eluded him for he was looking at a jewel with a microscope to find its beauty. From the sky, the far end of the port, or even the bus window, the town had held him spellbound. On closer examination, he was not absolutely sure.

He found himself inside the museum of Papathiamandis. The house was so small, there was hardly space for any visitors. Two mirrors, a trunk and a small desk recalled the famous writer's nineteenth century childhood. The floor sloped steeply downwards. He sat at the desk and the chair threatened to slide and skid about.

"Are you hoping for inspiration?" The voice rebounded gently from the walls with a soft Nordic accent.

He turned and found a Scandinavian face he had seen before, in passing. "Not in this particular position." He pretended holding on to the table-top for dear life. "Do you have any ideas for a story?"

An imperceptible smile. "I don't hope so. But you are supposed to sit at the other side and lean across so you can rest your elbows." She might have demonstrated, but for her rucksack.

"Say it again slowly." He feigned deep concentration. "If anyone wrote a single line in this room he *was* a genius."

"They do like to hide in small retreats like this; dark and secret." She came and stood near him. Surely the floor could not hold them both and the rucksack? This Nordic peak proved that mountains could be moved after all, with enough faith. It had climbed and clung to her shoulders, then rose two feet above her. And she had called it after herself with an embroidered tag: Ingrid.

He remembered seeing her at Athens airport, struggling to get off a taxi. Obviously the type who travel the whole world on fifty pence and rough it out. "Where will you be camping?"

She grimaced with tiredness. "Right here, if I can help it."

He laughed but with indifference, in subdued mood, for the house and its old furniture evoked another tiny room of lesser distinction back in Athens. Disturbed, he skimmed over everything and passed to the street outside.

Ingrid followed him along the cobbled alley. For a few moments he remained so deeply lost that nothing distracted him. Even the flower pots and geraniums went unnoticed.

"I'm off to Banana beach," she said at last. "Why don't you come along?"

Clearly she had been to Skiathos before. And he knew nothing better to do. Might as well then.

They ran to the harbour and jumped on a large caique just as the mooring rope splashed and the diesels roared. The vessel chugged powerfully through the blue, like a locomotive. Slowly, the harbour turned and floated out of view, and the island revolved past them.

The engine drone now came into its own. It seeped into the subconscious and conjured illusions of wandering over Elysian fields and seas of joy. Weary passengers attempted a few words now and then but they got mangled in the gears of the machine and, garbled, they evaporated. While the boatman, striding the tiller astern, had reached a sort of magnificence, masquerading as part of the grand landscape.

And so the canvas unfolded, just out of reach, with virgin seashores, beach after beach, mythical forests and sirens. He could watch it forever, gyrating while he looked for a landing strip, never stopping.

In a moment of deep forgetfulness his two hands stretched and held Ingrid's. She squeezed his fingers and both turned instinctively, but hers was not the face he had expected to see and gently he let her go.

Banana beach appeared distantly like a crowded mirage. Fenced by thick forests, almost inaccessible by land, it seethed with bronzed naked bodies. The boat approached and James Cromwell jumped joyously into the water.

Ingrid wanted a proper deck-chair but no parasol. She sat, modestly covered with a bikini, a picture of innocence. "Have some iced coffee." She held her flask out to him. "It's how the Greeks make it."

But he was thirsty for other things. He swam far from the shore, where the sea felt sweet like spring-water. There were moments when he wanted to drink this sea, until there was no more left and he was part of it.

Ingrid waited for him patiently to come out.

"The water is beautiful," he rebuked her idleness, gently. "So this is your sort of heaven. Thank you for sharing it." He stretched out on the sand to dry and she lay next to him.

"Mmm," she half-murmured. Nothing seemed to enthuse this icy maiden. "If only it wasn't so crowded." She had removed the bikini to show a good tan all over, her Nordic blonde curls almost white by contrast.

He sighed. "You are very hard to please."

"I get annoyed very easily. Why don't you take those ridiculous swimming trunks off?"

The truth was they kept his stomach cold and wet. "Is there anything to your satisfaction in this life?"

"I guess there must be, but I haven't found it. Probably never will." Then an afterthought. "I'm only sixteen, you know."

He sat up to look at her. She had looked and sounded years older. "How can you be such a pessimist, at your age?"

"Life is too hard, I think. Don't you agree? Too much pain. Am I right?"

"You may be right, but life doesn't look kindly on those who despise it. It is presumptuous for a sixteen-year-old to think the world is not good enough for her. Some god will get angry."

"If God made this place what it is, he must take the criticism. But I don't blame God or anybody. I just wish I knew what I could do to make me happy."

He placed his hand on top of hers on the sand. At least she had had the guts to speak. Still, it had seemed incongruous for such a young woman.

They had a whole melon between them for lunch and then moved under the cool shade of the forest. Lying naked on the ridge of the slope, above the beach, they watched the bathers from a distance.

He was the first to break the silence. "What would make *me* happy, would be to live on an island for good, removed from the multitudes - with the occasional guest, only."

"We have exactly the same tastes. Without the guest, only."

"Not one? Nobody?"

"No. I like to have things exactly as they should be. And guests tend to spoil them."

"I think the two of us should live in a glass ball, not on this planet."

"Balls. Separate balls. Please. Do not take liberties."

He rolled over her, and she fought him, in a mock struggle. "You should be a nun in a nudist abbey where no man could find you."

She lay pinned to the ground. "Let me go."

He rolled away instantly because his body was going places his mind did not want to.

She took a long look at the surrounding pine trees to avert her gaze. "You remind me of those pictures of randy Satyrs on Greek vases." Then, "What is your name?" She had come to rest her eyes on his, like Pythia in the mystical act of myth-making.

It struck him now how long it had taken her to inquire, and he had not even noticed. "James. I knew your name from your rucksack."

And she went for a dive in the water.

The rest of the day spun with extraordinary slowness until other bathers departed. They watched the boats go, one by one, until the water swallowed them up at the horizon. A handful of lingerers on the beach stood up and set off to cross the forest on foot before darkness.

"I fancy staying all night to watch the sky." She brought her knees up and curled into a naked cuddly toy.

"I don't think we have much choice."

Somebody combed the length of the beach for debris, stacking the deck-chairs into a pile. Then endless sands, totally deserted.

They moved into the middle of the vast expanse and sat facing each other. "How old are you, James?"

Her question confronted him like a brick wall. "Twenty-nine."

"Never been married?" She threw it at him like casting a stone, coldly.

"No."

"Got a girlfriend?"

Bricks came from everywhere. He considered several answers. "No."

"Get one," she said authoritatively.

"Is that an order?"

"It's your thirties depression. That's what my mother calls it. She's thirty-six."

Another brick. In a minute she would call him 'granddad' and find him somewhere to sit. "You don't sound like a normal sixteen year old to me."

"That's what my teachers said. I grew up prematurely." She cleared some pebbles away. "Would you like to try a game with me? What you have to do is pass your feelings and thoughts physically, body to body. You have to exclude the intellect. Sensation only."

"Please, continue."

"Stand and face me." She raised a finger. "I intend to demonstrate. The whole thing consists of six five-minute stages." She had a last look to make sure they were alone. "Tell me when you want to start."

"I think I have already."

"First the eyes. They are an actual part of your brain. Your brain is a sex organ." She dropped her voice to a whisper. "Five minutes. You must look at me for five minutes; my eyes only. Think anything you like but don't take your eyes from mine. It's the first contact. Good. Relax. Make yourself vulnerable. You cannot be loved if you are not vulnerable. Don't put barriers up. Let me see as deep into you as possible. Read my good thoughts. I think only of you. Think the same as me. I am your only thought. The closer we get to seeing the same thing the better. Don't try too hard. Stop fighting. Relax. Start again. Good. I can see you."

Minutes later he breathed out, exhausted.

"You are very good. Stage two: Close your eyes if you want to. Stand closer. Now toes to toes. It's a sexy part of the body. Let them touch, explore mine with yours, but don't break contact. You must try to lose yourself, until you can't tell which are yours and which are mine. Nothing else must touch. Resist the urge. It will be strong. Let your naked toes tell me what you have to say. Good. I think you've done this before. Relax. It's the most difficult moment. Let your mind come in if it wants to. Feel the powerful sexuality. Feel it raw. Don't analyze it." And she lapsed into silence for minutes.

"The next stage is in two parts. Chest, and fingers. Ten minutes. First the nipples must touch. I'll have to stand a bit higher. Sink deeper into the sand. Nothing else must touch. Lean forward. I said nothing else must touch."

"Sorry."

"Behave yourself. Chest only. Let them stroke, keep changing from one to the other. Slowly. Keep on until my fingers touch you. Then do the same to me. Use the tips, up and down the spine. Ready? No more talking."

His consciousness now faded and control loosened. Her skin had a primitive coarseness, the lighter her touch, the more the fever.

Then her finger-tips touched his back and shockwaves convulsed him. He shuddered but managed to stay up.

"Now." She still had some voice. "Lips and face. Together." She hardly whispered. "Kiss the lips and explore the rest of my face with your finger-tips. Don't wander. Let the bodies touch at every point. But hands on the face only. We'll start standing up, then bend our knees and fall on the sand. Lips together at all times. You mustn't lose touch or you'll lose the flow. At this stage control must go. When five minutes are up, you must lose all consciousness. Your mind must be part of the body. I'll give the signal to start. Come closer."

Five minutes passed and stages five, six - who counted? - this act had a pre-determined ending. Well, it was obvious. He broke off hastily and run to dive into the sea. Frustration ate him up, and he convulsed time and again underwater. This was cruelty, as cruel as any god could be to a fleshly human. He would not come up to breathe in case he caught a glimpse of her and burst into flames. Under her icy front, this nubile nymph was a blazing furnace which no ocean could extinguish.

But when eventually he surfaced, he cared much more for her than for his abstinence and absurdity.

"What is the matter with you?" She looked aghast, still in shreds, more in bewilderment than rejection. She cowered on the sand, looking devastated and alone, probably afraid of him now in the dark, but trusting him.

What was the matter with him indeed, if only he knew himself, or if he could give an answer.

Lying down again on his back, there was nothing to see but stars. Billions, like the sand, cascading down fast, never reaching. "Can you see," he muttered at last, "how much higher the sky looks in pitch dark?"

But she was taking no notice.

****

9th AUGUST   SKIATHOS

The shaver buzzed cheerfully over his cheeks, the sun-burned skin, the first imperceptible ageing lines. He checked whether any more had shown since yesterday. No matter. They made him look wiser.

It had been the early hours of the morning when they had made it back to his hotel. Ingrid approached unseen and passed a finger over his spine. He glanced at her in the steamed up mirror and continued uninterrupted.

"Why are you shaving?" She stroked a breast against his goose-pimples, casually.

"Because I'm celebrating."

"Oh, really?"

"Hm-hm! I always shave when I'm celebrating."

"Liar. You'd have had a beard."

He switched the razor off and beamed at her. "There!"

"Disgusting. What's the happy occasion?"

"Oh, it's nothing," he grumbled irritably and pushed passed her.

"Today we'll go camping," she chased after him. "We'll swim in a blue lagoon and then I'll cook you a soup, something Norwegian." She stopped and watched him fumble for clothes in the suitcase. Perhaps he looked different, nude in the confines of a small room, in daylight. Last night, she had compared him to a Greek satyr on the beach. Here his fleshly imperfections came to the fore, and the satyr became a man with flaws and bruises.

126

They sat on the open balcony and somebody fetched a single red rose with the bread basket.

"Look at me, James." She put the rose in her hair. "Do I look beautiful and attractive?"

"As a matter of fact you do. What happened?"

The bread basket hit him and everything scattered about. "Shut your mouth."

James kept cool. "Waiter, more croissants, please. We're celebrating."

The waiter came to an abrupt halt, swapped their basket to the sound of "bloody foreigners" and stormed out.

"Aren't you glad he didn't ask what we're celebrating?" she teased him. "We might have had to invent something."

"Whatever makes you happy."

"Whatever makes you shave. Right?"

"Ladies first." He raised the steaming croissant for a bite.

"O.K.. I'm having a baby. Your turn."

The croissant froze and refused to be bitten. "Congratulations. How long?" He exhaled slowly to gain composure.

"What do you mean, how long? They are usually about that long..."

"How long have you been expecting?"

"Nine hours; or maybe ten, I haven't worked it out."

He chuckled, then tore a bite. "This isn't funny."

"It's not supposed to be."

"I never touched you."

"James, I'm pregnant. If you don't believe me we won't talk about it."

"Ingrid, you are only sixteen, you play sex games on the beach with strangers twice your age, and now you tell me you're pregnant, probably, but do not remember how... I won't believe anything you say to me again."

"Don't talk like that, please. I wanted a baby. Why does it bother you so much? I'll bring him up in Norway."

"His country of residence is irrelevant. And how do you know it would be a boy?"

"You don't hate me?" She was forever metamorphosing between a woman and a child.

"Of course I don't. Now eat your croissant before it dries."

In the morning rush of port arrivals, Skiathos town was knee-deep with tourists. They waded through them, pushed them apart and stood on them, but they sprung up again, indestructible.

He had left himself entirely to her guidance on this island because she knew it. "I hope your camp-site hasn't been discovered. By all these marauding armies."

"I promise you, there will be nobody there."

But there were. After the long boat trip, the climb over a hill and a crawl through the thorns and thistles, a group of Germanic origin had beaten them to it with their private speed-boat. "Morgen, morgen." They waved big hands and laughed heartily.

"Fuck," she muttered and waved back, teeth clenching.

"I agree with you completely."

The place had been worth suffering for - a sort of lagoon, shallow enough for every pebble to flicker under the blue, with a small mouth to the ocean. He tossed her into the sea, exuberantly, then dived beneath her. They splashed and shouted like children in a playground, with forests and hills mounting the amphitheatre to watch them. The echo was extraordinary. Each little sound bounced and rose in spirals filling the vast auditorium, until nothing but cries of laughter surrounded them.

She stripped off completely and lay back on the sand as far away from the others as possible. James watched her uneasily. Today, it seemed everyone gawped at her and he felt very protective.

"I think you ought to put something on," he said. "You are being secretly admired."

"Tell me when I look dry."

"You look dry now."

"O.K.. Just ten more minutes."

"Wear your bikini-bottom, at least."

She sat up. "Give me one good reason."

"You'll catch a cold, that's why."

She laughed and her fruitful breasts shook bountifully. "Today I feel I can forget everything. Not a care in the world. You inspire me."

"Happiness is lying naked on the beach with an imaginary baby in your tummy; is that right?"

"You make it sound like I ate him." She pushed him off huffily. "Do you have a problem with sex?"

"At your age, yes. You are still supposed to be a child."

"Still? At sixteen? Wait for twenty-nine? End up an old maid like you, is that what you would like?"

"You know what I mean. Give yourself time. Time to develop and grow, and I don't mean your bra size. If you cut your childhood short, it's like abandoning school before you learn anything. It takes time, a very long time, to become a woman. Doesn't just happen because you slept with someone, overnight."

"That's ridiculous. I like to do it and then move on, as many people as possible. What's the big deal? It is like eating with someone."

A tall, blonde giant of a man walked over to them from the speed-boat group. "We have Greek cakes and coffee, would you like some?" he asked in his German accent.

Ingrid sprang up as if stung where there ought to be a bikini. "I'd love one."

She must definitely be pregnant.

"Yes, of course," the man bowed. "And coffee?"

"Two, please. James you'll have a coffee, won't you?"

"Yes, of course." He watched the giant strut away.

They came back, all four of them, and sat uninvited, handing out plastic cups and paper plates. "My name is Rosa." She was squarish, short and overweight in the

THIRTY NIGHTS FOR THIRTY ISLANDS

forward areas. "This is Gustav, my boyfriend, and those are Sabine and Karl." Gustav sat down so as not to tower over her.

Karl offered to shake hands, with a big enigmatic smile. "What business brings you to the great acid house party?" And they all had a Teutonic laugh.

"Why do you call it that?"

"Skiathos?" He handed cigarettes out. "Skiathos and Mykonos are legends for acid parties." Another laugh. "Have a joint."

"No thank you." James squirmed away from the unmistakable aroma.

"Stay," Gustav said and put a hand on his shoulder. "Have fun."

"If you don't mind." James stopped him with a flat palm.

Confused and frightened, Ingrid sat up and started to gather her belongings.

"Will you come with us on the boat?" Sabine addressed herself to James.

"I said, no thanks."

They stood up, clearly offended, and walked back to their own camp.

"What's the matter with you? Can't you put up with anyone for five minutes?" Ingrid was more flustered than irritable.

"I don't like them," he cut her.

"That's absurd. They seemed friendly and hospitable." And she lay back again, fuming.

"I wish they would... bugger off." His whole mood today was of a hornet at its nest.

A few minutes passed. "It's O.K.," she whispered to calm both of them. "I also wish we had the place to ourselves."

"We'll just throw your eggs and tomatoes at them. I hope you remembered to bring some."

"I have carrots and celery. Will it do?"

"That's O.K.. They wouldn't know the difference."

She pulled up closer. "You would make such a good father. Very protective. I used to wonder, you know. Whether to have any children of my own. Difficult to know."

"Ingrid, at sixteen, children are not what you have, it's what you are."

"I have this vision of getting married, with the white dress and the wedding photographers; and as I leave the church, a camera follows my whole life. Time-lapse photography. One picture every few days. And then I watch back the video. Minute by minute I grow older and greyer until, an hour later, it's over. That frightens me. Do you see? That's all life is. An hour."

"You need a bit of that soup you promised to cook. Let's have some. We'll die afterwards."

"And that is the reason I want to do everything as soon as possible."

He took a deep breath. "I'm hungry."

The moment of the great Norwegian soup arrived and a camp-gas appeared out of her bag. The rucksack had probably contained an oven. Now a saucepan, water out of the flask, and secret ingredients chopped up in a brown bag. The smell lifted up and German invaders fled off in the motor-boat.

She gave him a spoonful to try. To be fair, it tasted good. Anything would, after so much philosophising. Two more mouthfuls. A paper-plate-ful. The potion filled his hunger wonderfully, restored order to the universe, soothed him.

She put things away and curled up, listless. There was nothing to do but nestle up, luxuriate, and doze off.

They woke on the sand at close of day, the air still redolent of boiled carrots.

"It's getting late." He commented for something to say.

"Let's spend the night here, watch the moon, just like last night."

How he wished that voice had been someone else's, in a small room, a downtown hotel, and a sprung bed that creaked and rattled. For the moment all around him was stagnant and idle. Suddenly he craved the bustling crowds, fish restaurants, and the back streets of a faraway harbour.

He walked the edge of the bay to the far end of the lagoon, silent. There was the narrow inlet from the sea, peace, lifelessness. Only the sound of him pacing, crushing the sand and the pebbles. The sun had set. Soon there would be nothing.

"It's time we started."

"Will you have a last swim with me?" she begged.

They sank like into a mirror, trees floating upside down beside them. Overhead the grey twilight. Ah, to be in her arms forever, rolling up and down with each new wave, moving from a shade of blue to one deeper and more mysterious.

"I prayed last night," he said at last. "For the first time."

"I knew you did something weird. And was your prayer answered?"

"Don't know. How long do prayers take to get there?"

In the late breeze she heaved a weary sigh. "Last night I dreamt of spending the night here, with you, listening to the sounds of the forest. I didn't expect you'd be so difficult."

"Come on. We'll swim all around your lagoon once then make our way back."

"You swim. I'll get out that way."

It was not long before he realized something had happened. His swim had taken just minutes. And he had heard boats passing in the open sea. But it was dark now and Ingrid was nowhere to be seen.

He called her but knew there would be no answer. And so, he gathered their bags and made his way across the salt-baked fields and the sand dunes.

Midnight, and Skiathos town seethed with crowds. He followed the sound of disco music from a distance, knowing that he would find her.

He joined the queue at the cave entrance and bartered his soul for a ticket. This must be the place; the very earth shook to a subterranean drum-beat. A lone burning light said *"Dante's,"* and then a gaping abyss; and he plummeted.

In the darkest neglected corner, behind the DJ, he first made out a drum kit, some microphones and a keyboard. Edging closer, there was a *Stratocaster* and two amplifiers.

"Is the band coming?" he shouted into the DJ's ear.

"You are English!" Then pointed to himself. "Sunny Manchester."

"Wow!" James Cromwell echoed his enthusiasm. "Sunnier than Skiathos!" Every single syllable had to be shouted.

"Absolutely! No, no band tonight."

"Do you mind if I jam a few chords together on the *Stratocaster*?"

"On the guitar? Absolutely! What, right now?"

"There is never a better time."

The DJ nodded, James plugged into an amplifier and tuned up and, when he nodded, *Dante's* froze over and all hell went quiet. There was a moan from disgruntled dancers who stopped. And then James Cromwell picked a few notes on the pentatonic and kicked in distortion and whammy bar. And the guitar screamed the pain he had bottled up from London to Athens and Skiathos to Pireaus, for leaving a girl in tears in a back street in some downtown faraway harbour, for fighting the gods and gods getting the upper hand.

The DJ waved his head approvingly and set off the dry ice. James could see sweltering shadows dancing again like ghostly souls on smouldering sulphur and hellfire. Karl, Rosa, Sabine and Gustav stood in the middle of the pit, their faces hot and high. There was a holocaust of noise and cries of orgasmic suffering.

Then the guitar stopped and the DJ played another track.

There was a sudden stir and Ingrid threw herself at the stage. "James, here you are!"

He pulled away to stop her carrying him into Hades. "Ingrid. What happened?" The words fell on the floor meaningless.

"Nothing happened." She held him tight. "We've been trying to find you. Shall we go?" She put both arms round him. "We are heading back to the lagoon for the night."

The Germans beckoned her back and she wavered in agony. He placed a hand on her exuberant shoulder to stop her from flying, but she was already on a high. She just turned round and joined them and all trace of her vanished.

****

10th AUGUST   SKIATHOS

He lay in bed all night, waiting for her to return and collect her stuff and re-assessing his own attitude. What would he say to Ingrid, if she came back to him, to this sterile hotel room, his sterile life? What if she had been serious about having his baby? What if he had not stopped when he did the other night on Banana beach, and she had fallen pregnant, and she was bringing up his son in Norway without him ever knowing? The prospect was unimaginable.

But now that she had told him what her objective was, having a child together seemed like a feasible proposition. Julia would never have said such a thing to him. She was one for books and for her cello, not babies. Sonia, of course, would be perfect, if he was looking for a band manager. But, changing nappies? No.

Ingrid had pursued him for two days and really stuck to him. He was the one holding off, when he could have been a little more giving and affectionate. She really liked him. Ingrid was a good woman, after all. Ingrid represented the most tangible positive thing in his life at the present moment. A life that might yet be, an ordinary man's dream, to have and to hold, a homely woman, with dirty linen at her feet, an ironing board, a rucksack. Or even a conversation after work, "How was your day at the office, dear?"

Days at the office reminded him of Maxine and her happy marriage with children. His lowly secretary had ended up much wealthier than her boss in every way. Not she to gamble on diamonds from Liberia, so she never lost anything. Not she to haggle over mega deals like he could, but then again nothing to worry about after she reached home at the end of the day. Banks went bust and countries might default, but Maxine would carry on with her shopping trolley at *Sainsbury's* and would feed her children every evening.

Then there had been Elena Diamandithou who had said she looked for an Edwardian gentleman and had felt genuinely sad to see him leave Hydra. But Elena had her ships, had Sakis, and was still trying to get rid of penniless alcoholic suitors. The prospect of him and Elena getting together was as incongruous as her underwater gods. 'Mrs Cromwell? I am Greek. The whole country will disown me.' Pity; he loved her yacht and would have been good running her businesses now he had none of his own.

Just before Elena, he had had dinner at the same spot with a very different woman. What he had shared with Jenny was very little, but she was English and, much earlier, that would have counted for a lot to him. Sharing a life of simple Englishness had made some people happy. He could not dance like she could, but her mere presence had turned 'Little England' into an oasis and a haven - from man-eating French communists like Nicole.

And there had been Katia. She really had become the only affair of the heart, but Katia was unreachable in every way. 'Fancy taking a creature out of this earth and putting her through London winter nights.' Katia would have children one day, but they would not be his. Katia already had a fiance. What was the point of clinging on to a dream that could never be, and might in fact seem fanciful a few years down the line? As much as he loved her, would it not be sensible to put her straight out of his mind?

Women, women, he had found all of them captivating, each one unique, an island in her own right. Water, water everywhere but not a drop to drink. That shadow drifted past him again, his eyes darkened and he held his breath back. It crossed slowly like a stray dog, long ago driven from the pack, tongue desperate for water in the dazzle of the low sun simmering on the burning asphalt. None of these wanderings would have happened if Julia and he had married as had been planned. Strange how a straightforward love-affair could get mangled up and through and back on itself and all about. Beauty turned to

138

unnecessary ugliness.   Order and clarity into heaps of carnage.

The haunting image of Addie drifted past him. Was her father out to kill him really, waiting back in London for him, perhaps? How could a prostitute make it into his house without him suspecting anything the whole night? Was he responsible for her suicide?

And now there was bright, young, fecund, romantic Ingrid. A little bit icy on the top, but very much like a good cake. If only he had not been so 'difficult' - that was what she had called him. This loveable girl had liked him. A couple of children later their age difference would disappear. What was the problem with him indeed? What would he do when he run out of Greek islands to visit? What would happen to him when he run out of single available women?

Ingrid did not move him, it had to be said, but many good partnerships started like this. 'I have this vision of getting married, with the white dress and the wedding photo-graphers...' she had said. His mind went over each tiny incident since he met her. As the night drifted with him alone listening to tiny strange sounds and the dripping shower counting minutes, the four walls of this ghastly place kept telling him his entire life was meaningless. And Ingrid took on qualities he had overlooked. And he missed her.

> 'The next stage is in two parts. Chest, and
> fingers. Ten minutes. First the nipples must
> touch. I'll have to stand a bit higher. Sink
> deeper into the sand. Nothing else must touch.
> Lean forward. I said nothing else must touch.
> Behave yourself...'

He laughed out loud and then he remembered how thin these walls were, how she had loved watching him shave in this very room, brushing her breasts against him, how she had scattered the croissant and made the waiter furious.

Mentally now, he pushed her into the sand. Her top peeled off, her limbs unfolded and opened. The path from her breasts was brief, her warm incision intoxicating. He could see, smell, feel and even taste but...

It was daybreak when he heard her knock on the door. The sound triggered a surge of relief. But when he saw her, she was no longer the beautiful fecund woman of yesterday. She stood, ashen, several feet away, battered and bruised.

"Come in." He filled a bath for she was bleeding, the water turning to horror faster than it could pour in. He lay her head back against the rim and rinsed the injuries gently. And not a breath from her bloodied lips.

"You'll be all right," he said.

"Why don't you kick me out, hate me?"

He sighed in disbelief which she took to mean that he loved her and the misapprehension balmed them both.

"Somebody will have to see you," he whispered, but she refused with a gesture and held on to him. "You need a doctor and we must tell the police."

"No!" she cried. "Please, don't tell anybody. Please, James. I couldn't face it."

He held her mechanically, because she was there, wondering what would have happened if she had carried a Norwegian prince.

"Who did this to you? Those Germans?" he finally uttered the dreaded words.

"Oh, no. I went back on my own. Three men. They forced me," she said, her voice broken. "And it went on for hours."

"Let me call a doctor, Ingrid."

"No. I've stopped bleeding." The bath tub resembled a murder scene.

"Would you like to fly back home? As soon as possible?"

She nodded. "You'll come with me to the airport, won't you?"

"Of course. And I want you to write to me."

But their umbilical cord had been broken and her nod implied that she would not. It was a moment of liberation for them both. Something had threatened to tie them to each other and they had killed it at a stroke.

"It may be for the better," she said. "I didn't know what I was doing."

"You are very brainy and mature. You will come out stronger from this. I think you should dry now and lie in bed. You are shivering."

He carried her to bed gently, covered her gently, kissed her on the forehead and held her hand absently as he had done on that boat to Banana beach. It was like a father wondering what he could have done differently. And slowly she recovered enough to drink coffee and to get her proper voice again. She would be well enough for the flight, which made him feel thankful as well as foolish for those absurd night thoughts of a few minutes ago.

Then she got up and started to tidy her belongings.

He opened the window to a bright morning, the smell of the seaweed and a cool breeze. How quickly everything fell back into order again. He was alone, unattached, and his only pain right now was his sympathy for Ingrid. He felt glad that she would be going home to be healed and comforted. Yet also he despised himself for feeling free. A couple of hours from now he would be moving, risking more shipwrecks, voyaging.

Midday. They stood waiting at the airport and her rucksack looked unaffected. The flight to Oslo would be leaving soon. Ingrid resembled a schoolgirl on a picnic outing, with short pink socks, sun-glasses and a pink T-shirt. Two Greek policemen gave her an admiring, unsuspecting look.

Then everything happened quickly as they wished that it would. As the plane thundered on the runway and lifted, he gave a single wave to the sky, in case she looked.

Skiathos resembled a backwater today, dull, mundane, provincial noises filling its dusty streets. A horse and cart pulled up the hill to Golgotha, hooves struggling on slippery cobble-stones. It might as well have been the nineteenth century, their lives nothing but a moment in Ingrid's time-lapse photography documentary. From hell to earth and back again, he had lost sense which was where. This was no place to be, had no purpose. A mere few hundred miles up and the universe did not care who raped whom, or if a prince got flushed down a sewer.

He sat at a corner bar for solitude. A shaft of sunlight thrust through a missing brick in the wall, albeit without the harping angels. It only remained for Beelzebub to come in and list his evil deeds in damnation. The promise of paradise mauled and savaged to pieces.

Sod it, he thought, and drowned his whole philosophy in a cold beer. Then a breeze came from the east and it felt tolerable to be drifting. There was shade over his head, earth under his feet, the sea and its beaches at arm's reach... Ah, that was it! Something was missing. Perhaps a haven to shelter and to drop anchor for good.

As his own plane took off in the late hours of the night, he looked out of the window. Lights moving, stopping, turning, humanity shifting, grading and drifting. Dawn started to break. The sky looked so vast, so much space. He thought of the room where he first met Katia and it seemed smaller than ever, like a sepulchre.

****

11th AUGUST ATHENS

Wednesday. The beast's mouth opened and he was vomited to the shallows of the airport. Athens must have been very hot yesterday. He could smell the tarmac still melting, smoke from rubber tyres burning, jet and car fumes.

So there he was once more, in a place not of his choosing. Must get on and leave this great city before its past history caught up with him.

But the good gods had had other plans for him. His connecting flight to Thessaloniki had closed. He took back his ticket and carried his cases to a telephone.

"Mrs Diamandithou?"

"Yes," her sleepy throat answered a little hoarsely.

"It's James Cromwell. I'm at the airport on transit to Thessaloniki. Sorry to get you up early morning like this."

There was a few seconds' pause. "Stay there. I'll send somebody to get you."

The *Rolls Royce* with the cream leather seats and air-conditioning cocooned him. The chauffeur shut his door for him and suddenly everything seemed removed and unreal. He leaned back against the headrest and relished the surging power. Three cheers for the good god of hospitality, whatever his name was; Elena would tell him, no doubt. His clothes were not quite appropriate for the occasion and his unshaven face befitted a shipwrecked Odysseus. But Elena would see him right.

She was having a bath and shouted that he too should have one in the second bathroom. The third and fourth were occupied, perhaps.

She burst in on him while he dozed in the steam and the foam, and kissed him on the cheek very modestly. "I heard you are in a bit of a state. What has happened to you?"

"Your gods must have put a curse on me. My whole life is blighted."

"Small trouble. Soon see to it. Hurry up. Breakfast is served in half an hour." She strolled out, magnificent in her bathroom robes.

One could see the rest of Kifissia from the breakfast room. Her house ruled the entire suburb. And when it came to eating, she wanted absolute powers over him too. Have this, take that and better finish the other. But he endured it stoically.

Finally she pushed away her coffee-cup. "Tell me all about her."

"About whom?"

"You are boasting. There is only one. You can sleep with many but your heart knows better." She put a fist to her heaving cleavage.

"I've come to hear about you, and *your* troubles."

She looked at him sternly, then caved in. "Pedro is dead. He committed suicide. Sakis is taking it very badly. He had not wanted to meet him but he had the option then. Now he knows he will never meet his father. He thinks he's killed him by rejecting him." She looked away. "And I think I did."

"There was nothing you could have done, Elena."

"Yes, I know. But I feel guilty, no matter how I look at it. Perhaps I could have seen him briefly."

"You made the right decision at the time. One can't rehearse life. You do what you do."

"That's a very English thing to say. Very pragmatic." She was tranquil and pensive. "I'm thinking of Sakis. You can explain but it doesn't change him inside, does it?"

"Where did Pedro die?"

"That's what I try not to think about."

"Forget I asked."

"He turned himself into a statue. His last work. Dedicated to his son, he said in a note." She gave a strange chortle. "He told somebody he was making a body cast, then got drunk and poured the stuff over himself. They found him in a hideous mess. As always. He lived a destructive life. I couldn't let him ruin Sakis and me."

Yesterday's memories came back to haunt him. One could grieve for something different every day. For one could not stop loving, or one would cease to live.

He roamed the house while she dressed, losing himself in the innumerable vestibules. He opened a door and stared in horror at the mirror confronting him. So like Pedro! The face looked back at him. Then calmly he turned and slipped from the empty room.

Elena sat in the lounge, in a morning suit, checking her private mail. She would have to go into her office at some time and she wanted him to go too. He sat on the sofa opposite and looked round the room. A grand piano, paintings over the fire-place, an ageing man-servant tying the drapes with a cord.

She put the pile of letters down cheerfully. "Ready?"

"Who plays the piano?"

"I used to. Had to, as a child. Play the piano and paint." She came and sat next to him, and they kissed, making the servant extremely jealous.

"You are looking lovely and full of energy," he said genuinely, for it seemed that Pedro's death had liberated her. "It suits you to be happy."

"I was born happy. A mid-summer's day baby."

"Were you, now. What did it feel like?"

"Oh, I remember it clearly. Warm sun, blue skies, and then just me."

"That explains everything."

She laughed. "There were poppies everywhere. And thyme and pine trees."

"I keep hearing this story. It seems Greek women are born in fields."

"So. I'll ask you again. Tell me all about her."

He could not escape a second time. "Her name was Katia. Met here in Athens last week."

"You've been playing havoc here, haven't you? Was she as rich and beautiful as me?"

"A seamstress from Plaka. Yes."

"Forget her. She will meet a rich man twice her age and live happily ever after."

"She already has. Except he's not rich."

"Did you fall in love with her?"

"You don't ask an Englishman such questions. She meant something very special to me."

There was a hesitant moment while she scrutinised him. "You should have run away with her."

"How? Remember what *you* said? 'The whole country will disown me.' That was exactly her argument."

"She would have come with you. You were not forceful enough. A woman needs persuasion. I think she fell in love with you too. But my guess is you weren't sure. Like me, you always need a back exit, just in case. We make good managers but hopeless suitors."

She had spoken with some passion as if with personal regret. Perhaps she had never risked everything to gain somebody, probably never would. A life of glass jars, clean and sterilized, held from a distance with amputated finger-tips.

She got up, briefcase in hand, and led the way to the front lobby. Car and chauffeur waited outside. They rolled majestically through the gates, two nameless figures in a glass cylinder.

Her office was as only Elena's could. Plants, oil paintings and photographs everywhere, her furniture expensive, Italian, new.

He stayed with her while she made a few calls in French and English. Time to call Maxine he thought. "Can I ring head-office from here?"

"Absolutely." She loved him taking liberties.

"Maxine, it's me." As if she would not recognise the voice. "I'm calling from my new headquarters... Yes. You see, I've just acquired this shipping company... Pardon?... Yes, including the ships... The name? Hold on, I'll find out."

Elena rebuked him with her laughter. "Stop it. There might be people listening."

"What is a good Greek name for shipping?"

Maxine tuned in quickly. "I don't think it's funny. Now listen to me. Have you been in touch with Eamon?"

"What does he want?"

"I had this message to give you. It was marked 'Urgent.' Phone him, please."

"What did the message say?"

"I did email it to you. About that man, I think."

"No more emails. My laptop is on the seabed." He shortened the conversation to an update.

Elena brought in a new subject quickly. "I'm taking you with me to the wine shop later, for a little tasting. I want something special for dinner. I'm having a new chef in."

"Who else is coming?"

"Nobody. Just you and me."

"Such an honour. Trying to seduce me?"

"Absolutely. We both need a little pampering I think."

It was the late part of the day and they had just left the wine shop when something happened - something that neither of them understood. Elena had sat in the back of the car and he was preparing to join her when a stranger called him from behind, "Mr Cromwell," and, turning, he saw a knife thrusting inexorably towards him. He pushed at the thing instinctively and swung it outwards. The man faltered and run away among the crowds who carried on unsuspecting. James glared at the cut in his left hand while the chauffeur jumped out and pushed him into the *Rolls*. There was no screech from the tyres, just a surge of power, then seclusion.

Elena's colour had drained. "What happened?"

"He tried to kill me."

Her mouth dropped. "Oh, James." But the *Rolls* sailed on impassively.

She made a lot of fuss over such a small injury when they got back. "Who was he?"

"Don't know. Hardly saw his face. I wish I could have trusted him to do a good job of it."

"James, that's not funny. I'll murder you myself if you don't sit still."

"You would be doing me a favour."

"Don't tempt me."

But the servant announced dinner and postponed his summary execution.

They changed in separate bedrooms. Time must have spun very slowly for her alone in this place, with gaps as vast as her rooms. The evening itself drifted slowly over cocktails, the wine, exotic food.

"Best transit meal I've had, at any airport. My compliments to the chef."

"He works on the cruise to Egypt. They docked this morning. You are lucky. He's one of the best."

"I'd keep him here, if I were you."

"Why don't you stay, James? What have you got to do in Thessaloniki?"

"I have to catch the midnight flight. It's all been fixed."

She shook her head in despair. "When will you stop wandering? I don't know what you are running away from."

Neither did he. Something was drawing him like a dark void, calling him with a siren's voice, to an abyss.

"Are you afraid I might cast a spell on you? Like Circe?"

"Stranger things have happened."

She smiled vaguely. "I think your nemesis is female and a figment of your imagination. Because your mother did not love you. Look at me and say if I'm not telling the truth."

"I try not to think about it."

"You'll land in Thessaloniki when everything will be shut. It's a dismal place. Why are you doing this?"

"I need some time to myself."

"Some time. And then what? It will catch up with you again, this monster, whatever it is." She groaned resignedly. "I have friends in Halkidiki, not far from where you're going, with a lovely hotel. Shall I book you a room?"

"I want to see mount Athos, with all the monasteries. That's Halkidiki isn't it?"

"You want to become a hermit." She meant that to hurt him, with an appropriate smirk.

But he was not listening to her. "I don't believe they would let me stay. Far too intellectual for me. How do they manage to be Christian, yet also scholarly and Greek?"

The question shocked her. She gaped at him in disbelief. "James, I've never heard you speak like this."

"What did I say?"

"You have to be stupid to be Christian? Do not say this in Greece."

"Why don't they allow women in - not even to visit?"

"Women; that's all you ever think about. A simple Englishman who travels on business but likes to chase the girls."

"Their's is a contradiction, not mine," he persisted. "What's wrong with women in a Christian place? They make things up as they please."

"Athos is an island unique in the whole world; speaking metaphorically. It's very secluded, for contemplation. Don't go there. They might convert you to asceticism and that's not remotely you. You are right, you won't see women there, we are not allowed in. Your islands are female, you need the opposite sex." She led him to the blue bedroom and left both windows open to let her Greek gods back in. "Please, sit down here and talk to me. I find the blue calms me down." She pulled her feet up and patted a spot for him.

The bed was soft, the pillows deep, and there with him his own Calypso, Helen of Troy, everything a woman should be. One more sip of this potion and he would have stayed, forgetting who he was or where he was meant to be. Was he a fool to go? He had been indulged in every sense! But it made no difference. The sea was calling out to him.

The flight to Thessaloniki was delayed as usual. Inside the airport conditions resembled a refugee camp. It took an hour to prepare for the thirty minute flight. He sat and watched endless debates between ground and air staff. At one twenty past midnight, mercifully, the gates shut and the beast rose into the darkness. He would be arriving, as Elena said, at the dismal gates of hell, in the darkest hour.

****

12th AUGUST   THESSALONIKI

Northern Greece drizzled. He joined the mob for a taxi and was mobbed back himself. Thessaloniki was a dismaying city at night with weather like this. A long promenade behind a road, behind a forest of apartment blocks. There was a cargo ship at the extreme end of the harbour, derelict and alone. Nobody walked the streets, cars scuttled along, buildings stood solemn. And only the sea broke against the concrete. Never before had he seen such emptiness and sterility. It almost looked like a ghost-city, from the top of the hill to the haunted port.

He stood on the quay, suitcases either side of him, dazed. Nothing but darkness stretched out before him, wet skies and a black sea. The blackness was devastating. And the will to do anything, even to find a bed had left him.

He picked up his cross and trudged along. Several hundred yards on, the buildings gave way to a wide open space and there he sat on a park-bench, defeated. His eyes could only focus on the black vastness, absently. Now the one thing he wanted most was to sleep.

Then, out of the Erebus, Katia's ghost rose and lit up the harbour with dazzling light for him. Her spirit drifted from the sea and glided towards him benevolently. He buried his face in her two hands and she consumed and enveloped him. He made to hold her vision but she kept slipping through his fingers.

Katia's magnificent eyes smiled, a mere few inches away from him. Yet she was flying, remote, unreachable, her delicate figure fading before he could talk to her.

The next thing he knew, he woke on a park-bench to a bright day and he looked round him. It was several minutes before he remembered where he was meant to be. Above and behind him, ugly buildings of every species occupied every square inch. In the port nothing moved yet. Its black waters stagnated with garbage and oil slicks, threatening to rise and flood this city to oblivion.

He walked into the first door he found as road sweepers charged down the street. "A room, please."

Locked up, shutters closed, he lay on the dirty mattress staring up at the ceiling and the sprung bed just creaked and rattled with every breath he took. Sea-gulls kept calling him to come out and fly with them, but he could neither speak nor move. For both his wings had been broken, and he needed miracles to heal him, to get his strength, to suffer the seas ahead.

****

13th AUGUST   HALKIDIKI

"My son, seek for thyself another kingdom, for that which I leave is too small for thee."

Onward to Macedonia, kingdom of Alexander the Great, who went on to conquer the world before the age of thirty. Well, seventeen days left for him to break that particular record.

His bus wound a path towards the three-pronged peninsula of Halkidiki. Here the mountains gave way to a flat plain of golden wheat, ripe and ready to be harvested. From barrenness to fertility and beauty. Yesterday's memory was fading fast, its darkness had set over the horizon. This was a different kind of sea, bright and auspicious. Its simmering surface concealed no sepulchral mysteries. He felt an overwhelming desire to ride through it on a galloping thoroughbred, letting his hands stroke its velvet smoothness - the entire plain his, his conquered kingdom.

But the old man next to him snored heavily through the whole scene and the driver spat out of the window. Perhaps they had a better claim to its earthy beauty.

As the clouds cleared over the mountains, a breath-taking light filled the landscape. The sun shone and there was nothing to see but gold and yellow from one corner of the earth to the other.

"Stop," he cried.

Nothing happened except some curious looks from passengers and the driver.

He left his seat and stood by the front door looking at the endless fields of wheat nuzzling to the breeze like waves.

"Stop! Stop, stop, stop." And he fled through the door as they slowed.

The bus stayed and they watched him through the windows, laughing at him, then sombre and silent. He ran through the fields, arms spread, palms brushing the whiskered tops, riding the farrows.

Someone was shouting at him and he heard the engine rev up. "Your bags! Eh, take your bags, mister!" But it did not matter. He ran farther and farther from the road, scattering the nesting sparrows, frightening the scarecrow. All that silk to swim through, bobbing up and down over the ditches, moving from a shade of gold to another, deeper and more auspicious.

Then, looking back, he saw his suitcases thrown in the air, opening up, and all his belongings flying against the sun like chaff at a summer threshing. "You bastards," he shouted and ran back, but the bus accelerated and vanished. He lay on the ground panting, jubilant, watching his shirts and his underpants nestle on the stalks, flapping. This was his kingdom, at last, his own warm, promised island.

He swallowed the smell of the earth in gulps, drunk its potion. And when he had drunk enough, he gathered his scattered rags and made himself respectable. Hm, maybe not quite a conqueror: There was a risk Alexander would crop up at any minute and challenge him to a duel. The great pretender was just an eccentric Englishman. He was already heading in the opposite direction to Athos, a serious dereliction of religious duty, no matter how he looked at it.

He stood, very modestly, with his suitcases repacked, hoping to hitch-hike.

What rescued him was a different thing altogether. A luxury coach with air-conditioning, it had "ALEXANDER PALACE" written all over it, and double-glazing to prevent spitting through windows.

"Can you take me to Kalithea?"

Well, they could not leave him there in the wilderness. "Get in."

Back to a more tepid civilization, then, and his surge of exhilaration dwindled to tranquillity. He settled into the seat and relished the silence.

His guidebook mentioned a few villages where he could stay. He asked the nearest passenger which was which, and how much longer before they got there. She said she was a local girl and an archaeology student at Athens university, returning to see her parents. Spoke and acted too much the blue-stocking for her age, a very serious young woman indeed. She read his *Baedeker* and showed whether she agreed or disagreed with certain comments. A brief nod here, a grimace there, her eyes examining rather than expressive. Kept a certain distance, without aloofness, inscrutably.

Her educated hands skimmed over his map stopping on Kalithea. "Why have you put a cross here?"

"It's marked as a place of special interest."

She gave the hint of a possible smile. "These maps are fictitious. They tell you what's in somebody's imagination." Her voice weighed heavily like a marathon university lecture. "My parents live not far from Kalithea."

"How long will you be staying with them?"

"The rest of the summer. It's our holiday together." And she moved along on the map quickly.

"See if we bump into each other, then; in our imaginations."

"If you hover around the hotel, I am bound to see you." But hers was not the casual comment one makes. She said it as if she would be observing him, from heaven.

They had been talking across the corridor and now turned to look through their respective windows. The picture had changed, with people and houses scattered more frequently on the landscape. "Why did you do that?" she asked distantly, looking away.

Her question was so disjointed, it was disconcerting. "Did what?" He was genuinely unsettled.

"You ran through the fields with your arms spread, like a bird, and then lay flat on your back, unmoving." He laughed, unnerved, and she turned to look at him sternly. "I saw you from the other side of the river."

He had not seen any river. "You ought to try it," he deflected her, getting goose pimples.

"You haven't answered my question."

"I don't like being interrogated about my secret past. Why do you want to know?"

"It is my job to dig deep, to know past secrets."

That sounded frightening. "Well, I am not your archaeological treasure yet. I'll tell you all about it some other time." The driver shouted something which meant he had reached his destination. "Might see you, then."

She just bowed as he got off, with no particular significance.

Kalithea did not turn out to be an exalted place. If there had been glory here once, the shops and the houses had trampled and overgrown it. They must have been bricked and plastered quickly while he travelled from Thessaloniki. A short distance away some steps led down the cliff to the beach which contoured the whole peninsula. This was the one redeeming feature of Kalithea. An endless beach, gold, stretching all the way to the cape and round it.

It was there that *Alexander Palace* hotel had hid. Big, modern and out of place, it lay behind thickets of poplars, palm trees, willows, rhododendrons.

Two girls were selling watercolours on the pavement in the bustling street and he stopped to take a casual look. "Pictures of Germany?" he ventured to say something.

One of them looked up and smiled diffidently. "No. Denmark."

He nodded. "It's a good way to see the world while earning some money. If you are an artist. Where else have you been?"

"We're doing a tour of Greece. First Macedonia; then the Peloponese."

"Business must be good."

"Yesterday we sold two. We need to sell two a day."

"Come to dinner with me. Both of you."

"Where?"

"Anywhere. We'll meet here when you close shop. I'll come and see you."

"O.K.."

They sat across him at the taverna of *Alexander Palace,* next to the beach. The waiter came and tucked the table-cloth under the elastic. "Carnations for the ladies!" He plucked two from a nearby flower-pot and scattered them on the table. "What's your names ladies?"

"I'm Tine and this is Marie."

He then twirled to the music once and banged the cruet and the serviettes at their precise place.

"I have been told to look after you, real special."

"What does that mean?" Tine teased him.

He cried "*Opa*," and repeated his dance step. A thousand smells of roasting meats and herbed delicacies accompanied him.

Then dancers in folk dress shepherded all of them to view the foods on display. Wine was thrust into their hands by a costumed Dionysus.

Tine and Marie were completely transformed under the influence of *retsina* and Greek waiters. It was a job to keep them seated. They tied the serviettes round their heads to mimic the dancers' costumes and Tine removed the cloth from the next table and draped it round her bottom.

"Here is to Zorba," she cried.

"Who is Zorba?" Marie scowled at her. "What has he got to do with this?"

But Tine was dancing on her chair and did not care to expound.

It was not nine yet, when they all felt overfilled and worn out. They tried to leave the unstopping revelry, unseen, and to walk barefoot along the beach. But the waiter chased after them. He thrust a bottle of wine at them. "Here, take it. Compliments of the *Alexander Palace*."

"Are you sure?"

"Take it. I was ordered you take it."

"Who by?"

"Someone high. Don't ask." And he stared strangely at James.

"All right. Thank you very much."

"I'm getting married; tomorrow." There was all the heat of the mediterranean sun on his brow. "Will you come?"

They were taken aback. "Congratulations. Where is the wedding?"

"You know the church? Small church, on road from Kalithea? But come home first. By the sea, on the other side, over there. You'll see other people and lots of cars. Can't miss it."

"Great," Tine jumped. "We'll be there."

"Thank you," and he fled, kicking ecstatic heelfuls of sand after him.

"What shall we do with this, folks?" Tine raised the bottle high, then tried to suck the cork off suggestively. "I fancied that Greek waiter. You don't think he's really getting married?"

"Tine, how can you?" Marie always supplied the considered aspect to each occasion. "You should be ashamed."

"Imagine having his kids," Tine persisted. "Lots of dark hair, big brown eyes."

"Yes, hairy chests, moustaches."

"I'll keep that bottle safe while you two fight it out," James announced.

"No, no," they both stood in front of him. "Sorry," Tine said and leaned forward knocking him down and snatching the bottle back. "Now, you stay there and we'll open it for you." She pinned her knees to his shoulders. "Open your mouth and wait." And she sat down on his face.

He struggled away from Tine's crotch regretting he ever met them. The quicker they got rid of that wine, the better for him. In the tussle, the bottle broke and frothed on the beach with relief. The sand felt warm and they crouched together in the dark babbling inconsequentially.

For James Cromwell, this was the most brainless company he had had for years, and time passed by slowly. All went quiet at the taverna behind them later, but more crowd noise came from elsewhere. His mind drifted to other things. Must find that strange girl he had met on the coach, who knew everything. She would prophesy, maybe, what would be the end of this voyage, and of his desert island incarnation.

****

14th AUGUST   HALKIDIKI

The waiter's wedding day arrived with James Cromwell waking late. He went over to the Danes' bedroom and found the door ajar letting the breeze in. He pushed and the curtains blew through the window opposite. And he stepped in. The sight of them together naked in each other's arms amused him. They had missed breakfast by now, so he might as well let them sleep on.

He closed the door behind him and sat on a chair to watch them. What had come over him to end up spending last night with them? There was something erotic about two brainless fun-loving nymphs with vacant faces, and it was getting to him all over again. Love's musky perfume, the picture of liquid lithe flesh. Take Tine's features, a sort of unpolished beauty, just before ripening to the core. Beauty had always come with innocence and callowness. Not with experience or knowledge. Once, in the distant past, he had had personal experience of the stigma. Now that had changed. His face had become more care-worn and rugged.

Tine bore an uncanny resemblance to the small blonde who had stolen his youthfulness. She used to pass across his open window at college, hair flowing, setting his virgin spirits aflame. He smiled now but it was not funny at the time. On the third encounter they had seduced each other to his bed, putting him out of action for two days. Ah, he remembered it well. Almost. Time was flying inexorably.

Tine opened her eyes first and told him to come and have a lie-in between them. Marie flopped on top of her, oblivious to everything. Dawn on the battlefield. Time to get up and count the dead and the wounded.

For one mad moment he wondered what it might be like waking up with each of them every single morning. Why did he automatically exclude them from eligibility? This was humanity - short-sighted, trifling, ephemeral. Nothing greater drove the hordes of Macedonian youths to descend from the distant mountains onto the fertile shores of Halkidiki. Here they sought, not knowledge, nor happiness, but the flesh of a girl and a few minutes of ecstasy in her vagina. The concrete sensation triumphing over abstraction and philosophy. Flesh over the mind.

As the wedding approached, the girls began to take it more seriously. Tine insisted she would turn up naked and wrap herself round the groom like a cherub. Marie snubbed her and searched for something respectable, like a jeans shirt. They had a fight and stormed out together to some boutique.

Back in his room, he sat alone and waited. A soft breeze came through the window and the curtains heaved a little. 'Have a lie-in between them,' indeed. Suddenly he laughed. This girl was crazy. Maddening in her whirlwind mind, a month ago he would have consumed her in an inferno of lust. Mentally now, he pushed her onto a table-cloth but it was just memories from last night. Memories of a bubbling bottle, her soft pink lips on its cork, her golden locks flowering to a parting in front of his mouth and nose. The breeze then died signalling a hot day ahead. Nothing else moved and the silence was only tempered by distant holiday-makers.

"Now, what did he say about that bloody church?" Tine burst in noisily. She slammed the door to his bathroom and continued talking incomprehensibly, then re-emerged, sedated, in blouse, shorts and sunglasses. "James, hurry up," she shouted.

And so the three of them set off under the blazing sun for the short stroll to the groom's house, and when they got there he came out to meet them. The gathering relatives crowded under a palm tree. "Good morning, good morning," they all chorused and stood up hospitably to give their seats to the foreigners. Three cool lemonades were ordered forthwith. Two men came out with instruments, and spirits rose. "Wine! Champagne!" the groom shouted, and several children scattered. The place bustled like a carnival.

Only a priest, sitting back, had remained tranquil through the chaos. His face serene, haloed by his hair and beard, all in black, he smiled at the proceedings.

Mid-afternoon and the procession formed behind a horse and carriage, and an old open *Chevrolet*. James and the girls were put in a taxi which marked the occasion by winding all windows down. Tine was uncharacteristically quiet, subdued by the stifling hospitality. He held both their hands on the back seat, to keep them behaved. The cortege proceeded forward as the whole town joined in, new converts by the minute. Cars lined up the arterial road, until the *Chevrolet* veered off and everything halted.

The church was so tiny it seemed hardly able to hold the wedding couple. They saw it, almost by accident, hemmed in by an olive grove, dwarfed and uncannily pretty, its tiny Byzantine dome no taller than the willows round it. And nearby a campanile, freshly whitewashed, each roof-tile a sparkling red, its door varnished.

The groom got out and started distributing button-holes. White gardenias scented the peninsula of Halkidiki. Two each for the foreigners. They shoved him into the church before he squandered everything. The man had been on cloud nine since last night.

Next, the bride, coy and self-conscious, as customary. The most elaborate, dazzling white train was lifted by small girls in folk costumes. Because of the crowds, she had to stop and put up with countless blessings and kisses from well-wishers along the route. Tine and Marie ignored conventions and thrust themselves forward and through the church door.

As the Byzantine doxology rose, James climbed a stone fence to look inside. The ground sloped downwards from there and the flood of worshippers sprawled below him and away towards the entrance. The heat was too much and some of them scattered about. Others stayed in clusters and talked quietly.

Then a lone figure in black satin approached towards him. She cut a bee-line for the church, stopped and looked round her.

He stepped down and she pushed forward into the sanctuary of the church. He reached the door but the cool air and the dimness shrouded her. Closer and closer now, although he had lost sight of her.

Then suddenly she confronted him with that unnerving look of hers and slipped a few paces towards the altar. One or two recognized her and made room, courteously.

In the dimmest part of the church, in front of her, the priest conducted the ceremony. He raised his voice and everyone went forward to circle the couple. Two crowns were swapped repeatedly over them. A bevy of old grandmothers chanted and danced round the bride. She bowed reverently, her whiteness softened in the half light. In this simple world, everyone would know that this girl wore her white by right.

He wandered out, back to the street, and waited for the ceremony to finish. Then the bells rang and joyful cries lifted from the crowd. The bride and groom emerged from the crypt into daylight. Cars hooted and clouds of jubilant dust rose as they started.

Tine and Marie came up last, smiling. "What do we do now, James?"

"I'll catch up with you in a few minutes."

"We'll be at the *'Captain Nemos'*. What drink would you like?"

He pushed slowly against the crowd, towards the church, deserted now. Big flowering rhododendrons covered what little view remained of it. Across the large open yard, through the olives. Nobody. Inside, the candles flickered by themselves in clouds of frankincense. And in the middle a prostrate figure, praying, her black dress spread in nuptial rituals of another kind.

He stayed a moment to watch, unseen, her dark mystery enthralling him. Then he turned and tip-toed out.

With the wedding crowds and his two companions gone, this was a great opportunity to snatch some peace and quiet. He let the afternoon drift on his own, but could not stop thinking how unreal everything that happened in Halkidiki.

In the evening, he went to the *'Captain Nemos.'* Tine sneaked up and pounced on him. "Got you," she growled then slammed her bottom onto a bar-stool. "Why didn't you come in to see the ceremony? It was great." They had consumed some cocktails between them and were a little merry.

"I can't find my own god in there, Tine."

"How many different gods are there?"

"More than dreamt of in your philosophy."

"Phil who? What are you talking about?"

There was no point in explaining. "I saw somebody outside and got distracted."

"Man or woman?" she interrogated him.

"None of your business."

She eyed him viciously. "You are not gay, are you? Are you? Are you gay?"

"None of your business."

"Nothing wrong with being gay. Is there, Marie?" She chuckled once. "Just wanted to know, that's all. Where is your boyfriend then, James? Why did you come here on your own?"

There was an ugly vein to her questioning. He glared at her.

"Sorry. Just a joke. O.K.?" and she stormed out.

"Ignore her," Marie calmed things again. "She does not mean it, she's just frustrated. There is a barman over there who makes exactly the *sangria* she likes. I think she fancies him."

Tine returned with drink in hand as if nothing had happened. "He's taking me out," she announced. "Tonight. I think he's the cutest man alive."

They reached the wedding house where all doors and windows had been flung open and light poured out onto the beach. Silhouettes moved carrying food and drink, musicians circulating among them. Wine and champagne were freely distributed; and the music hastened to keep pace. Suddenly a rag-curtain parted and trays of roast meat came out to feed the thousands. More trays, with bread and whole tomatoes. It was such a warm, mellow night. The groom saw them and threw his arms round them. He ordered more food and wine for his foreigners. The music drowned him out.

"My first Greek wedding," Tine exclaimed when the groom had left. "Wouldn't have missed it for anything. That poor bride. She can get screwed now, at last. About time."

"Tine! Shut up!" Marie gasped in shock, but could not help laughing. "It's not all about sex, stupid."

"Do you think that barman would marry me?" Tine took a very long sip from his *sangria* with no sign of feeling censured. "He wouldn't mind, would he? He's been around."

"No man will ever marry you," Marie crushed her. "You couldn't sit still for five minutes, let alone settle for life."

"I will settle," Tine said. "What's wrong with trying a few drinks before deciding? That bride has never lived, and now she'll be a slave to him for the rest of her life."

"No, no," Marie felt guilty by proxy for her outrageous partner. "Don't talk like that. She's happy."

They fell to silence because the object of their discussion had re-emerged from the house, having changed from bridal gear to a normal dress, a few decades out of fashion but colourful and respectable. Her first excursion into the status of a married woman. She had risen now, and could command some respect, a gulf separating her from the previous day. Her words would count as more knowing to the younger girls when the night was out. Everyone wanted to talk to her already, and she relished it, and gave back generously from a good heart that never knew upmanship or pretention, or any guile.

"And she's got love, I envy her that," Marie added in a lower voice.

Tine went and stood a few paces apart, seemingly to be alone, and watched the bride from the darkness like a ghost, bleary-eyed.

"Tine, what's the matter?"

No answer.

"Are you all right?"

"I've got to go," she told Marie. "Are you coming?"

170

She had little choice. "We'll catch up with you later, James," and they made off hurriedly.

That night, he lay in bed under the open window and counted stars to get sleepy. The noise, the rhythm, the celebrations still reverberated inside him. He thought of that praying figure, prostrate in the dimness like a bride in black. Must find her soon. Has to be tomorrow. Before she metamorphosed again and he lost her.

****

15th AUGUST   THE AEGEAN SEA

It was the noise that woke him early this morning. First the cleaning maids, then thuds from next door. Finally he heard shouting and screaming in the corridor.

He went to see and found three men tearing another to pieces. More screams from a woman and some hotel staff ran about madly, too scared to intervene. And when the slaughter had finished, the executioners pushed past them and fled.

People gathered round the victim, out of macabre curiosity as there was nothing they could do. And by then two policemen came and James Cromwell withdrew.

It was to prove a short-lived uninvolvement. For the next hour, messages pursued him from his room to the breakfast table and back again. They came in written form, asking him to call reception as soon as possible. Finally a grim-looking manager came to escort him to the proprietor, in person.

Mr Koudos rose from his seat and shook hands across the desk. "I believe you were the first to see it, Mr Cromwell. I want to put myself in your confidence and ask for discretion."

"How do you mean?"

"The woman had taken three strangers to her bed. Her husband had gone off with somebody else. He came back in the morning, drunk, and started the fighting." Then came the point. "I don't want it known abroad that this murder happened in my hotel."

"Aren't the police involved already?"

"The police will do their duty."

"I see."

"I knew I could rely on an English gentleman. Once I lived in London myself."

"Rely for what, Mr Koudos?"

"All the circumstances, the grim details that you witnessed, can give a bad image in the international press."

"You thought I was a journalist?"

"I'm told you travel alone to study the local area. I did not know what to think."

"Well, I am not here to study anything, but I can't promise silence, let alone lying, if journalists come to me."

"I'll offer you some hospitality, if I may. I want to..."

"That won't be necessary..."

"No, hear me out. My wife is leaving for Crete this evening. With my daughter and a manager. He is in charge of my other hotel. Go with them and stay as long as you please. Be my guest. Crete is beautiful, and the hotel at Ellinika one of the best in the world."

"I'm afraid I couldn't. I am intending to visit Athos tomorrow."

Koudos gave a frustrated chortle. "I want you to think about it. It would be a pleasure for me to treat you as my guest, and a real pleasure for the ladies to sail in your good company."

"And if I did accept, it would not be to keep me silent."

"It would make it easier for you to avoid undesirable consequences for yourself."

That sounded like a threat. "I will let you know as soon as I can."

"The yacht is leaving at eight. Come to lunch first." He stood up and opened the door. "I'll be waiting for you."

So this was to be the bloody ending of his Macedonian reign: exile to the antipodes of Greece. He would be sailing with Mrs Koudos and company, in the lap of luxury and some mysterious girl.

The prospect intrigued him. How tall might Miss Koudos be? As short and stocky as her father? Perhaps the mother had compensated. It seemed strange that Koudos should trust a stranger on his boat with the female members of his family, but not to keep silent about the murder. Obviously, business came first. Or perhaps the daughter was unmarriageable; Greeks were notorious matchmakers. The thought of being trapped with unattractive company for such a long journey frightened him.

In the event all speculation proved irrelevant for he had met Miss Koudos before. It now seemed fated that he had sat next to her on the coach two days earlier, and seen her praying after the wedding in church. Perhaps the forthcoming journey with her across the Aegean had been predestined as well.

Seeing her now in her father's office, she showed no inkling of surprise, just confronted him with that inscrutable look of hers.

"I am sorry," he greeted her. "Your father has tricked me into this. I hope you don't mind having me."

She nodded, serious as always. "I think you'll like the yacht."

"Will you be coming to lunch with your father and me?"

She put that familiar hand to her chin to suggest scepticism. It was as if she shrouded her every move in enigma, while examining openly everybody else. "Father had to leave for Thessaloniki and I'm holding the office for him. Can we skip lunch and just have dinner?"

"As you please."

"I'll be on the yacht from seven."

"You haven't told me your name."

"Catherine."

"You know mine already. I have been your unwitting customer for the last two days."

"Yes." Her look indicated that she had business to do and he felt obliged to leave. As the door opened he knew his measure was being taken, if not dissected. This girl had the eyes of a black leopard.

He arrived at the quay on time and Catherine greeted him. Then mother appeared in a panic and introduced herself in his direction while shouting orders at the crew. Just as he had guessed. A tall, thin woman with long legs and a peculiar elegance. But neither parent accounted for the daughter's looks.

A speed-boat came to take them offshore to the yacht.

"Welcome on board," the captain saluted him with a thunderous voice and a huge grin. His hand shook him to the soles of his shoes. One foot on board and he felt totally at ease.

A uniformed boy showed him to his cabin and then disappeared and was never seen again. Strange how anyone could disappear on a boat but right now everyone had. As they sailed, at dusk, there was nobody anywhere to be seen.

He stumbled upon Catherine in the bar and she served him her own mix. "What do you think?"

"It's good." He contrasted her evening dress to his first impression of her. "I thought you were going to spend the summer in Halkidiki."

"Well, stop thinking. No thinking, please, on this trip."

He swallowed the rest of her brew in one go. "All right. What do we do instead?"

"Anything that doesn't require the use of brains. I left mine at the university and won't be needing them till I return."

"Nothing else for you to study all summer except me."

She never acknowledged any humour. "I like to dig very deep."

"Are you suggesting I'm a suitable subject for archaeology?" he retaliated with more facetiousness.

"Just interesting."

The yacht picked up speed quickly and land floated distantly through a porthole. Any chance of visiting Athos was drifting away from him.

Dinner on board the *Nausicaa* was a party for six. Mrs Koudos and the captain sat at opposite ends, the hotel manager and his wife either side, and Catherine facing James.

"Captain Stathis, Vicky and Nikos." So much for the introductions. "Pour me some wine, Nikos. I'll toss that waiter overboard. He's never here when I need him." That was Mrs Koudos, naturally.

The waiter came with a big dish, to which the captain and Nikos clapped and cheered. "Over here!"

Vicky slapped their hands. "Women first." The dish was offered to Catherine. "Make sure you serve Nikos last."

"Well said, *agape mou*. Carry on. I'll eat everything that's left."

Mrs Koudos remained aloof from the frivolity, without discouraging it. "Nikos, have you got your guitar?" she asked, as if used to all this.

"Yes!" he thundered. "Waiter! The guitar, immediately."

"Not now, you idiot."

"Why not? I'll be drunk in a minute."

"Nikos!" Catherine delivered her first public warning. "We have to show Mr Cromwell, here... some manners, please."

"No, I don't mind," James protested for fear of seeming snobbish. "I love a good dinner party; and I want to see the real Greece."

"Real Greece?" Nikos went even louder. "Mr Cromwell, you are not in Greece right now. Real Greece is bankrupt. People are starving in the streets. The government cuts the electricity, then the taxman takes their house from them."

"Shut up, Nikos. No politics at the dinner table."

"But this isn't politics," he persisted. "A little bit economics, maybe. I get tax bills every day. There is nothing else I have to give. Next time the bailiff knocks, I will open the door completely naked and say, 'Here, that's all I've got; take me.'"

Vicky winced at the image. "You've got nothing there either. And you are exaggerating. Not everyone is as destitute as you. And stop shouting. Catherine was right. Tell James about the real Greece."

"Catherine will teach you," he feigned sobriety, softly, to a great roar from the captain.

"Play something jolly to cheer us up. Not one of your dirges," Mrs Koudos broke up the argument.

"He always dirges," Vicky ganged up against her husband.

The captain slapped Nikos's back, heartily, to which the latter feigned a dislocated shoulder. "That's it. Finished. Waiter, cancel the guitar. More wine, immediately."

They passed the distant lights of some island at midnight. Nikos had drifted back to his dirges and Vicky nudged him to stop. Mrs Koudos went to bed for reading and the captain sat in the cockpit to light a cigarette.

Catherine lay her head back, her eyes closed. James poured a gin and tonic and stood on the other side of the deck.

"James, sit down, you are bothering me."

He went over and stared down at her. "Look here, Miss Koudos..."

"Don't call me that."

Another enigma. "Catherine?"

"That's better."

"Don't like formality."

"Don't like the name," she whispered quickly and looked away.

He pulled up a chair closer, sipped some gin and said nothing.

"They are not my real parents, you know that," she had to say eventually. Another minute went by. "We get on all right." His silence was forcing her hand. "They couldn't have any children. I was a substitute." The engines throbbed reassuringly. "They love me, you know. I can have all I want. They spoil me. They irritate me."

"What would you rather they did?"

"I'd like to pay my own rent, sell newspapers in the street, if necessary. Just be myself."

"They do not let you be yourself?"

She looked annoyed by his questioning. "Don't know. You lose your bearings with all this luxury. What is the real me?"

"Don't despise money, Catherine. Life can be very cruel without it."

"I despise nothing; except myself."

He reached over and held her hand. "You are a formidable woman. I think you'll get what you want eventually."

She listened unstirring, then looked at him. "Can I trust you to be honest?"

He nodded.

"Don't I look like either of them?"

"I don't think you do. Are you not related in the least?"

"No. They were friends of my father's. He is dead now. I have a vague recollection of him."

"And your mother?"

"I can't remember. It's terrible being adopted."

He glanced at the cockpit where the captain sat alone, smoking. More lights drifted in the distance, disappearing. "They've tried to make it up to you."

"It's all right for you to talk. The great wanderer. No chains to shake off."

"You are making a false comparison. You are not chained to these people, and my wandering does not mean that I am free. It's not as good as it seems. There's no time for roots to grow. Just long lonely gaps in between."

"I'm sure you compensate for those when you can." She looked at him pointedly.

He guessed she had seen him frolic with Tine and Marie, and had sent the bottle of wine to them the other night. "It depends what you mean. You say 'wandering;' maybe I'm looking for something better. But there must be purpose to freedom. It cannot be meaningless."

"And what is it you are looking for? I get the impression you do not need anybody."

"I do not know exactly what I need. I called it 'looking for something better.' Something permanent. Didn't you envy the simplicity of that couple yesterday? I saw you at the wedding. Just a poor waiter and his village bride. But they do know exactly how they stand every single step of the way. Such absolute certainty."

"I've known the bride my whole life. I could not be like her."

"Naturally. You are more complex. And you have been educated. But what a price to pay, yes? A life of floating on unsteady ships, not knowing where you land next. I speak from personal experience."

"Me too. Personal experience is such pain."

"You and I think we can be like God, knowing good and evil. While that girl, well, not even a hint of guile in her. I'd never seen such goodness, such purity."

"I told you, I do know her. She will die happy one day, but hardly ever set foot outside her kitchen and her village. You don't envy that, surely?"

"She does not want to change the world. She's happy. Why disturb God's universe? She likes it as he made it, with solid ground under her feet and just enough food on the table."

"I have a mind to feed, also."

He left a long gap of time. "Am I right to think she had never slept with anyone before her wedding?"

Catherine look startled. "Who, the bride? Yes, absolutely."

"You know her that well?"

"Everyone would know. They live very close to each other, those village people. A small world. In cities it's different."

His mind went back to Katia, but he would not mention her. "Do the actual traditions change when you get to big cities, or just for the educated?"

She came the nearest he had seen her to laughing. "Educated!"

"I mean, for example, did your mind broaden while still living in Halkidiki, or when you went to university?"

She turned round sharply and fixed her eyes on him. "Are you being personal, Mr Cromwell?"

"Oh, no. We are discussing Greek customs, and you said the difference between villages and cities. Is it just the size of the place, or do ideas change from here to there?"

She continued staring at him. "I don't care, if you ask me." There was a split-second hesitation. "Twice, if you must know. Same man. I loathed myself for doing it. Didn't like him to start with." Her eyes darkened. "It was like surgery. You know, precision timing. With half his clothes on. Just lay there, never touched anything. Then in it comes and out it goes. An endoscope."

"Why the second time?"

"I thought I must have missed something. Done it all wrong." And she let her skirt blow carelessly.

And that was that, no more information offered nor anticipated. The boat moved on, the sea-swell rose and fell, while the engines throbbed relentlessly. Nothing except the waters of the Aegean gushing deep below them.

Yet this revelation seemed to have soothed her, or some suppressed monster inside her. Her body relaxed, her eyelids drooped, her voice softened. "You know, it was I who told father to get you?"

"Yes, it all fits."

"You don't mind?"

"Not now. Not anymore."

At dawn they docked at Naxos for fuel. Breakfast on board the *Nausicaa* was over a white table-cloth, very different from the taverna in Halkidiki. Mrs Koudos spoke little and did not eat. Nikos and Vicky cooed softly over a hot pot of tea; Catherine drank a full litre and ate half the supplies on the ship.

Then she turned to James and kissed him, in view of everyone, on the lips. "I think you'll find Crete has a surprise for you."

****

16th AUGUST — — — — — — CRETE

They reached Ellinika in the evening after twelve hours of cruising relentlessly in the heat. From breakfast to Crete it had been a long, long journey. And now it was dark again. Mrs Koudos pronounced that they must look presentable before entering the hotel. Catherine took him through a back door, up to her own suite and to the bathroom. And by the time he came out, she had made sure there was nothing for him to wear except a Cretan folk costume, its baffling components spread on the floor.

"What is this?"

She gave him a sacrastic look. "It's a business suit. What do you think it is?"

"Of course." He hit back with more sarcasm. "Just the sort of suit I wanted."

"You won't find this in London. They have no taste in clothes."

"And just who is going to see me wearing it?"

"Come on. Do it for fun." She helped him with it. "It's your passport to maleness and comradeship in Crete."

"This is ridiculous. Can't I appear as simple James Cromwell, my humble self?"

"Your self is too humble, James."

"Do people actually wear such things in Crete? They must live in the middle ages."

"I wouldn't repeat this outside these four walls or you might have to defend yourself. A frightening prospect."

"You haven't answered me."

"Only on national holidays and celebrations. But do be careful what you say. Cretans are easily roused to passion - a proud people. When it comes to honour, each man is a law to himself. Even the courts show sympathy to murders of honour."

"Barbarians. Will I be challenged to a duel?"

"Yes. Tonight I shall be choosing a husband and he who survives to the end, wins."

"Not much of a choice, really."

"It suits me."

He put on the buggy breeches, a flowing pleated garment, huge. The black shirt, also ample, crossed his chest twice with an inside and an outside row of buttons running diagonally across. A red band tied his waist, gripping top and bottom together, its colour the mark of war. And there the knife was tucked, its blade bare, the white handle protruding casually.

"Is this legal?"

"Depends how you use it. Don't kill unless you are crossed." She fastened his black head-band. "There. You are a man's man now. You could walk into any place and your fellows will be proud to welcome you, ask you where your village lies, whose daughter your father married. Men will invite you to their houses and lay a meal for you. They will offer you gifts before you go, and walk to the edge of the village with you. Being male is a great privilege here. Treasure it; you'll feel sexless when you get back home."

"How can you stomach such brutal chauvinism?"

"It feeds my fantasies."

Ever since arriving in Macedonia, he seemed to be stumbling from feast to feast, but this one was different. Three hundred guests had been gathered and a folk band played, dressed like himself. Fasting in celebration of the Blessed Virgin had finished yesterday and people intended to make up for it. The most extraordinary scents wafted from the kitchen.

Things run informally, however. He joined Mrs Koudos's table who had sat there drinking with the captain alone. They talked in Greek while he listened to the band and watched the colourful crowd round him. It was noisy, boisterous and spirited. This could easily have been the wedding banquet of some king in Knossos four thousand years ago.

Catherine made an entrance with a costume to match his - a black shirt heavily embroidered, her skirt a mixture of red and gold.

"In that costume, I would fight a thousand men for you."

"Good. You might have to."

He poured some *raki,* pure and clear, like one hundred per cent alcohol, and pushed it towards her. "What is the big occasion?"

"I don't know and I don't care. Personally I'm celebrating my return to the land of the Minotaur."

"Can't say I know him personally."

"You will, if you are not careful."

The rule seemed to be that there should be four times more food on the table than was possible to eat, of more varieties than could be tasted. People escaped to the dance-floor, men women and children, in a large circle. Everyone danced the different complex rhythms from age zero. Catherine dragged him to the floor, broke into the revellers and proceeded to show him up as best she could. He felt his breeches about to fall to his ankles, tying his legs in a knot.

The tempo changed and people fanned out to fill the platform. A large Cretan seized his chance and snatched Catherine to partner him at the front. The crowd cheered him with every leap in the air and punctuated every other beat with applause. It was a dazzling exhibition, as much from the audience, as anything. And all the while, not even a ripple of expression, but furrowed fury on his face and total inscrutability from her.

Then it was over and Catherine made to return but the Cretan held her hand forcefully and James intervened.

In a flash, a knife shone in the air and his black eyes burned angrily. The dance-floor cleared and people watched.

James stood still. The Cretan moved in provocatively. They faced each other squarely in stalemate. It was to be the longest few seconds ever, before a crowd of men came over and stood between them. James took Catherine's hand and walked back to the table.

"I think we'd better go," she told him.

"I can't see why."

"I would have got away eventually. You've insulted him."

"I am sorry, I had to stop him. I would do the same again."

"Let's go for a drive. I'll call a taxi. The car would be recognized easily."

"What is this, all-out war?"

"It will blow over in the morning. Follow me, we've got to change first."

In the back seat of a taxi, she put both arms round him. "You'll be the talk of the town tomorrow." She took a fresh look at him. "Men here get jealous of strangers. They see me as a local girl and there are several local suitors. But you were brave and they respected you. The way you stood without drawing your knife. That caused a stir. They'll place you very high. A hero."

"You mean I've made a fool of myself."

"He wouldn't have dared touch you. You intimidated him."

"Sarcasm."

"You'll see."

They stopped about an hour later near a cliff and let the driver leave. Nothing but darkness, the sea, the sound of breakers coming in.

"This is the end of the earth for you and me, right here. There is nothing further south, you know. Africa, Egypt, different worlds altogether. And a huge gap from us to them."

"Come on." He held her and led her down searching for footholds. As they got lower the roar of the waves got louder. Clouds of sea-spray filled the air, and white foam dotted the ocean. They sat on a step and gazed at it. "Wild," he said. "This is as wild as it gets."

"You like Crete now, do you?"

"I can see where the Cretan character comes from. It's this landscape. Place and people, both part of the same thing. They have a compelling beauty, these people," he murmured. "I remember his eyes now, hating me. They were passionate and beautiful. The power of brute strength over pointless etiquette. Captivating."

"You weren't supposed to fall in love with him."

"I see his point of view. The beauty and ugliness of it. Each blurring into the other. Honour and pride. Splendour and savagery both."

She kissed him. "You are not English. Not anymore." They listened to the waves pounding. Each drew a different echo from the shallow cave underneath. One near, the other distant, like spirit voices in the wind. She was like a siren calling him to stop his journeying and never leave. Deep black waters surrounded them, a dark horizon, her voice casting a spell on him.

Time to get on the road and hitch a lift. The driver looked at them and offered sympathy. Yes, he knew what it was like. Being lovers and destitute. Having to fuck on the pebbles and getting your arse all bruised. Catherine held a straight face and kept translating.

In the early hours, back at the hotel, they sat looking over a different coast. It was the darkest possible night, without a moon. There was a thick volume of hand-written pages on the table in front of her.

"Do you see that reflection on the sea?" she pointed. "I have spent most of the summer under those waters." She touched the dossier. "For this."

"What is it?"

"My thesis. I am doing research on the Late Minoan Stage."

"What do you do underwater?"

"I study the ruins of ancient Olous. It sunk in a subsidence over there. Two thousand years B.C." She looked at him briefly. "There's an underwater cave - and a storage room," she added casually. "I was the first to discover it." She looked again. "No one else knows it. A fisherman took me there and we both swore secrecy."

"Are you betraying your oath?"

She put a hand up to silence him. "I took my aqualungs one day and went down with him. It was pitch black but the water was clear and the torches carried. Frightening. Like a tomb. We came out and planned how to open the jars and catalogue everything. This lasted a few weeks, sometimes well into the night, without anyone knowing." She sounded eerie.

"Should I be hearing this?"

"Wait, I've nearly finished..."

"But you said he..."

"He's dead!" she cried, "Listen; for heaven's sake. He went alone one day last April and never came up again. I've looked everywhere; there is no trace of him. No trace whatever. And I dare not tell anybody what we did. There must be another cave down there. I've searched and searched but can't find anything. God knows what happened to him."

"Has nobody ever asked you?"

"Never. He obviously kept the secret. Nobody knew we had been doing this. He couldn't have told his wife, even. I see her regularly and she greets me like everyone else. No suspicion."

"You ought to tell her."

She feigned horror. "Too dangerous. I could be held responsible. They have their own justice here."

"Weren't you frightened to go and search for him?"

"You get used to it. I'm going down again tomorrow. You can come too, with me."

It sounded like a dare. "Maybe."

"You won't get scared?"

"Probably."

She left her chair and lay on top of him. "Me too."

It seemed a good moment for him to yield. She had cast her net round him. "Do you think they'll ever find us?" he said.

This made her shiver but she shook her head. "Doubt it. There's a whole city under there."

Then ancient Olous fell asleep and made her caverns ready to receive them.

****

17th AUGUST   CRETE

They pushed the boat and jumped in. It was six o'clock, the break of dawn, and the sun just tinted the surface pink. Catherine steered to the open sea and deeper waters, away from the first ruins lying submerged.

"It's so calm," he breathed.

"It has to be to come here."

There was deathly silence apart from the oars splashing languidly and the slip-stream. She circled, slowly, searching. "Here we are. Do you see that patch at the bottom? It's seaweed covering a reef. Could be part of a wall, I don't know." She dropped anchor. "We'll have to swim its length before we dive below."

They checked each other's gear, picked up the torches and plunged in.

The reef stretched for a few yards, then plummeted to a sheer drop. It was as if the bottom had fallen out of the sea. Nothing but blue-black all the way. Catherine looked back to make sure he followed. Minutes later she headed vertically down.

The hole was frightening. It looked so small he wondered if anyone could get in. He saw her swallowed up inside it and he followed. The passage became wider like a cone, and it was longer than expected. For a moment he lost sight of her, then discovered that she had stopped inside a cave at the widening end. She pointed to an opening, then swam towards it. He hesitated at the solid darkness, his head pulsating.

Catherine had crossed the threshold already and beckoned him. He saw her face behind the glass, her eyes a little dilated under the pressure. Somehow his feet propelled him and he pulled through.

Here the roof was covered with barnacles and tiny fish hovering, combing for food. They had reached a cubical room with huge jars along one end, the size of a human. Catherine stopped and shone into them.

He tapped his hammer against one and it gave a muted echo. She gestured he should be delicate. It still stood in one whole piece, unbroken. Layers of dead crustaceans cemented the lid and they set about freeing it. Then it slipped and floated down: Nothing. Totally empty.

A conger-eel surfaced from under another jar and eyed them curiously. James poked his knife towards it and it snapped at the bare blade before retreating. It seemed hardly possible there was room for it there, and they decided to pursue it. James shifted the jar and Catherine pushed it. Then they sprang back.

There had been little flesh left on the skull, no eyes, the sockets hollow. Part of his diving gear was still intact, the mask enlarging his face. Small fish had got even there. They gnawed his bones leaving contemptuous tatters floating, then swam amongst them.

A chasm opened underneath, black like Erebus, and a strange current shifted the body gently. It felt as if the floor would crumble any minute and they would fall into an abyss.

James pulled her strongly towards the exit. She turned slowly. His flippers had to kick for both of them and he wondered if she was breathing. He pulled her through to the outer cave and found the narrowing vestibule. She would have to cross that by herself.

He shone his torch into her eyes to get some response. Bubbles still burst from her regulator but no movement. He had to push her.

He put her head forward and through the narrow gap, kicking desperately. Then, at the critical moment, her waist buckled and she became embedded in the tube. He pulled her back, then realized she was trying to turn. Some madness down there lured her and she had fallen for it. Suddenly her muscles tensed up and she fought him, pushing him back towards the cave, that room, and Hades.

He stuck his torch to her face, blinding her, but Catherine had lost her senses. Disorientated, she now kicked strongly towards the exit and pulled herself out - then tried to come back in.

He raised his hammer to block her, getting himself wedged in. Coming through finally, he seized her arm and pulled. She kicked too, and they broke through the surface.

He jumped on board and tore her mask off. "What the hell are you doing?" She sat down breathless. "Catherine?"

"He's dead," she whispered.

"But you knew that."

"How did he get there? With that jar on top of him?"

"Stop thinking about it."

"Somebody killed him."

"I don't think so. His gear was in place. He died suddenly."

"Somebody pushed the jar on top of him."

"No Catherine. He found some other way into that cave. Then trapped himself."

They beached the boat and unloaded. "I've never seen anything like it."

194

"Forget it," he screamed and she burst to tears.

They got back to the hotel and sat down, dazed. "Do we tell anybody?"

He buried his head in both hands, the picture still haunting him. "You can't leave him there."

"I couldn't tell his wife. She might think there was more to it. She will accuse me of killing him."

He shook his head in despair then got up and opened the French window. It was mid-morning and strong sunlight flooded into the room. In the distance the sea spread calmly, like satin over a sepulchre.

He pulled Catherine to her feet. "Let's get away somewhere. I can't stop seeing him."

She glimpsed the view outside, tentative, in case some phantom rose and came at her. Her feet staggered without purpose, then she held on to him.

In the car-park, her two-seater open top roasted already, under a tin roof. He took the wheel and screeched off. She looked alarmingly ashen, and yet there was an undercurrent of power, her eyes inwardly focused, intense. People waved at them from the roadside, but she was seeing nothing ahead of her.

Twenty minutes along the road to Heraklion, she stopped him. An old man came to greet them and called his wife in the highest of spirits to set the table immediately. They sat on a rickety construction built like a balcony and jutting over the sea.

"Fresh fish," the woman gesticulated at James, bursting with eagerness. "This morning." She pointed to the sea. She would have done anything to please them. Catherine replied with a few words in Greek.

He hoped that lunch at eleven was out of the question but negotiations ended without consulting him and the woman dashed to her kitchen forthwith.

He watched Catherine closely, still dazed by this morning's gruesome finding. It did not seem to be her behind that face anymore. Some power had taken hold of her and she was going through the motions, disjointedly, metamorphosed yet again. Subdued, she hurtled from one odd thing into another, acting strange, her eyes alert but looking inwards. It was not just a dead fisherman she had seen in that cave, but something deeper within her own self. And he was trying to shut out the same dark image that he had thought would never surface inside him.

The old man wrapped himself round Catherine, patting her on the back affectionately, while glancing polite acknowledgements to him. His wife returned with a pile of fried cuttlefish and cold beers. Her lord and master issued further orders which she rushed to execute unquestioning. More food, tomatoes, cucumbers, fries and feta cheese. Soon everything floated in olive oil and herbs and onion rings.

They left two hours later in an awkward mood. "I felt sorry for the poor woman. What was that about?" he said.

"James, this woman does not need your sympathy."

"Is this what happens all day? He sits people down and she's got to cook for them?"

"You sound ungrateful. It makes her happy to be generous. It is her reason to live."

"Why didn't he get up from his chair and do some of it?"

"There you go. You are missing the point. They loved doing it as they did."

"What a waste. Who were they, anyway?"

"She's the local match-maker and he is a church chanter; brother of the priest."

He laughed and she growled angrily at him. "Wonderful!" he exclaimed. "One stop shop. The complete service under one roof."

They took a narrow road now, through a valley, crossing the river-bed. The earth became red and dusty, the trees tall, sparsely leaved, emaciated. A sign said "Knossos Palace" as they turned off and stopped.

She walked ahead, climbing the portico, and stopped at the main entrance. Two pillars supported a roof, a half wall and a fresco. It was the picture of male youths in ceremonial loincloths transporting vases of gifts to a wedding. The scene was elaborate, beautiful, extraordinary.

"Watch this," she said and hid in the ups and downs of the ruins. "Now you see me, now..."

"Are you a ghost, Catherine?"

"Of course. Did you know that Minos, the king of Knossos, sat judge in the underworld?"

"Where are you?"

"His favourite punishment was to send you wandering back here, under the gold sun and the sky, so you could see what you had wasted when you were alive. And so his ghosts meander, invisible in the daylight, and memories of this life torture them."

"He's a cruel bastard."

"Your turn will come."

His eyes circled the area. More tourists climbed the stairway to the palace. On his left, the storehouse, with some of those same store jars. He stumbled and paused for a brief moment then took the north entry, looking for her. A door between two pillars and a deep shadow: "Catherine?"

In the deepest part of the darkness, something flickered. He thought of turning back, then lost himself among the red columns and the passage-ways. A dead end. More columns, this time black, and countless secret openings, each one a refuge and a trap. Someone trod the next vestibule.

She must be a ghost, then, if she can vanish like that, yet still follow him with eerie footsteps. Any minute now she would emerge through the stonework, transformed and reincarnated. Not for the first time today. "Catherine?"

"James!" Her voice came from further back. "What happened?" she whispered, and pulled him deeper into the shadows.

"Where did you go?"

"This way. Quiet. Keep moving."

They cut through the central court and into the open throne room. His eyes adjusted from shade to glare and back again. A Greek priest waited for them disconsolately. Catherine kneeled and he placed a fatherly hand on her. Then over to James and a handshake. He could speak a few words of his language, he told Catherine, but would not try. Instead, he smiled benevolently, saying little, his beard omniscient but untidy.

"Father, will you marry us?" she asked him aloud, in English, suddenly.

The priest rose. "Yes, of course."

"Here in the throne room?"

He bowed devoutly. "Where you want."

"Thank you."

James frowned. "What are you doing, Catherine?"

"Come on, James," she said sweetly through clenched teeth. "He is a godsend."

The priest smiled more broadly, then burst into chanting. They stood there, all three, hands joined together.

"I will translate," Catherine muttered to him. "'Do you, James Cromwell, take Catherine, to be your wedded wife; to make her fruitful with children as Zeus did Europa...'"

"He is saying nothing of the kind."

"Shut up darling. It's nearly over. 'May the gods bless us and our children - .'" But the priest had finished and started folding his stole from the chin downwards while she carried on. "That's it. You may kiss me."

There was quiet applause from a small crowd of tourists gathered behind them. They buzzed excitedly, thinking, perhaps, they'd seen some ancient ceremony. The priest laughed too and hastened off, before other, more exacting, rituals were demanded of him.

"Let's get out," she whispered grimly.

"That was no priest, Catherine. Where did you get him?"

"He comes instead of a guide. As a free gift."

He wanted to grab and shake her, and get some sense out of her.

She drove all the way back herself. They took a different route, and reached the hotel unspeaking, in half the time, before early afternoon.

A grim receptionist gazed at them and waiters leaned over the balconies. They hurried into her room, but there was to be no sanctuary.

Mrs Koudos burst in, with Nikos the manager a step behind. "Catherine, what is this?"

"What is what, mother?"

"What exactly happened in Knossos today?"

"Nothing."

"And what else besides?"

"I told you, nothing that I know of. What did you hear?"

"Catherine, are you mad? This is Crete, do you understand? You can't play this sort of joke here. Papa-Yiannis insists the marriage was binding."

There was a moment's silence, then Catherine laughed. "The fool," she cried.

"Stop it, now. This could mean disaster for your father. One scandal and it would ruin us. What explanation do you propose we give out?"

"None at all. It was all done on the spur of the moment. Not a proper marriage."

"The priest thinks differently. He says he had his robes on and spoke all the words of a proper service."

"This is absurd," James cut in. "What service are you talking about? We didn't sign anything. No witnesses, nothing."

"He says he's got witnesses. His brother the chanter and his wife."

"It's no use, James," Catherine stood up. "We'll have to consult a lawyer. Please, mother. I'd like to talk with my husband."

Mrs Koudos gasped loudly and stormed out. Nikos shut the door flamboyantly, then reopened, put his head through and winked a smile. "I wouldn't wait for the lawyers," he said. "Make the most of it now." And he slammed the door in feigned anger.

"I don't believe this place," James cried.

"It's that stupid priest. He takes himself too seriously."

"Do you think they'll make it stick? He's even got false witnesses."

"See if I care. What difference does it make?"

"Quite a bit, I think. Why did you do this, Catherine?"

"There you go again. It was good, wasn't it?" She glimpsed his expression. "James, look at me. Suppose the lawyers declare the wedding valid."

"That would be a serious problem. For you and your father."

She looked angry. "Would it, now? It takes two to get married." She stuck up two fingers to his face. "We stood there as bride and groom at a proper ceremony. You were the groom, remember?"

"Nonsense. I was sightseeing."

"I'm not entirely sure I can vouch for that. There was the priest, the chanter and his wife."

"That was no priest. He was a pagan charlatan."

"Don't worry, then. It's hypothetical. You don't have to fret; I thought you said you wanted to get married."

He gazed at her dumbfounded. Hardly knew whether to fight her head on, or let go. He put his belongings together, calmly, and sat back. "Catherine, you've gone a little too far. I think, for both our sakes, I'd better go."

"No," she cried, then brought her voice down. "Don't leave, please. It was just a joke, really."

"Everyone will know tomorrow. Better for you I wasn't here."

"Stay for the evening, at least. For the banquet."

"Not another banquet!"

"Don't leave now, James. They'll laugh at me. They'll think I have been jilted."

"I think otherwise. Get your priest to change his story before people start believing him." He stood with suitcases at the ready.

"I'm not letting go of you."

He opened the door and went down some stairs, then stopped half way to look back at her. But she was no longer there.

Two hours later, at the airport, he had been stranded already. They could not get him on to any flight. No place to go but the transit lounge and a formica bench.

He had to chance it. "Was there nothing reserved by Miss Koudos?"

They looked him up, strangely, top to bottom. One seat to Rhodes just might be possible. It would be flight OA-five-twenty at half past eight, give or take the usual margins.

He had no other option. "Yes."

Then some over-zealous official decided to check his credentials and the familiar two-seater soon roared into the car-park. Catherine strolled in and stood over him.

"I could have cancelled your ticket," she said looking down on him. "But didn't."

"Thank you Catherine."

"I thought you were a man of honour, James Cromwell. But you stormed out of my place without speaking to anyone and now you sell my name for a ticket. Is there no limit?"

"I'm sorry but I had to."

"Do you think I would have refused you a lift or helped you to get a seat, if you had asked me?"

"I know you wouldn't."

"Don't I look like a lady to you?"

"Yes, Catherine."

She sat next to him, almost in tears, and softened. "Will you write to me, at least?"

"One day, maybe. From London."

She stood up and walked off proudly, her mystical spell hanging over him like an omen.

Well, he had not seen the last of Catherine. He knew she would track him down, haunt and follow him, with no respite, for ever, Amen.

As the plane lifted, the sunset burnished the sea in the same pink twilight as this morning. They might have passed over ancient Olous, who knows. It certainly seemed very tranquil, the water that same silk, shrouding its darkness.

> *"As for your departure, when it visits you, Death will come to you out of the sea, in his gentlest guise."*

That was not such a bad thing. All mortal life must finish. The question was what would happen to him between now and then. It was worth considering.

****

18th AUGUST   RHODES

It was a balmy summer night, fanned by the eastern breeze from Asia Minor twelve miles away over the sea. He walked close to Mandraki harbour and the air felt soft, wakeful and exciting. Rhodes became a mixture of modesty and glamour after midnight, as the private yachts glittered alongside inexpensive cafes, and crowds of tourists drifted between the casino and the breakwater, munching sunflower seeds.

In a back street, sophisticated shop-windows poured shameless luxury onto the road, everything from ice-cream to fur-coats branded *Lacoste*. Designer labels had taken this town over and had become synonymous with Rhodes. This was a whole world away from elemental Greece. All the simplicity expected of an Aegean island gave way to slapdash opulence, albeit a little mediocre; there seemed to have been no buyers to take an interest in Parisian fashion accessories while the locals suffered for lack of more basic necessities. Global austerity had reached even Rhodes. And so the shop windows looked dusty, with objects toppled here and there - no effort was made to put anything right again.

Rhodes town was a patchwork of contrasts. The boutiques and galleries held centre stage in the new sector. But inside the old city walls, the flea market, moments before closing, was selling curios from as far back as the Ottomans, or from the Italian occupation before the war. He lost himself for a few moments puzzling an old pistol until the shutters came down and he moved on.

Three o'clock in the morning and people still filled the bars and restaurants, mostly Scandinavians migrating south once a year for a good thaw. Two of them bumped into him asking where the *Pink Panther* was. Time to make his excuses, go to his place, and to take stock.

He had asked for a simple bed to stay the night but all they had available was the bridal penthouse on the third floor. With a bouquet of flowers thrown in, of course.

Inside, the place glowed in semi-lit sumptuousness with a huge bed, private bar, jacuzzi and a pink telephone. Piles of cushions filled up every corner, in satin and silk. More like a padded cell should be. One could float weightlessly around it without risk of self-injury. He picked up a cushion and threw it. Missed. There was too much of everything in this prison - two bidets, two basins, two New Testaments by the headboard. The only escape was through the balcony door over the street.

He watched the passing traffic below and the waves lapping the beach beyond. Had Catherine followed him, this would have been their honeymoon. The thought of it!

Then he halted, for he had seen a blue shadow crossing the road below, glinting discreetly and vanishing at the top.

He jumped to his toes and stared. That was her *Rolls Royce*, surely. How could Elena be here? He paced the floor galvanized, back and forth. Did she have somebody with her? In the morning he would call her office in Athens to find out. Better ring her house, perhaps.

He fell on the bed as his last energy left him and feather cushions piled on top of him. Wonderful, lovely, wedding-night bliss.

They woke him with a gentle knock at day-break, and he opened the door. "Breakfast, Sir; champagne and caviar, croissants, a double profiterole." Was this compulsory? He tipped the waiter and sat there staring, still asleep. Screw your caviar. There were silver trays everywhere sprawled at his feet. Catherine would have wiped them all clean. He promised himself not to think of her.

Today he would re-trace his steps to the flea market and take a look at that pistol, just out of curiosity, again. It had had a hand-carved inscription on the handle and came complete with a pocket tin-box of ammunition. The object had fascinated him.

Up and through the old castle gates, then past the Suleyman Mosque to Sokratou Street, looking less sinister in the day. The pistol had not attracted buyers yet. He picked it up, almost gingerly, and felt it - each small detail - captivated. What a peculiar object, deceptively peaceful, beautiful, half-asleep.

"How much?"

"Ten euro."

He paid and the man box-wrapped it, discreetly, like a freak thing.

The act of buying it resolved some tension in him. He walked down this old Gothic street on the cobbled surface conscious that something had happened to him.

Just short, at the bottom, he turned for the Hospital of the Knights, now a museum, and came face to face with Elena Diamandithou. They looked at each other, speechless for a few seconds.

"Are you running away from somebody again, James Cromwell?" she spoke first.

"Yes, but I thought here, of all places, I'd be safe from you."

"Not likely. Where can we find a shade to sit? I want to interrogate you."

"I have nothing to say."

"I know; over here; in the museum."

She led him into the courtyard, and up the stairs into the Hospital vaults. The Knights had died in the Middle Ages, of course. He would be the first patient since then to be operated on and hopefully cured of whatever his malady was. Their steps echoed in this most extraordinary chamber, feet counting its huge space like a slow funereal drum-roll. Here the air had stayed cold, and light reached dimly through medieval glass windows. It was an imposing, aristocratic and deathly building, the Knights of St. John observing them from the catacombs. He slowed down to absorb as much as he could of its atmosphere, feel the tranquillity and awe it put into him. Everything about the place evoked that underwater grave - the echo, the timelessness, the semi-darkness - a floating underworld.

They came to the terrace at the other end. "We'll sit here," she pronounced. "Now tell me what happened to you since I last saw you. No-one married you yet?"

"That's debatable. Can I come back to you on this?"

"Typical of you. What is that you're carrying?"

He hesitated. "An old pistol."

"A pistol! What for?"

"Things haven't been going well lately."

"I don't like it when you make such jokes. Let me see what you've got there."

"Not now; later." He put a stop to her. "I saw your car yesterday. Who did you have with you?"

"Friends. Are you jealous?"

He fixed her with a cold stare. "Maybe."

She stared back but then yielded. "You're all right, you'll do." Then seriously. "I want to hear about your current marital status. Tell me all about it."

"You brought me up all these stairs to ask me this?"

"I brought you here for a confessional."

"Let's change the subject. Have you brought the yacht with you?"

"I've come here on business, James Cromwell, and I'm flying back to Athens this afternoon."

"Do I get to keep the *Rolls?*"

"It depends what you want to do with it. Do tell me, what fate brings you to Rhodes?"

"Does it matter? I can hardly remember myself."

"This is your interrogation, you understand." She looked at him sternly. "Why did you run away from my friend, Catherine?"

That hit him like a left hook, and yet he took it like a true Englishman, stiff-upper-lipped, without flinching. "Pardon?"

"She rang and told me what happened. And I said 'I know him. It doesn't surprise me at all.'"

"You know Catherine Koudos?"

"I ask the questions. What exactly did happen in Crete?"

"Well, if Catherine told you, you might be able to enlighten me."

"You break girls' hearts, James Cromwell. The gods will get angry with you."

"I never got on with your gods in the first place. Ever since you introduced me, they keep shipwrecking me."

"These are just warnings. Ignore at your own risk."

"I should have guessed all Greeks would conspire against me, mortal or otherwise."

"What would you have done different? Nothing," she answered the question for him. "Catherine wanted you badly. It was the first time she really fell in love with somebody. Why did you leave her like you did, alone to face the consequences? Last night she took her father's boat and wandered the seas all night until they found her this morning, exhausted, broken, half-dead."

"I can't talk any more about it. It was disastrous to get involved with her. Better to leave early than to prolong such things. It was regrettable but necessary."

"I wish I could understand you, James Cromwell. Why is it a mistake to get close to someone? You keep doing this again and again."

"You should know, Elena, better than me."

She looked away. "Have you any idea how much pain you left her in?"

He looked away himself.

"You do it deliberately; seduce women and then abandon them."

"That's not true."

"You charm them, you don't discourage them. Then suddenly you just leave."

He circled the floor once like a trapped animal in a cage. "Well, if you must know, some strange things happened in Crete."

She smiled knowingly. "Catherine is a girl of many secrets. But she's good looking, intelligent, and very, very interesting, isn't she?"

He kept watching her closely to see how much she knew.

But Elena showed nothing. She pondered, sober again. "There *is* a woman, isn't there, James?" Her head dropped a little. "That girl in Athens?"

The phrase startled him because, for one second, Katia had slipped from his mind. But he said nothing, his face hardened, lip just as stiff.

In the afternoon, Elena asked him to drop her at the airport in her *Rolls*. He then came back to his hotel in it, alone. If driving a *Rolls* made a social statement in London, it made headlines in Rhodes. Perhaps that was why it had been brought here, to clinch some shipping deal for her owner, no doubt. People felt compelled by the symbolism in a way they would not by a yacht or a house many times the car's worth. Word soon spread and he was viewed with a certain attention, welcome or otherwise he could not tell. He had to submerge beneath the surface as soon as possible, so for the moment he parked out of sight and sat in it. From one padded chamber to another. Luxury always had been both a comfort and an isolation cell. Silence; not the smallest sound could seep in. He had shut all windows - cut the world off. Three o'clock midday, and the heat peaked. Must start the air-conditioning. The *Rolls* put up sail and he set off.

In the south, at the other end of the island, he stopped for the first time. This was the village of Embonas, four thousand feet up on a mountain, and a few centuries back in time. Here the villagers still walked the streets in folk dress, women swept unmade roads and hang washing in streets. Their men-folk sat at small tables drinking coffee and playing worry beads. They all gazed back at him, mocking his sort of existence, from their straw chairs under a plane tree.

He wound a window down and let the rustle of leaves and the smell of pines replace the air-conditioning. A warm aroma from the bakery called him away from his glass cage, to taste some hot bread and drink with his two hands from the mountain spring. He smelled the wild herbs, flowers, and charcoal ovens roasting lovely meats. Ah, that he could stay here forever, bereft of meaningless adjuncts that suddenly seemed so burdensome and unnecessary.

But the *Rolls* beckoned like a desert island, floating up and forward, never stopping. Fingers amputated and sterilized cocoons. Elena's sea-gods had risen up and set their faces against him. The more he fled, the sooner they caught up with him. They simply fished him out and damped him on yet another dead reef.

He reached the Valley of the Butterflies and climbed on foot uphill; over the cliff-hanging bridges, deeper and deeper into the shady green. Trees soared and joined branches, vaulting the valley. It was like an endless avenue, and butterflies covered its every inch.

He looked up as park attendants urged the last visitors to leave. Soon there would be nobody here but these crea-tures. He lay on the carpet of brown leaves with butterflies swarming around him. Katia. What made Elena remember her? Katia had been different. Only she could fly, exuberant and unfettered, a butterfly herself. As dusk fell, she reappeared and lingered over him. Ah to be in her arms forever... That's right. That was where he should be.

"Surprises and sudden movements are not permitted in the Valley of Butterflies," the notice said. "You are welcome to admire this natural phenomenon without disturbing the peace and silence of the butterflies. Do not violate their tranquillity by causing them to fly unnecessarily, as this is very costly to them. They are nocturnal creatures and need to sleep by day. And because they do not feed, once they reach maturity, they need all their energy to complete their life cycle. Every unnecessary flutter depletes their small reserves irreversibly, until they lose all strength."

In the clear mid-summer night, he floored the accelerator, claws hanging over the precipice. Faster and faster, and the tyres screeched. There was no sense of danger or purpose in doing it. Just a thrill from the rampant madness that had seized him. The more the car groaned, the harder he pushed it. Round and round the island, stretching it to the very limit. Until he could go no further and, having come back full circle, the lights of Mandraki harbour greeted him. He slowed down, spent, and the car secluded him, like an inflated caterpillar in a cocoon, in that dream. There were no fish tavernas here, no table for two strangers who had just met in a small room over a pile of fabrics and a worn-out sewing machine.

That's right. That's right. That was where he should be.

****

19th AUGUST   NAXOS

Dawn painted the frosted glass yellow in the corridor skylight. Having parked the *Rolls*, it was time for him to get some sleep before leaving Rhodes later today. He was turning the key to his room, when he heard laughter inside. Two female voices talking animatedly. As the door opened they stared at him.

"Would you like us to make your bed, Sir?"

"I thought it was already made."

"We'll make it better," one said and they started to giggle.

He took a few ponderous steps towards them but nothing intimidated them. "Perhaps you can run the bath for me and leave quietly," he said.

"Certainly." They crossed paths with him in the hall, their eyes lowered, still giggling.

He shut the balcony door to trap some coolness in, removed the previous night's clothes and sat on the bed with a brochure.

"It's ready," they both shouted over the sound of the jacuzzi.

"All right, you can go now."

"Will there be anything else, Sir?" They were making funny noises to each other and probably could not hear him.

"Yes, there is. Can I have the London papers, please?"

"We don't know, Sir."

"Will you, please, go and find out?"

"We don't work here, Sir."

He jumped up and confronted them over the swirling jacuzzi. "Who the hell are you?"

"I'm Lina and that's Fabiana."

Something made him push her into the water and he regretted it instantly. She made sure the splash was much greater than called for, and her clothes unnecessarily soaked.

He threw a bath towel at them and slammed the bathroom door, but they both came out soon. "Would you like some English tea with your bath, Sir?" and they convulsed uncontrollably.

Then the phone rang.

"Yes?"

"James, it's Elena. I want you to do me a favour."

"Of course. What is it?"

"Go to the harbour and see if *Helena* has come in."

"Just a moment." He stepped out to the balcony. "Yes, Elena. It is here."

"Have you seen it?"

"I have."

"You'll need to sit down for this, James. I want you to bring the yacht to Piraeus."

"What?"

"Not on you own. Panos, the chauffeur, will navigate. But he takes people on board, sometimes, and I don't like it; women, you know. Just keep an eye on things."

"What about the car?"

"Leave it there. I'll be coming to Rhodes later."

Back in the bathroom the girls had disappeared under the foam. One of them raised an inquisitive toe and he fished it out. "Get out of here." This time he saw them through the front door and locked up.

Panos greeted him with the assurance of a Lieutenant Commander. The man looked as much at home in the yacht as he had done driving the *Rolls* back in Athens. Captains and chauffeurs always exuded a careless ownership over their masters' belongings.

"We sail as soon as possible." Gloriously vague. In Greek it probably meant he had no intention to move.

"I need a couple of hours," James said.

He weighed the pros and cons on the palm of his hand. "All right. We sail this evening."

"Oh, no. Noon would be fine."

"Noon!" Panos agreed with a jerky nod that could have crippled him. There was no pleasing this Englishman. He shook his middle-aged head wearily. "Noon," he repeated.

Back in his flooded jacuzzi, James pulled the plug and had a hot shower. Monday morning, time to call Maxine in London.

"Hullo, can I help you?"

"Hullo, Maxine. I miss you."

"Oh, yes. How is the shipping company?"

"I will be sailing to Athens shortly. From Rhodes."

She laughed. "Stop making up stories. When are you coming back?"

"Any problems?"

"No. Just fed up. It's busy here, you know."

"I'll make it up to you. Have you heard from Eamon?"

"I told him I gave you the message. Has nobody killed you yet?"

"Somebody tried."

"Oh, yes. Can I go now? Some of us have work to do."

"Bye, Maxine."

He packed his luggage and put it to one side. Downstairs, in the breakfast room, sleepy waiters balanced trays precariously over fingertips. "Good morning." "Good morning." He went straight past them. The car-park looked strange. No *Rolls Royce*. Surely that was where he had put it. Nobody would try and steal a car on an island, would they? Not this car?

A frantic search revealed no keys. Those girls had vanished with them. Panos must be told immediately.

But Panos had vanished also. James asked at neighbouring boats and was sent to the coffee-shop. A woman informed him that Panos had gone to see distant relatives. She wrote the name of the village down for him. "That way," she pointed to her back wall.

Incensed, he raced on a hired moped with nothing but sunglasses and shorts. The road began to climb and he had to push the useless thing uphill. It must have been twenty thousand feet high on this bloody mountain. And not a soul to see.

He found Panos sat on a door-step by the village road, sipping *Coka-Cola* majestically. "Welcome!" he thundered heartily as if to a long-lost friend.

"Panos, I was looking for you in Rhodes town."

"Yes, don't worry. We'll be sailing soon."

"Panos; the car. It's been stolen."

The man's eyes darkened. "Oh, never! When?"

"This morning."

"This morning?"

"Yes."

He laughed loudly and ostentatiously. "Don't worry, Sir James." And he slapped him on the back.

Sir James would have renounced the title immediately but Lina and Fabiana emerged from the house to interrupt the procedure and dangled the keys in front of him.

"It's them," Panos protested his innocence. "Bloody Italians, typical. They took me for a ride."

Rage turned him blind. "Tell me what happened," he demanded with assumed superiority, struggling with that upper lip.

But Panos called it no contest. He kept grinning and said, "They came out, opened the door, tried to start it and then I saw them. 'This is what you do,' I said. I just showed them."

"I'll see you in town," James Cromwell announced flatly and push-started the moped downhill.

"Are we in trouble, Sir James?" Panos mocked him. "They're coming with us, but only as far as Naxos. Please," he shouted after him, but he was out of hearing.

And so, at noon, or near enough, the yacht emerged from Mandraki harbour and out onto the open sea. The Anatolian mountains in the distance appeared more ominous today. *Helena* trod precariously between Turkey and Greece.

Panos resumed his authoritative look, proud to be captain. Lina was in frolicking mood, prancing from prow to stern, naked. She sat in the cockpit watching for possible icebergs while Fabiana made up lost sleep. The journey frittered away slowly, without peaks or lulls, at its own rhythm. Suddenly there had been nothing to do. Penthouse jacuzzis and soft cocoons seemed a whole world away, and the senses suffered monotonously in the heat. The sea had taken over while everything slept or idled, and only the engines droned sedately to it.

Somebody put the flesh of a peach to his lips but that too had lost its taste. Tantalizingly out of reach, Lina sat tempting him to yield, whisper a word, touch her. Heat was an insidious aphrodisiac. It gorged blood into the most susceptible parts, surreptitiously. He lay on his back and watched the sun get bigger and bigger until it swallowed the earth up like Charybdis. Head, brain and mind felt dead, weightless, insignificant. All he could do now was linger in limbo where voices reached distantly.

When he opened his eyes at last, a cascade of Mediterranean houses greeted him as if he knew them. This was where he had had breakfast with Miss Koudos on board her yacht three days ago. Twilight over Naxos was beautiful but undramatic. The place bobbed up and down rolling dangerously, and there were faces on the edge of the quay. Midway point on the journey to Piraeus. The island jolted and came to rest, tied by a mooring rope.

Naxos was a different world altogether. The town itself had been off-loaded on a hillside against a backdrop of mountains. He got off the boat and across the promenade into its nooks and its burrows. The place was reminiscent of Plaka, with white-washed houses, pot-gardens, the scent of geraniums and jasmine.

Up to the castle and back down the crooked lanes and cobbled streets. Small tortuous paths snaked between the houses, narrow, twisted. He came back full circle, and as he approached the *Helena* he stopped.

She must have known he would be coming for she had stood on the quay watching the yachts manoeuvring. Miss Catherine Koudos stared at him. "Hullo, James." Her voice had ridden on a sudden swirl, as if to encircle him.

"What are you doing here, Catherine?"

"I'm going back to Halkidiki. You know we always stop at Naxos for fuel."

He saw the *Nausicaa* in the harbour and recalled the journey to Crete. "I'm off to Athens," he said. "Must be careful not to miss the boat."

"Yes, one tends to do this."

He sized her wind-swept figure against the sea. "We both live dangerously, Catherine."

"What else is there for one to do?" She looked very vulnerable in the early evening, her face no longer so inscrutable.

"I think it's something in the earth here," he nodded.

THIRTY NIGHTS FOR THIRTY ISLANDS

"Naxos is a dangerous island. Women always get abandoned here, ever since my distant friend Ariadne in ancient Greece."

The mythological reference was blurry, but hints to events in Crete inescapable.

"Have you been unfaithful to me already?" she continued.

He chuckled but with displeasure. "I would consult your other friend, Elena; both you and she know everything."

"She tells me there is another. A girl in Athens, no less."

"That's partly true. There are many girls in Athens."

"I wreak revenge, Mr Cromwell." This would have sounded chilly, if he could take it seriously. "No-one escapes from me. Tell that girl of yours, I will soon find her." She was pausing for emphasis. "You've heard me."

He looked at her and it seemed comical, but nothing coming from Catherine would surprise him. "You know, my dear Catherine, you amaze me. But that's a good thing. I would have hated our brief friendship to be boring."

Captain Stathis and captain Panos now held a conference and decided to celebrate before continuing. The two boats, *Nausicaa* and *Helena*, followed each other to Apollonas which was on the north tip of Naxos and therefore a justifiable detour.

James Cromwell, already feeling responsible for letting the two Italian girls on board, now remonstrated with Panos. "We will not be back in time. How long to Piraeus from here?"

"It's not a problem. Mrs Elena knows. We always eat at that taverna; it's on our way, not a problem."

"You have arranged for the two girls to find transport afterwards, I take it."

"You don't like them?" In the absence of his mistress, he was a little impudent, but in a manner difficult to object to. "They are so pretty."

"Looks are not the issue."

"You like girls, I know." This sounded a little insulting.

"Panos, if anything goes wrong, I will take control of the boat away from you. I have been given authority."

If that threatened him, Panos did not show it. "We'll eat at Apollonas then sail to Piraeus," he reassured him. "Celebrate! Worship the god, you know?" He laughed and raised his hands heavenwards. "Apollonas!"

They booked a table at the small taverna on the pavement under Apollonas temple in the village port. "Sit down, sit down," they clamoured, which was the Greek equivalent of "Good to see you and be my guest."

The chairs did not stay empty for long. Passers-by were looked out for and everyone was invited. The captains went in and raided the kitchens of everything; eating degenerated to rape and plunder. More tables were added and voices had to stretch farther and farther. The noise became incredible.

James turned to Catherine who treated all this with indifferent familiarity. He made polite conversation. "I should have phoned Elena. We'll be late in Piraeus tonight."

"You won't get to Piraeus tonight."

"Oh, yes we will. I'm giving Panos an hour, then we set off."

"Pity. You won't see Naxos at all."

There was a scramble to clear the plates and make room on the table. "What are they all saying to each other?"

"The same things people do."

"Such as?"

"Do you want me to translate for you?"

"Briefly, yes."

"Right. 'In Cyprus meat is cheaper. And plenty of meat. Lots of meat. Pork!' 'And cheese?' 'Goat's cheese!' 'The best tomatoes and cucumbers come from Galaxidi.' You want more?"

"Sounds delicious. How far is this other galaxy from here?"

Suddenly heaps of cooked meat - huge chunks, on the bone, on skewers, in pots - arrived in quantities to match the crowds. Two Greek females, young and coquettish, found themselves in the laps of Stathis and Panos out of the blue. They put more wine to their lips, kissing them, letting their breasts to be fondled. The taverna owner emerged from a crypt dressed as Bacchus, inciting lechery and debauchery. He managed to find three musicians, live, and everyone rose from their seats. Street-dancing broke out spontaneously by the side of the road. At first, their instruments lacked practice, a little. But then a cry of hedonism went up and back came merrier tunes and more wine.

In the midst of the pandemonium James realized that Fabiana and Lina had gone missing, but when he tried to ask Panos he could not find him. He rose to look for him and Catherine gripped his wrist and tried to hold him down.

Then, as he stood up, the whole world spun with extraordinary speed and reeled from side to side. It was a curious feeling of being perfectly conscious and in control, but with his body cut off. He could not move at all.

He broke her grip, steadied himself and staggered to Apollonas harbour. Inside the *Helena*, Panos was impaling a temple prostitute, her cries just drowned by the revelling on the shore. He slammed the door, eyes blazing, but the crowds laughed and bawled incomprehensible exhortations.

The door re-opened and Panos put out his face to see what was happening. Something alarmed him and he came out naked, shouting hysterically to Catherine.

"Get in," Catherine said and pushed James forward into the boat. More roars from the drunken crowd. Panos came back and bolted the cabin door. The rioters outside had got closer and cheered louder. A light came on and there lay captain Stathis with the Italians and several more females previously smuggled on board.

They cut adrift and Naxos slipped away with the current. Far out on the benighted sea, the two yachts rendezvoused for an exchange of passengers. Stathis would take all the girls to Naxos town, leaving Sir James alone with Panos on the *Helena*.

He grabbed Panos's sleeve. "Tell me what happened!"

"They've all been drugged," he bellowed. "That Koudos girl. She put too much in."

His face darkened. "You knew?"

"We planned to stay overnight," he said sheepishly.

"Panos this is dreadful. It's unacceptable."

The captain-combined-chauffeur was not as ebullient as he had been. "We always eat there," he repeated. "I told you, the god Apollonas."

"Never mind him. You lied to me; and you went against Mrs Diamandithou. Apparently you do this often."

"Love," Panos said. "Love! Eros! *Erotas*."

"Never mind translating. Please, find some other euphemism."

That last word lost him and he was silenced. He made a gesture of resignation. "I am a man," he said with Greek contrition, "I like doing it."

James now felt secure enough in victory. He stopped responding to him and pursed his lips tightly. He watched the *Nausicaa* drift off with Catherine and all on board. The girl was unbelievable. Her plot torpedoed at the last moment, she had not got the retribution she wanted. But she had served notice. Medea was incensed and he would be hearing more from her.

****

20ᵗʰ AUGUST   ATHENS

Sunrise had a Homeric quality in Athens. The mood was not of a city waking to work, but of expectancy for something magical to happen.

A shaft of light had crept through the curtains stirring him up, his head adrift as if a great gap of time had passed by. What had really happened last night during those hours in Naxos? He had a clear picture of the revelry and the banquet, but then very little.

He pushed a shutter and peered through the window. There were noises coming from the ground floor. He put one foot in front, carefully, and went to find out.

Elena was making coffee. "Are you glad you came?" she said.

"Don't know yet. Things turn out to be eventful in Athens."

"I wanted you here for Sakis's engagement party tonight. He's rather taken to the idea of you being around."

"When did he get engaged?"

"Yesterday. That's why I had to be here. We had close families last night, young friends and his business links tonight. Small and informal. That's how they wanted it."

"I'm going out to see someone this morning but I'll be straight back."

"Someone I know?"

"My former fiance's sister. Her name is Sonia."

"Someone I don't know. I didn't even know you'd had a fiance. Why don't you ask Sonia to come this evening?"

"If you think it's a good idea."

"And don't be late for lunch. Half past one."

It was ten o'clock in a humid morning when he pressed Sonia's door-bell. She let him in, fresh from sleep and surprised. The flat was exactly as he remembered it, with Sonia reclining on the bed as if being painted, her buttocks the only threat to proportionality.

She was wriggling her naked toes and spoke to him as if from the other side of a mountain. "James, you have a sun-tan! Aren't you glad I put you under the grill for a few hours?"

"I was in pain for days afterwards."

"Serves you right for leaving so abruptly. Thanks at least for leaving a note," she added with irony. "What happened to you that night?"

He lay stretched back on the armchair and momentarily reminisced a long night stroll in Piraeus, fish restaurants and *bouzoukia*, a deep conversation and a boat trip with Katia. "Nothing."

"You look strange," she went on after some shallow reflection.

"Hm," he snorted indifferent.

She frowned with scepticism. "Who did you sleep with last night?"

"Don't know that I slept at all, if my memory serves me right."

She leaned forward. "Was it a good fuck?" she whispered slowly and emphatically.

He stretched his arms in a big yawn. "It was massive."

There was a puff of disappointment. "So much for putting 'all that' behind you. What *have* you come here to tell me?"

"I've come to see how you are. And ask you to a friend's party."

She scrutinized him. "What friend and what party?"

"Her son got engaged and you are invited."

Sonia resented this sudden diversion from cross-examining him. "She wants to look me over, does she?"

"One more question and I'm going to hit you, Sonia. I don't think there is a sinister motive, frankly."

"Does she know you nearly married my sister in London? She's bound to want to know."

"I shall explain in advance that you don't look or act like your sister. All she said was 'Ask her to come.' Will you?"

"I might. Give my congratulations in advance."

"See you later and good bye."

He got in a taxi and thought how small the world would be, if he had married Julia as then planned. Would he be journeying, right now, a shadow in a grey taxi, the great Odysseus, shipwrecked but knowing and humbled? It must be the thirtieth of August coming up that chastened him. Pre-birthday tension. He had thought he would never be thirty. Might as well treat Saki's engagement as his own party.

Katia too would be getting married soon, in five days, if they could still afford it and Greece had not sunk. Her wedding would mean confirmation, if any were needed, that he could never stroll hand-in-hand with her again. The one speck of colour in this endless greyness was about to vanish. He wished the pain was deeper so he could mourn with dignity. Anything but this perverse detachment that gripped him now.

Elena opened the door and kissed him. "What did Sonia say?"

"She's coming."

They went to the sitting room. "Good," she breathed sinking into a pile of cushions. "There will be about thirty people tonight. Which is a relief after yesterday's mayhem. I find large numbers tiring."

"Thirty can be a good number. Now, tell me all about Sakis's young lady. What is she like?"

"Very nice. I met her when I flew back. Didn't know what to expect. But she's pleasant and unassuming. And very shy. I can't believe Sakis is getting married."

"He's beating his own mother to it."

"Oh, I haven't given up, James."

"Still looking for the Edwardian gentleman?"

"I've actually met one. English, upper class and a pauper. True gentleman."

"How old is he?"

"He looks young and he has a certain style that I like."

"Hm. Time you settled down."

"Oh, yes? Look who is talking. How much longer are you going to wander the oceans, running away from your inadequacy? I suppose tomorrow you're off to another island just to look her over quickly, find her deficient and dump her."

"Yes, actually. Corfu."

"It's about the only one left, isn't it? And then what next? You'll never find what you are looking for, James."

"Perhaps. I don't know."

She looked away. "We'll have to start planning the wedding soon."

And his mind faltered between the two contrasting forthcoming nuptials.

"I think we'll have the reception on board a liner. And sink it down with people. They can take *Helena* for the honeymoon and go where they like. The more I think of it, the more thrilled I ought to be: Sakis getting married. Perhaps I feared he would follow in my footsteps. And yet, now, I hardly feel the excitement."

He focused on her elegant features, the mature, subdued expression, her Cleopatran eyes.

"Tell me," she said, suddenly decisive. "Have you ever had a premonition?"

"How do you mean?"

"That something awful is about to happen. I've felt it ever since I got back to Athens."

"It's anxiety, Elena. Put it out of your mind."

230

She shook her head. "I hope all this lasts." And she shivered.

Lunch drinks were served with olives and anchovies to stir the appetite. *'Beware of Greeks bearing food.'* They bound and force-fed you in stifling hospitality. He just picked an olive before being ordered to down stuffed aubergines and a *souvlaki*.

Afternoons in Athens passed slowly and this was meant to be his last in the city. At a time people took shelter in blacked-out bedrooms behind their French windows, this mad Englishman wanted to go out and see the sights.

Elena finished her drink in no hurry. "Do you realize we'll miss the best time for making love?"

"You stay here and make love, if you want to."

She laughed. "While you roam on your own like a stray dog in the midday sun," she rebuked his English absurdity. She had spoken as if they had been lovers all their past lives. "I'd much rather sleep and wake at five, wonderfully relaxed, to a whole new part of the day. Now, come five, I'll be stumbling into the furniture."

What was he to do with such blatant propositioning from a hostess with considerable power? "Tell me how to get to the Parthenon and you won't have to come."

"Oh, damn you."

"This is my last day in Athens and I've seen nothing but streets full of scooters and protest banners."

"You've seen Plaka."

He observed her closely, his eyes on fire. "Does that mean I've seen everything?"

She stood up angrily. "Oh, you and your Parthenon."

"It's not mine," he shouted after her.

"It's where your lover lives. Or one of them. Right over Plaka."

"Just tell me how to get there, dammit. I don't want an argument over a pile of broken marble."

"Ah, there you are," she came back. "All you see is the broken marble. Why don't you try and look a little beyond? Not with your head all the time. There, at the heart. That's where beauty lies."

"I know where she lies, Elena. Just go and get dressed now." And he watched her proceed majestically through her palace.

There was a terrible calm after this outburst. They had cleared the air as well as each other's minds. She now knew he had no sexual interest in her, and he knew he did not want the Parthenon, but to be near that street in Plaka for the last time.

She reappeared, hair tied back under a kerchief and with sunglasses. "Ready?"

He studied her. "What is the name of your Edwardian gentleman?"

"Smith."

"You are lying."

"Of course I'm lying. Didn't it make you wild?"

"Hardly."

"Liar. Who is that woman who stole your sanity? She may be sitting on the doorstep waiting for you to pass by."

The picture of Katia waiting on the doorstep was unappealing. "I'd rather we stayed clear of that particular area, thank you." But he was lying to himself now.

They reached the top of the Acropolis and looked down. The city sprawled like a sheet, spreading to the far dimness. Just a speck of green here and there, then nothing but seas of concrete. Clouds of smoke lingered over it, refracting the heat, turning the sky to slate. He tried to pierce the cloud and look through the ugliness.

They circled the Parthenon once, half-blinded in the sun, hardly seeing. There, to the south, was the coast, with Piraeus next to it, and he could see sails dotting the sea in the far distance. Beneath the other end of the hill, Plaka. His eyes searched for that well-known pattern in the streets but it looked different and unfamiliar.

It had been an ill-timed expedition and Elena not in the mood to be guide. She started the long climb down the slippery steps and to the west side. They passed the rock of Areopagus, to the foot of the hill and the first houses.

Down through the crowds of tourists to a cafe' bar which, instantly, he recognized. Disturbed, he looked round to get his bearings. He had sat at that very spot at the bottom of her street, twice, waiting for Katia to emerge. There, in the shadows, a stooped man gesticulated, his back towards them. And sitting next to him, Katia.

She turned and saw James and their gazes locked consumedly. Elena stood a step back and watched, enthralled and immobilized. Suddenly the landscape shrunk round them. James reached for Elena's hand. She followed him expectantly, transfixed by the extraordinary moment.

From speaking distance, Katia looked older, mature, at the peak of womanhood. Her eyes had changed and become knowing and sombre. She seemed infinitely more serious, her vitality bridled. And there was the trace of a mask over her extraordinary face. That innocence he had fallen in love with had vanished.

The fiance perceived the presence of the two strangers and turned slowly. He was immediately judged to be unworthy. He looked grim, unimaginative, lethargic after his lunch, his dominant facial expression overbearing. And something about him seemed familiar to James.

"This is Stavros," Katia said with admirable control over her inner upheaval.

"My friend Elena," James responded and stretched his hand.

It was as if the two gentlemen were about to remove their cloaks, walk back ten paces and fire. Just a single shot and Katia would be free, exuberant once more and unfettered.

"Pleased to meet you," Elena said formally. She too had been captivated by Katia.

"You are still in Athens?" Katia said.

"Just one more day."

She smiled. "You must like it."

He nodded vaguely. "It seems very festive at this time." It had been the most stupid thing to come out of his mouth.

So far the fiance had stayed remote, but now he murmured something in Greek and Katia replied briefly. "We come here to talk," she said finally.

And James took Elena and withdrew after a simple good-bye.

"What did he say to her?" he asked.

"I couldn't hear him. She told him she would explain."

"He wouldn't believe her."

"Probably not. Her voice had trembled. Do you think it was a good idea to speak to them?"

He shook his head. "I don't know."

"What a captivating face she has, James. She reads into you, like a book. Fascinating."

"Please, don't."

"I wouldn't feel sorry for her. She's intelligent and knows what she's doing."

"There are other forces too that shape our lives, Elena. *You* should know."

But Elena just said nothing.

For today's party, Mrs Diamandithou renounced every extravagance. There was only a buffet, a servant mixing cocktails and someone looking after the barbecue. Sakis had dressed casually and his delightful fiance floated beside him being self-effacing and charming.

Sonia arrived "late-ish" with a small gift for the couple and James felt it his duty to partner her. There was no rivalry in the air. It took only a second for Elena to see what was happening. "James, do talk to Sonia while I get her a cocktail."

"Thank you, Elena. He's such a gentleman he was about to walk off and abandon me."

"He's out of practice."

"Perhaps not quite your Edwardian gentleman," he countered.

"My gentleman-friend is not perfect but he makes me feel desirable."

"Her Edwardian friend is a figment of the imagination, Sonia."

"Sonia, I'm told you are happily married," Elena changed the subject.

"Partly true," Sonia replied. "To an airline pilot."

"Don't you think James ought to be getting married at his age? Look at him. Another week and nobody will have him."

"I think he will die alone in a cold bed, one night," Sonia ganged up against him.

"Poor James. As a matter of fact, he's just met somebody, haven't you, James?" Elena turned a sore knife. "But she's already engaged."

"Don't know who she's talking about," he tried to stop them.

"I think he should whisk her off, don't you, Elena?"

"Absolutely. But he's got no nerve. It's against his principles. He likes things clear-cut, properly labelled, in glass-jars and sterilised."

"Do you think I should turn up at the church and snatch her?" He was fighting hard for his ground.

"Yes!" exclaimed Elena. "That poor girl. And that man. Tragic."

"Wouldn't she be better off, though, Elena?" Sonia persisted. "Better any old man than James?"

"On second thoughts, yes. Do excuse me." A guest had arrived and she wanted to see him in.

Sonia laughed. "Trust a Greek woman to talk about nothing but marriage. They are inveterate matchmakers, you know."

"Mr Koudos!" Elena was heard in the front reception. And James's glass froze to his fingers.

The stocky figure of the hotel proprietor entered the room accompanied by a dazzling Miss Koudos. Catherine had transformed herself for the evening with sophistication and glamour. She smiled congratulations to Sakis and his fiance with her usual mystery and detachment. Elena accompanied Mr Koudos to another small group for introductions.

"There," said Sonia. "What did I tell you? Your match has arrived. Do you know who that is?"

"Do I know who *who* is?"

"That! The rich girl. Talking to *Daphnis and Chloe*."

"Her?" James gasped. "No thank you."

"Don't worry. She probably wouldn't have you."

But Catherine went to a side room and made out she had not seen him.

They did meet up, eventually, outside the ground-floor bathroom.

"Catherine!" he said. "The last time I saw you must have been back in..."

237

"Last night, you fool."

"Yes, I thought it was getting rather a long time."

"Sorry, I didn't get a chance to say I'd be coming."

"Presumably, your friend, Elena, thought it better not to speak either."

"All right, I told her to keep quiet."

"I see. Well, no point in standing here, I suppose."

"Are you suggesting we both get into the bathroom?"

Elena materialized through the hall and smiled. "Do excuse, if I'm spoiling something. I see James has lost no time."

"Is he in the habit of cornering ladies into bathrooms?" Catherine pretended innocence with her two raised brows.

"It wouldn't surprise me if he tried, Catherine. Still, must leave you to it. Excuse me."

"No, do stay, Elena," James stopped her. "I was on my way back already. Why don't you two gossip?"

"No, James. You are far more capable of entertaining Miss Koudos. As a matter of fact, I had been hoping you two would meet each other tonight." And she disappeared with a false smile.

Catherine chuckled. "The world is against us, darling."

He drifted back to the buffet and surveyed the scene. Groups had stabilized in semi-permanence. Sonia was proving popular, raising a lot of laughs from a small audience. Elena had taken her own confidants out to the patio. And the newly-betrothed had vanished.

He went over to speak to the Greek hotelier and his entourage. Mr Koudos had kept aloof but now welcomed the initiative. All dark secrets had been forgotten.

"I am told you met Catherine in Naxos."

"Only briefly."

"Pleased to hear it. I got a different story."

"You must be confusing it with a previous incident," he raised his brows. It was just as well the balance of terror remained equal between them. The best deterrence - mutual assured destruction.

Catherine re-joined them, forcing an end to the dangerous subject.

"How much longer will you be staying?" Koudos asked him.

"I am not quite sure just now. Another few days, possibly."

"I think it might be safe for you to come back to Halkidiki with us. News of that murder has died down. And we are flying tonight."

"Thank you. But I've got a ticket for Corfu."

"Scrap Corfu," Catherine blurted. "You won't like it in the summer."

"He hasn't liked any of our islands so far," Elena had crept up from behind.

"He likes Athos," Miss Koudos proclaimed, thinking she had delivered the coup de grace. "He should go there and live with hermits."

"Yes," James said. "A refuge from mythological vengeful wives."

There was a scream from the patio. Elena froze and several men dashed out. "What is it?"

"There's a man in the garden."

The servants re-grouped and run about the house. Lights flooded the outside grounds but nothing more could be seen. Elena formed a small war-council and gave instructions. There was a general disarray with most male guests joining the action. Then, just as quickly, the buzz died.

"Did anyone see his face?" he asked her.

"He had it covered."

"What was he doing?"

"Hiding."

He stole to his upstairs room for an overview of the garden. There was a cabinet in front of him with his suitcase on top of it; he pulled a drawer out. He held his pistol mechanically, broke it and looked through the muzzle. It augured power and security but also foreboding. A curtain rippled lightly to the breeze. The crowd was still a little excited. And there, in the middle of the lawn, looking up at him, Catherine.

The guests all had left by early morning. Catherine had stolen a kiss from him before departing, an honour everyone else reserved for the hostess only. Sonia had declined his offer to accompany her in the taxi. Sakis had gone with his young love to her parents' and would not be returning. James and Elena went to separate bedrooms.

In the dead of night he looked through the window at the garden once again. Was there somebody or something? Elena's uneasy premonition was infecting him.

But the heat and the soft breeze just whispered silently, reassuring and enigmatic.

****

21ˢᵗ AUGUST   CORFU

Flight six-zero-four looked promising to land on time, but this was judged out of character and things slowed down awhile. The *Airbus* lingered over the coastal hills as daylight began to dim, and water, sky and earth turned to scarlet. Suddenly a welcoming asphalt strip and James Cromwell stepped onto the Phaeacian island of ancient times.

Baggage claim, a brief chaos, then hardly anyone in the airport lounge. The *Avis* girl sat behind her diminutive desk and smiled. Isabel, from Hampstead.

"Do you like Corfu?" Her voice could have floated out of a car advertisement with keys tinkling in the background.

"Give me a chance, Isabel, I've just touched down. What is it like?"

"All the English are here. It's like being at home, but with the sun and the beaches."

"Oh, no. Where does one hide?"

"I like it on the beach. Any beach. As long as it's hot and crowded."

"I was hoping for peace and quiet."

"Come to Messonghi. I work there at nights." This time she did hold a pair of keys out to him. "Don't forget to bring it back." And she gave another commercial smile.

Outside, the grand approach avenue glittered under a declining sun, with hardly a car in sight. It stretched parallel to the runway, and a lake hemmed in and surrounded both tarmac strips with only a verge of grass on either side.

He drove to the top of Kanoni rock and looked down. Good place for surveillance this, with a view of the east coast out of town. A forest of pines and cypresses tumbled over the precipice to the magnificent bay, and then a tail to Pontiki, the tiny mouse island, reflected upside down.

Then the sun plunged into the far end of the basin and began to fizzle itself out. For a brief moment the sea and sky united. This was where Odysseus must have stood before his very last crossing. The old Phaeacian ship that took him from here to Ithaca had come back without drama. It now stood rooted to the bottom of the sea, no more than a reef, stranded and overgrown. Such was the price for the fulfilment of a humble dream; nineteen years of wandering for a single moment of arrival.

A chorus of voices rose from the foot of the rock, about a hundred feet below. He looked but saw nothing except bathing sirens crying that he should cast himself down. He stood unmoved, for a moment, observing the grand tableau, then took the path downhill to Pontiki island. In its courtyard, under the belfry, two ageing nuns waited for another Ulysses, their stale virginity preserved in sackcloth. The horror of shipwrecks, against that of withering unpollinated in a window-box, each more terrible than the other. Humanity was divided between those who wandered and those who waited. There was no permanence or arrival.

Something possessed him and he fled back up the rock, to the car, and racing, racing without knowing why. He hit Corfu town, down Constantine Avenue, and cut along the water front to the old palace. The trip could not have lasted minutes yet darkness had fallen and the evening began to cool down. From one exile to another, banishment to banishment, yet one more island, which way, God, now?

> *"Brother James, do you swear by the holy scriptures to live a life of poverty, removed from worldly goods and fleshly desires?"*

God forbid. Those long, long days of asceticism seemed like a lifetime. Would that this were his very last shipwreck before arrival. But the darkening sky looked at him and thought not; not yet, anyhow. Out of town, the prospect of beauty again weakened and died. Litter, slovenliness, and an indifferent shore-line. Just another island; a few days closer to Ithaca, perhaps, but - just another island.

An old Venetian building, its shutters locked, looked down on him, dumb and blind. For the gods it must have been difficult deciding whether to make this hell or paradise. Never anything in between: either perfection or ugliness.

He took a fresh look at the extraordinary muddle. Something about this place was gravely amiss, everything about it breathed uneasiness. The earth had shrunk and the sky crashed down like a lid, barring exit. He raced across the wilderness southwards.

It was late and pitch black when he stumbled across Messonghi and stopped for the night. The strain of chastity had brought his *Fiat* to a complete standstill. He sat in the car and thought of turning the stones to bread, well turned out loaves the shape of Isabel. Mentally now, he pushed her onto the back seat. Her top peeled off, her limbs unfolded and opened. The path from her breasts was brief, her warm incision intoxicating. This was too much for flesh and blood to endure.

He found Isabel playing Chopin in the hotel-bar, with as much sensuality as renting cars out.

She stopped and came to sit next to him. "Hi."

"Hi. I had expected to see you pulling pints."

"These are summer jobs. I have to pay my way here."

"Business and pleasure."

"Yes. I come to Corfu every year."

"That leaves a lot of the world still to travel."

"Is that what you do? Keep going round?"

"Round the islands."

"Don't you get homesick, alone in foreign places, night after night?"

"I'm not alone right now."

She turned away. "I like to be where people speak my own language, eat sensible food, like I'm used to. Don't like foreign things much." She spoke in short simple sentences, her red lips a constantly moving target.

"If you had been with me for one week, you would have changed your mind."

He watched her brow rise indifferently, her fickle face, her mannerisms. The smile he had judged superficial, became transparent and seductive. So much for the monastic habit.

"Any requests?" And she went back to her piano.

By half past ten, restlessness had given way to strong anxiety. Must do something to stop this tension rising. He held Isabel's hand and stroked her fingers to calm his inner storm down. Were it not for her he might be screaming now.

He opened the passenger door for her. "Shall we go for a drive?"

"Let's go to Corfu town."

"You just want a lift back, don't you?"

"Why, what did *you* have in mind?"

He shrugged his shoulders. "A restaurant? I'm so hungry I could eat you alive."

She burst into laughter and there was warmth and richness this time.

Corfu town resembled a huge village fete at night. They joined the crowds swarming the old Venetian alleys, the shops, the cafes. Now holding hands with Isabel seemed the strangest thing to do, but she swept him along like a tide. She knew a particular night-club, complete with English DJs, straight out of Covent Garden.

"James," she said. "You are not all here. What's on your mind?"

Strange that she had asked him as he was beginning to forget Athens. "Nothing."

"Then eat your food before it gets cold. Don't you love chicken n'chips in the basket?"

"Of course I do," he said obligingly, or he would betray King and country. Must not upset Isabel. She was a surrogate friend in a port of call, a fellow sojourner.

They danced until two o'clock, then he took her home and let her talk trivialities. He must phone Elena tonight. They sat in bed and drank tea together, in celebration of being English and Englishness. Then he got up, and after a chaste kiss, they parted like brother and sister, happy not to probe or be probed deeper tonight.

He phoned Athens the minute he got back to the hotel in Messonghi. "Elena, is everything all right?"

"Yes, of course. What makes you ask?"

"Nothing. Couldn't sleep for some reason."

"Oh, guess who rang the office this morning."

"Who?"

"Katia's fiance. Must have recognised me, despite sunglasses."

He pulled a stool and sat down. "Oh, no."

"I shouldn't have told you, perhaps. Don't worry, he sounded quite sane."

"As sane as anyone who takes the trouble to track you down. What did he say?"

"He wanted us both at his wedding, he said. I think he wanted to know if you had gone back to London."

"You refused, I hope. But why check on my whereabouts?"

"I don't know. What does it matter?"

"We should have stayed clear of them. So stupid."

"By the way, did you leave an old pistol in my cabinet?"

"Yes, sorry. I should have told you. Didn't want to carry it from flight to flight."

"It's all right. I'll keep it safe for you. How is Corfu?"

"Depressing. I want to get away but flights must be full for some time." He paused. "What do you think will happen to Katia?"

"Don't worry James. I told the man you had left. It will put him off for now."

"Unless Katia herself has blown it."

"She looked too clever for that. Go back to bed. Have a drink. Call back in the morning."

"Elena, you know that premonition of yours?"

There was silence then she said, "I've never seen Sakis happier. It must have been you who put me on edge. Sorry, it's late; I don't know what I'm saying."

"Sleep well, Elena."

"Good night."

He sat on the balcony and looked at the stars in the clear sky. They were making love-sounds next door and had left the door open. Maddening.

Then nothing but rustling leaves in the breeze, and a distant party of revellers wailing strange cries.

****

22nd AUGUST   CORFU

Except for the hotel complexes - and they were not much to look at - Messonghi village presented nothing extraordinary. Smudged rather than cleansed by its Ganges, the sea-shore quickly turned into grass, scarcely distinguishable from an English school play-ground. A string of beach-bars, canteens and restaurants shut out the view between the sea and the monolithic white blocks behind. Large paving stones run circles round pointless trees and arrows marked every alley like traffic signs. So this was Isabel's paradise.

In the sea, several bodies swam or floated, watched indifferently by others. And further back, more rowdy hordes, crudeness and mediocrity.

There was a stream cutting them off from the tavernas and the native life, and a queue waited to cross to the other side. Just a rowing boat and a ferry-man collecting coins on arrival. Several yards down, the small estuary had clogged with froth, the Ganges avenging man's insolence and depravity. Here the sea settled everything, what constituted ugliness and what beauty. People could do little except protest feebly at its immensity. Only the sea had the power to cleanse or defile.

He disinfected himself and showered before heading for the dreaded canteen. The food was average even by Isabel's standards. Beef, ketchup and chips had been imported from Gatwick, although the gravy had missed the flight.

Marooned in total futility he aimed pebbles at a plastic bottle floating by. A couple grinned at him amicably, with a tinge of sympathy which, at first, he despised. "Do you live locally?" he challenged them.

"No. We're Italian."

"Italians in Messonghi? What did you come here for?"

"We have a boat. Sailing on to Peloponisos. Just stopped overnight." His girl companion pointed a camera at her boyfriend and said something in Italian. And as she released the shutter, he reached out and pressed her nipple in reprisal.

"Mario!" she protested.

"Renata," he countered.

She ran off indignantly and Mario got up and chased her into the sea, laughing. They stood on a reef splashing each other.

He tried to piece his thoughts again but the plastic bottle had floated out of sight. This day was turning into the fiercest attack yet from the Aeolian sky. Eyes, ears, the five senses, were subjected to rising apprehension. Something had taken hold of him and loomed larger and larger in his mind.

He left the beach and took shelter in the air-conditioned lounge. A mere three days left, counting to the big occasion. Was he mad, clutching at straws, dreaming improbable dreams, infantile? Too late, perhaps. Waves rose inside his head, beating him senseless against the rocks, drowning him.

A touch on his shoulder and Renata spoke to him in Italian. *"Ti disturbo?"*

"Not at all."

"Why are you sitting here alone?"

"Waiting. Just waiting. Where is your boyfriend?"

"Husband. We are on honeymoon. Do you come to Corfu for holidays?"

"I go where-ever the winds blow."

She looked puzzled. "You haven't booked anything?"

"It's no use planning ahead," he baited her, for she had pointed the finger at his asceticism and it had piqued him. "Only the gods can decide."

Mario turned up to rescue her from total incomprehension and she took shelter in his embrace. There must be some other route to Ithaca, without chaos, trauma, drama. As long as the lull would hold, he pleaded inwardly. For the gales of Aeolus, gift-wrapped tentatively in an old skin, were rumbling.

He got up and called Sonia in Athens.

"Sonia, one ticket please."

"What's the matter?"

"Never mind, just get me out."

"Don't you like Corfu? I thought you might meet the woman of your dreams there."

"Must have missed her somewhere along the beach. It's easily done. So many women."

"Where would you like to go now?"

"Just out of here. Anywhere. First flight tomorrow."

"All right. Give me ten minutes."

They called him to the switchboard. "Telephone for Mr Cromwell."

"Already?"

"From Corfu town."

Back to the call-box. "Yes?"

"James, it's Isabel."

"Isabel, how are you?"

"Fed up, really. I've got to do overtime."

"Come down and join me afterwards. Will you be playing here tonight?"

"No. I'll be dead tired. I'll see you about seven."

He called Sonia the second time. "Is it good news?"

"Come on, James. Do you think I can pull no strings here?"

"What did you get me?"

"Seven thirty-five a.m. to Athens and direct connection to Santorini at half past nine."

"Good. Make it two."

"Pardon?"

"I'm taking someone with me. Two seats please."

"Who might that be?"

"The woman of my dreams."

"That was quick. Let's check the computer... Yes, all right. You'll have to get your tickets from the airport. Be there at six in the morning."

Late afternoon and a long stretch to kill before Isabel would arrive. On a last minute impulse he went off to see Paleokastritsa on the other side of the island. The famous bay, sheltered like a port, opened out to an endless Mediterranean. And there the ghost of Ulysses, yearning for home, weary but unbowed. Would it be morally right for him to steal Katia away from her forthcoming marriage? What if Katia herself agreed to be stolen?

For three weeks now, although it seemed ten years, he had been travelling. He pictured himself at his London desk, leaning out of that window at the usual closing time.

"Do I dare
Disturb the universe?"

The train of thought startled him. He had been about to renounce his Greek existence for good, but this sudden glimpse of the past was frightening. For, no, he did not belong there either. He was more knowing now. He could not pretend to un-know, once the experience was inside him, any more than one could go back to innocence after committing a crime.

It would not be right, he kept repeating. All practical arguments must come secondary this time. What right did he have even to try? Katia belonged to a different world, his falling for her the grandest delusion of all time.

He pictured her once more as a bride. Who was that man in a suit, with only his back in sight? Voices rose again from the foot of the rock below him, but he saw nothing. The young Phaeacian maidens had gathered their dowries and tip-toed into the shadows. They crossed his path and dropped their linen as if startled. Then one stepped forward and waited for him to turn, in silence. But how could he? This was not Ithaca. And so she moved on, saddened. He stayed and listened until the voices turned to mist and evaporated on the other side of the night.

Isabel arrived at Messonghi as he got back, dressed for eating out. They might as well be going to an Oxford Street steak house. "Tonight it's my turn to eat you alive," she announced. "What's on the menu at the canteen?"

"I don't know what's on the menu, Isabel. We're not eating there, thank you."

"Why not?"

"I'd rather have some nice imaginative taverna by the sea-front."

"Whatever. I'm so hungry."

They joined the queue to cross the short English channel and saw the Italians on the other side. "Jump!" Mario shouted, but Isabel disapproved of excitability and felt embarrassed.

The foursome wandered into the maze of souvenir shops and open-air barbecues. Mario led them to a place with folk dancing and found a table on the veranda. "Waiter, four people. How many vouchers?" It was a torment exchanging jokes between three languages.

"What, these?" the waiter shook his head profoundly. "One beer," he pronounced glumly.

"One beer, twenty vouchers?"

"Yea. What do the ladies drink?"

But Isabel ignored their banter and concentrated on being nice. Must show these hot-blooded foreigners how to act properly on British sovereign ground.

"So when are you coming sailing?" Mario asked James.

"One day, maybe."

"Come with us to Peloponisos now. We know this secret place on the north coast; Kounoupeli. Pine trees all the way to the beach. *Magnifico!*"

Suddenly folk dancers invited them to the dance-floor. Mario began to tango with Renata who tried to be obliging. But he got a cheer from the crowds and returned to the table a hero. He kissed his wife on the lips, then kissed Isabel Mafia-style. "Waiter?" And he waived his vouchers.

It was late when they headed back, Isabel hardly any less hungry or tired. They reached the channel and Mario debated various sailing methods for crossing it. It was dark and Renata's foot could not find the boat. She reeled and the boat swung away from her. A stoical ferry-man helped her, obviously familiar with the ceremony. Mario kept singing, "England, oh England," and held the prow end steady. In the confusion nobody paid the man but he waved and drifted out again with a smile.

They saw the Italians to their room and walked slowly back to the sea-side. Isabel looked almost drained. This was not the carefree creature of yesterday. She shook visibly, her cheeks had sunk and even her sensuous red lips looked withered and fireless. He held her close and she curled up, digging her chin to his shoulder. Here, at night, the beach resembled a tropical shore after a cyclone. Litter and wreckage lay scattered about, the earth felt slithery and things floated on the new edge of the waterside.

They sat on an upturned boat and she cried. It was like coming back home after a journey, to find it wrecked by the storms, a battered wasteland of destruction.

"You know what I wish right now," he whispered stroking her tears away. "That I did not have to move anymore, didn't have to go. That I had come to a safe port, arrived. Then I would climb up the mountain and see the shore, and miles and miles of meadowlands all around." He turned to find her eyes watching him, her tears dry.

"Shall I tell you what I miss?" she said. "There was this ugly boy at college, fat and short, with an evil, crooked smile. He used to kiss me whenever I cried."

They looked at each other and laughed in self-mockery.

"I meant to tell you," he said. "I'm leaving tomorrow morning."

That stopped her. "Why?"

"There is nothing here for me. It's barren."

She chewed his every word but could not see the significance. "There's me," she said bravely.

"Yes, I know. But the place - the place is ugly."

She stretched her hand out. "Nice meeting you."

"You are coming with me, aren't you? To Santorini?"

This startled her. "But James," she sat up, "how can I?"

****

23rd AUGUST   SANTORINI

Room service knocked at four thirty. He sat up in bed until the steps died down the corridor. Some gale had risen during the night and stormy breakers had come pounding at his door. Santorini's volcano had erupted and all the world's seas were rushing in to put it out. Death by water and fire.

Ten to five. Still totally dark but the nightmare held off. After the storm, stillness, silence and foreboding.

Isabel had slept on the spare bed and now sprung to her feet with a smile. "I dreamt we missed the plane!"

"Eat your tongue, Isabel, and cross your fingers that it leaves on time. There's a connecting flight to catch in Athens."

"I'm so excited!" Her bouncing breasts swung exuberantly from side to side.

"Cover them up, please, or we *will* miss the flight."

"What, at six in the morning?" She laughed. "Sex-maniac. We'll need time to get my luggage and write a message for the office. And to check your car-return in." Her high spirits had come back with a vengeance. "I'll be crucified, you know that. Hope there are some jobs in Santa-Rene. They'll never have me here again."

"Santorini," he corrected her. "We're not going to South America."

If only he flew to London instead, and took up the old routine once more. He had a house back home, and, thanks to Maxine, still had an office to go to, and now a woman willing to leave her Corfu and follow him to unknown parts of the world - he could have everything most people dream of. He gazed at Isabel, now as excited as a child, and relished her simple openness. Would she not share that priceless Englishness with him her whole life? He was presuming, of course, but it was worth considering.

Time was running out. They got to the main road in a hurry and it was still dark, with not one motor-vehicle in sight; except the municipal workers' bus. And so the journey began, with just a little romance, up to Corfu town. Slowly, painfully, the night-scape slid by, its empty beaches half-lit and exotic-looking, for once. Such would have been his dream island, spotless, uncrowded, beautified. And he was stealing a glimpse of it, unexpectedly, on his departure.

The light hardened two hours later when the plane took off, yellowing, purpling, then brightening against the clouds. He turned to look at the sleepy face beside him, her utter vulnerability endearing. A lone girl wandering on a stranger's borrowed pass, trusting him. He would not have thought her capable of leaping into the dark. There was that fractional hesitation before each movement and every word or laugh - the brain struggling to keep ahead, and checking and choking each tiny pleasure before it budded. But he kissed her forehead and held her close, pretending that he, at least, knew exactly where they were going.

"Mr Cromwell, passenger to Santorini, is kindly requested to come to the information desk." The public address at Athens airport sounded like God was observing him.

"There is a call for you, Sir, on that telephone."

He picked it up. "Yes?"

"James Cromwell, where art thou?"

"Who is that?"

"Thought you could hide from me, did you?" Magnificent Sonia. How could he have presumed such a thing?

"I heard thy voice and I was afraid, Sonia."

"How is Isabel?"

"You and your computer have been spying on me. She's in the transit lounge. When am I going to see you?"

"Don't put yourself out too much."

"I'll call you from Santorini."

"Oh, guess what? Do you know somebody called Thomas?"

"No; why?"

"He's booked himself on every flight with you. To Corfu and back; and now to Santorini."

He breathed relief for he had feared different news. "Some coincidence."

"I know. You can go now. Bring me a bottle of the local red, will you? From Santorini."

"Everything thou commandest I shall surely do." And he wound his way back to the lounge.

Isabel looked strange from a distance as he approached. Disarmingly pretty, absorbed in her own thoughts, she stood out among the crowds, as if from another continent. Suddenly she saw him and smiled. "What was it?" she asked.

"You rival, darling. Checking me up. Come on. We'll miss the plane."

Her high heels clattered hurriedly on the tarmac. Then the plane lifted and Athens was falling, falling off the edge of the universe.

Santorini. The gates opened to a hush and a soft zephyr from the mountain. Here the earth had been born of volcanic fire and it breathed fertility and muskiness. Stepping out from the plane felt like arriving at an ancient pre-historic settlement of no more than a few fishermen and hunters. The air was light, the tone humble. Donkeys would have seemed appropriate to shuttle the passengers into town. And James Cromwell would have been happy with a single palm-branch.

Isabel was absorbing her new experience with detachment which he took for profundity. Then she mumbled that it seemed too quiet, and wondered what night-life there would be and how to pass all day in such a small island. The taxi-driver shook his head and said nothing.

They reached Kamari and gaped at its wildness. A massive rockfall to the right, black sand on the beach, black waters. Here hotels turned out to be spare rooms in private houses, small, manageable, on a different scale altogether. And their proprietors mended fish-nets and hauled small boats.

It was this air of primitiveness which disturbed and enthralled him. Even the sea looked primeval and awe-inspiring. One only had to dip one's foot at its very brink to find oneself in the middle of the ocean. This was a different sea, ambivalent, distant, with arms fisted to a hard breast. Her dark womb had opened and glared, unmoved, unyielding, indomitable. It brought back images he had left behind. Pursued by her, he could not master the stillness that must necessarily precede Ithaca. "Damn you," he growled confronting her. "Damn you..." and he let his voice be gusted to her on the wind.

He hit the waves, deep into her, as far as his breath would take him. And there he looked and saw the blackness beneath him, terrible but irresistible. On the crest of a huge swell, he caught a glimpse of Isabel, sitting alone on the beach with a newspaper. How much less painful it would be to paddle in the shallowness which she preferred, with the rest of the multitudes. To end all journeys, give up on Ithaca, settle wherever he found himself vomited out.

She watched him come out of the water and brightened. "You've been so long I thought you swam back to Corfu."

"I did, but then I came back."

"The waters look very dark. What is it like?"

"It's deep. Very deep. I've never seen such blackness anywhere. But the waves don't break. Why don't you try?"

"No, I'm too scared," and she drifted into a shop to leaf through the magazines.

In the afternoon clouds gathered, making the beach less desirable. He thought they should go to town and see the volcano before dark. Isabel's face had metamorphosed and her impeccable skin had paled. She had found the masculinity of the place oppressive, its primitiveness overbearing. The fertile earth, bursting with sexuality, oozed some threat out of its every pore and pothole. The bus trundled on and its pretty white houses shook and threatened to tumble.

On foot for the last few steps and to the edge of the precipice. The eye first plunged into the chasm, across the strait, and there, on a separate island, the birth and death-place of Santorini. Dark, awesome, mysterious, its shadow rose as the sun sunk and turned the universe red, till there was nothing to see but water and fire.

Then Isabel vanished from his side. At first he waited, unconcerned, then he strayed into the criss-crossing alleys, looking from shop to shop and getting lost in the crowds. Houses jutted in and out, narrowing here, extending there, with numerous crypts and passages. It was now he realized how thin the thread had been between them, how very little they had shared and how ephemeral. They had stood across a gulf looking from different angles, seeing two different islands. The rumble of the volcano, almost ripe, had escaped her altogether. What she had longed for had been safe familiarity.

In the distance, he saw her laughing in somebody's arms, untroubled, leaning against a bar, happy. He was not angry; confused perhaps, but not angry. If it were not for the shared room and suitcases, he would have cast her adrift without a thought. Yet tonight she would return, still cheerful and unthinking.

He turned his back and climbed an alley, took a sharp left through an arch and almost touched the red sky. A figure barred his way and backed him onto the parapet. At first he thought this might be some drunken tourist pulling a prank, then possibly a mugging for money. But the attacker said nothing. His buggy clothes seemed to suggest at a Greek folk dress like those in Crete or at Embonas, with the headband pulled down to cover the face. And through two gaps, his eyes and breath like fire from a dragon's mouth. James Cromwell would have to fight or fall into a steep chasm. Behind the parapet the sheer drop plunged to the sea crater, already bloodied by the sunset. And so he lunged forward in desperation. The man gasped, staggered, and disappeared as suddenly as he had come. And James covered the knife-wound and stumbled down the steps to a drug-store.

The scene had lasted but one moment, yet instantly, the world turned upside down and several mysteries linked up.

Two hours past midnight he still run the incident through his head over and over. He had come back to their

262

guest house on the same bus, finding the crowded passengers comforting. And now he stood on the balcony watching the night scene beneath, the sand and the sea stretching beyond into total blackness. A loose-footed Isabel alighted from somebody's car while the last revellers scattered. She crossed the drive to the guest house, came up the stairs and slipped into her own single bed quietly. He decided to stay put for another hour, letting the tension drain itself out. They were yards from each other, but not a word from either. His wound hardly ached but he still struggled to remember something. Sometimes it surfaced to the brink, then plunged again to the back recesses with no hope of recovery. That had been the second time a man with a knife had been so hateful yet incompetent. Such blind hate. How could anyone hate so much. That hatred had been of infinite depth and power. He could hear hate in every breath that man took as he lunged at him. And now he found the time to hate him back with as much savagery. It clouded his very core and left him anaesthetized. He paced the balcony, puzzled that such a force should have risen inside him.

Still sleepless, he stepped in and lay down, but every inch of the ceiling sprouted gargoyles of an improbable likeness. He watched them calmly until, some hours later, they submerged in the water and died.

Isabel turned restlessly over and over.

"Why did you bother?" he said at last.

There was a moment's silence. "Bother what?"

"To come back."

"I just lost you in the crowd." She curled up in self-protection, hardly knowing the strange affection he felt for her vulnerability and callowness.

More silence. He listened to the sound of her breathing, half-asleep, trusting him like a brother. A lone female, unwooed and unharvested, scorning the vain sterility of maids waiting unpollinated at their window box. He had denied her essence, yet she had come back on top and triumphed.

No more was said. He lay awake watching her body loosen, arms limp, head slack, legs drawing provocative diagonals on pure white. There were so many stars crammed over the balcony and the smell of herbs grew stronger and stronger by the hour. Her breath turned calmer, whispering now. The breeze had turned cooler, from the north, searching out this stark wasteland. Perhaps it lingered inside the sultry bedroom, but then slipped out again and fled, in fear of some volcanic eruption.

****

24th AUGUST   SANTORINI

At first light he went over and showed her the blood-stained dressing crusted to his chest. She glared at him accusingly as if he deserved it. Then she got up and locked herself in the bathroom, pointedly indifferent.

"I'm being followed," he shouted through the door, pursuing her. "First to Corfu and now here. Someone called Thomas. I think it is a false name." No reply. "Flash the toilet if you don't give a shit."

She came out and started tidying the clothes in her suitcase, pushing his to one side, disdainfully.

"I'll try to slip out of here on a regular boat," he continued. "I take it you plan something similar."

She turned sharply and eyed him with a vacant look.

"We'll show up at the harbour and hop on. I can't book anything in advance. He's always known which flight I'm going to be on." He was still puffing after shouting and the dressing stung. "I've got an idea who he is but it's too incredible."

"You are not afraid, are you?" she said mockingly.

"A little afraid, yes. And intrigued. I think he's mad."

She studied him a bit more, then sat on the bed, her naked feet towards him. He duly obliged and looked at them. They were perfectly good feet, to be sure, with ten toes and freshly cut cuticles - no reason why they should not be put forward. But he was making her self-conscious and she tucked them under and sat on them, which made her look adorable like a child. She put her hands over what was visible of her thighs and they were a pianist's hands, long-fingered and elegant. An old picture surfaced, of a Greek girl curled up in his arms, her face glowing. She too played the piano and had supple erotic hands. Katia materialized in devastating clarity to take her place on the sprung bed in front of him. And he was torn apart by the mirage.

But this was Isabel looking at him now, her trifling sneer no deeper than her smooth skin, eyes endearingly wide. "I wouldn't have given it a thought, if I was you. Such a small wound." So there she was, take her or leave her, impulsive, capricious, superficial. The mystery lingering on her lips had been lipsticked over, and there was nothing else under her make-up.

On this morning's beach, tourists took much longer to appear. Sharks prowled the seas of the mind, keeping swimmers at bay and voyagers to the shore. Yet this had looked like an auspicious day, with the donkey-man and the small boy plodding the length of the beach selling grapes, and the tavernas preparing for midday libations.

They sat together on beach-towels sunbathing because there was nothing else to do, and he wanted to act as normal, in case that Thomas assassin was watching him. His eyes then caught a dark-skinned figure with a gipsy kerchief round her arm. Suddenly their glances met and she fixed him with provocative arrogance. Chin down, lips pouting, she traded heavily on the security of the male body embracing her, to flirt wantonly with another. She started to stroke and kiss her boyfriend, boxing him, teasing him, in a display seething with carnality. This was eroticism pitched to perfection, subdued yet ferocious. She was bewitching the man watching her and she knew it, raising the fever with sexual posturing - limbs limp, thighs open, hands brushing the narrowest part of her bikini casually.

He found her glance disturbing, this whole unexpected game mesmerizing. This was the kingdom of Circe, dark, fecund, and sexy, each grain of sand a speck of lava from her burning gush.

And then she got up and pulled her lover to his feet, strolling into the distance with silent laughter in her throat, her hair flowing. He watched her vanish, leaving the wreckage behind her strewn, scattered and overthrown. Isabel, unaware of the whole incident, then got up to wet her toes and her navel with a small splash.

At about noon, rumours reached them that the volcano had rumbled and boat-trips across to it had been banned. The story was being considerably enlarged as it travelled. Some talked of thick smoke, huge tremors and even lava streaming down the island. James's first thought was whether his chances of escape would be endangered, while Isabel exaggerated her calmness as a mark of superiority over the fussing local populace.

He left her there and went to pack his suitcases, inwardly debating what to tell her, even though there was little to discuss. He had only hours to spare. Instead of a boat, he would catch the late flight to Athens, then put together some plan. Katia would be married tomorrow. The Italians had said they would be in Peloponisos with their sailing boat: "Kounoupeli;" weird name but could be the perfect secret place. Time to ask for some help at last.

From the balcony he caught sight of Isabel talking to someone, then getting into his car. Could it be Thomas? Santorini's blackness was getting darker by the hour. He stood for a moment and followed the trail of dust on the road, then wandered down to the shops, nonchalant. In the green-grocery's narrow isle, someone tried to squeeze past him, the unmistakable feel of breasts pushing him into the canned peas and tuna chunks. There was no apology forthcoming and, turning, he saw the dark gipsy girl. She pushed him again then opened a tiny door, where her little shop backed into the mountain. There was only a ten-foot courtyard with stacks of crates and craggy volcanic rocks. Such naked sex, so brutal. So much untamable black hair. Loose skirt gathered to her knees, then up to her stomach. No longer the kerchief-armband, no shoes, no bikini, no chain to her soft ankle. He pushed her onto the jagged rocks.

Her top peeled off, her limbs unfolded and opened. The path from her breasts was brief, her warm incision intoxicating. Earth parting, rocks drawing blood, crates strewn, scattered and overthrown. He kicked the thorns and the brambles, and the scratches stung and made him stop.

Late afternoon. The rumbling volcano no longer seemed to bother anyone and scooters zoomed exuberantly here and there. He looked from his balcony at the sprawling sea-front and the water beyond. Ithaca seemed as far away as it had ever done. Only this time he knew where he headed. It was just a question of making it in time. And if the good gods determined that he must die before getting there, so be it. But there was no question of turning back.

A last-minute seat on the late flight felt like ticket to heaven. He looked at the rest of the passengers behind him just once. He was losing Thomas and Isabel at last.

They landed at Athens airport. Twenty to eleven now. Which meant an all-night journey for the taxi driver to Kounoupeli and back. He felt sympathy but paid a fare to match.

"We have two hours to get there. Fast."

"Three!" the driver shouted. "I don't want to break the car."

Now past midnight. Nothing to watch but a clock on the dashboard. Faster and faster. His brain raced; wedding tomorrow. Despair and urgency, and a plan.

Town of Varda. A sign post: *Kounoupeli*. Cart-road, tall reeds, unearthly, otherworldly. The jolt of a level-crossing, the trough of a dry river. A forest of pine trees. "Tomorrow," he kept thinking.

Then the end of all the world's roads. A half moon floated becalmed mid-seas. Now sinking, fish jumping all over it. Speechless driver. Taxi rear lights disappearing in a dust cloud. He lay back on the beach.

Wedding tomorrow. And the red sea parted to show a path.

****

25ᵗʰ AUGUST   KOUNOUPELI

Dawn. The brightest whitest day. A thousand-odd jubilant church-bells awoke him, quickly to become discordant and dissonant. The sound had drifted from far away but it had ceased as soon as he had opened his eyes and gazed around, disorientated. There was no breeze, no ripples on the water, not a single creature scampering on the beach.

Dawn. Warm, blushing, naked. Overhead a sky so clear he could see through it, elusive and shifting as the light changed by the minute and temperatures rose degree by degree.

The sky dominated everything. It dwarfed the long parabolic bay stretching to his right and running farther and farther until it faded in the morning mist. Pine trees hemmed in the sea, guarding it from all sides. They left a narrow strip for the sand to breathe, and then trampled it and rooted themselves in it, and soared above it.

To his left, the bay was halted abruptly by a giant rock plunging to the sea, then rising to a sharp summit. He ran and clawed his way up it, inch by inch, to the very top, the sun climbing just as fast behind him. And there he stretched his arm and scraped a finger against the sky.

Never such blue. Its depth consumed him, its span took him off his feet, absorbed him into its vastness. He looked down at the earth's circle, half of it sea, the other forest, a thin gold line in between. This was beauty as he had always imagined it, hidden from those who would have trodden it rough-shod.

Then, at the foot of the rock, the sea swirled uneasy, like a startled crowd, confused, agitated. But the sky calmed it like a lid, stopping it, for this sky stamped all disharmony. Far and near views coincided. The eye found no need to enhance deficiency. Never such blue. And he had thought it only existed in his mind.

The beach continued on the other side and in the distance a sailing boat, still, just yards away from the shoreline. He ran downhill and through the forest to reach it, and wading in he shouted until a face peered curiously back at him.

"Renata!" he waved, hardly recognizable, "Hi." Another face. "Mario!"

"James! Wait there. Wait."

But he swam and waded and climbed on board.

"How did you get here?"

"I got a taxi; last night."

"Your luggage?" Renata asked practically.

"It's on the beach. On the other side."

"We'll sail round to take it."

"This place is beyond dreams. How did you find it?" He turned to the sound of an approaching diesel engine in the open sea. The first caique in a line passed them, chugging stolidly, returning to shore. Worn, brown faces looked benevolently and a weary hand sent a greeting.

"*Buongiorno!*" Mario waved back at them. "Isn't that beautiful? We sit here and watch their fishing lights all night. They always bring us something at dawn."

"They know we are on honeymoon," Renata said.

"What happened to that girl of yours, in Corfu?" Mario said cautiously.

"We weren't together. Not for long."

"That's O.K.. We'll have a honeymoon for three," Mario pondered and Renata lifted a plastic buoy and hit him with it. Another mock fight broke out and the newly-weds rolled from one end of the deck to the other, then fell off. Renata screamed in Italian to the effect that he was brutal and the water too cold. She climbed back on the boat and Mario swam out to the shore.

"What is he doing now?" she said, drying her hair out. "He's not normal today. Never is."

"We'll give him ten minutes and then just go, shall we?"

"*Two* minutes," she cried. "Mario! James and I are going."

But Mario splashed enthusiastically and waved them off.

They met him some time later on the beach, together with two fishermen gathering dead branches for firewood. He lit it and they all settled there for breakfast, roasting a handful of prawns. "Today we entertain an Englishman," Mario told the fishermen, "So mind you P's and Q's." They could not have understood but laughed heartily nevertheless.

Around midday the party split three ways, with only James deciding to stay ashore. He walked back to his starting point and sat in the middle of the beach. From the centre of the huge bay, the coast looked too serene, almost sinister. Echoes returned of a distant crowd, and the heat turned it into a chorus of wailers. Suddenly the landscape darkened, the wind strengthened, and trees bent and hissed venomously.

At the southern foot of the rock, edging the forest, there had been a miniature church, like so many all over Greece, hardly big enough for one worshipper. He had glimpsed it when running past this morning and now decided to visit it.

Deserted yet freshly white-washed, it languished in the smell of incense and a single candle close to extinction. He blew it out and watched the dying smoke vanish, then kneeled on the bare floor. Silence. The strange echo had stopped. He looked up and it was roofless - just some pine branches and a sky empty of angry gods.

"Father forgive me, for I know not what I do."

He wandered out again and beat a path up the rock, to the very summit. The water beckoned and a soft breeze drifted seawards. There he could see her, across the strait, a journey's distance, no more. The decision was taken calmly, like knowing the next port of call. He knew, for the haze lifted and Ithaca appeared on the horizon.

He lay on his back and watched the undisturbable sky. Never such blue. It seemed so near, arm's distance, a mere short hop, if he reached out to it.

"You are thoughtful, James," Renata leaned over him. "Do you miss England?"

He came to, startled to find himself on the boat, her face a silhouette against the midday sun. "It seems a long time back," he answered. "But no. I don't wish to be there either."

"Come to Italy. You can spend some time with us. When do you have to be in London?"

The question hang in the air, irrelevant, almost comic. Should he tell her now, he wondered. But the moment lingered and cicadas drowned out whatever he might have said.

It was mid-afternoon when they put up sail and set off. The wind was south-easterly, perfect for crossing the Ionian sea. Zante, Cefallonia, Ithaca. They hoisted the blue and white spinnaker and the hull heeled leewards and raced forth.

Now only the sound of the sea marked the minutes. Amidst the ropes and the fairheads, each of them found their own secluded corner. Renata, on her back almost naked, soaked up the sun and the spray. Mario hardly busy, steering. Down on the foredeck, James, almost hanging over the prow, half-slept, half listened to the silk sea. He opened his eyes and the mast soared, infinitely tall, slicing the sky, magnificent.

"Are you glad you came?" Renata's silhouetted face again, and it was the first human sound after much journeying.

He nodded.

"Come and hold the helm for a minute," Mario said and sat with his wife astern.

James now piloted, not yet knowing where he headed. Here at the cockpit, the universe curled and shrunk round him into a glass ball. The sea rose and fell with a gentle swell, the deck glimmered, the sails burst full of fecundity and promise. He became drunk with beauty and the world stopped, never to move forward out of this moment, his grand plan on hold once again.

"Land approaching!"

Mario jumped and looked ahead anxiously. "What do you mean 'approaching?' You've nearly beached the bloody boat!" He faked panic convincingly for they were miles off. "Where have you brought us to, James?"

"Some Greek island, I think. Undiscovered, for sure."

They looked ahead at the drifting land-mass, rising higher and higher, darkening as it got closer. The yacht sailed into its shadow and suddenly it became evening. In the cockpit, the radio came to life in incomprehensible crackling bursts. The sunset dimmed and mountains changed into a wonderful chameleon. A wedding day was ending, the night to come as yet. Long before he could get to her, some sword had already bloodied earth, seas and sky.

In the farthest corner of the harbour they lit up candles and spread enough food and drink for a banquet. Hot cooking was brought on board from the tavernas, freshly sacrificed on some Greek altar, and wine for the libations. The small fishing town, removed to the other side of the port, had gathered its own people indoors, each tiny house feasting quietly.

Well past midnight the wine run out and Mario got up to his feet. "My friends," he started with a lisp...

"Oh, not again," Renata tried to intervene. "He likes speeches. Sit down and shut up."

"...Many years ago I wrote this bloody speech and ever since I've been waiting for a bit of silence to give it." He sipped a triumphant mouthful. "This dinner tonight was very special to me. Tonight I sit in company with my wife, my lover and my best friend." He made a dramatic pause. "So, I hear you ask, James, where the hell do you fit in?"

James nodded agreement vigorously.

"...James, to you I say that few people have we loved as we love you. You became a real friend within an hour of meeting you."

Renata smiled with grudging enthusiasm.

"...And so we have decided to ask you to come with us to Italy. This was never meant to be just a day-trip. We have no plan to return to the mainland. In the morning we sail north and then west, up the Adriatica and to Venice. We'll stop at many beautiful places - you tell us where you want to stop. You be captain."

James chuckled and shook his head with sadness.

"...But, please, I beg you, don't refuse until you sleep through the night and think on it. And then, if you cannot come, we'll take you back to Peloponisos." He paused and sat down to the sparse applause of four hands, his face excited and mischievous. "Now where's your bloody ticket?"

James stood up and raised his glass to each of them. "My friends," he said, "you are very generous and Italy irresistible."

"That's right," Mario thundered.

"The ship is good, the captain is good, and the hostess beautiful. But ..."

"No, no," both Italians clamoured loudly. "There are no 'buts.' Sit down; finished."

"But!" James silenced them - and they waited - "I can't find my bloody ticket."

Roaring and shouting now, the Italians heckled him.

"I've looked in every damn nook and cranny..."

"It's not there," Mario shook his head knowingly.

"... and I can only presume that the gods are not willing."

"New ticket tomorrow. For Italy only," Mario shouted.

James brought down his voice. "You've been very good to me and I'll never forget it."

Renata eyed him curiously.

"Yet tomorrow I must be in Athens."

"Why?" Mario challenged him, but Renata's face had sombred and she beckoned him to be quiet.

"You mustn't ask me because I can't tell you yet."

"A woman," Mario persisted. "We'll wait. Why don't you steal her? Bring her with you."

The deck keeled from under his feet and he almost fell over. "Yesterday," he tried to say - but had to pause. "I don't know what happened. I meant to tell you... That's what I came here for..."

They sat next to him, either side. "What? Anything. Just tell us what."

But his voice would not come out. And suddenly the party broke up with James Cromwell disembarking to leave the honeymooners alone.

In the middle hours of the night the harbour slept, its lights near extinction. The feast had ended, the wedding couple had nested down to bed. He walked the deserted town uneasy, irresolute. This eerie stillness, the silence - so strange. Not like a proper wedding night, full of ecstatic small sounds, whispers, half-breaths. The bride had stripped her diadem and kneeled barefoot on the nuptial bedspread.

> "Oh father, in a shameful bridal
> I am joined of thee."

He stopped to listen, alone, tormented, possessed. The moon had set, the stage empty. At last he yielded and he unknotted the old Aeolian gift-wrapped storms.

277

"Elena, it's me, James. I'm sorry to get you out of bed."

"You didn't."

"There's been a small complication; I want to reach Athens tomorrow; early."

"James, where are you?"

"I can be on Peloponisos about six in the morning, then get a taxi to Athens..."

"What complication did you say there is?"

For the first time he noticed something in her voice. "I've got myself stranded on an island I did not mean to," he said.

"Nothing new there."

"Don't be cynical."

"James, did you know it was Katia's wedding today?"

The sentence charged up his spine like an electric jolt. "Why do you tell me?"

There was a silence at the other end. "You haven't heard anything?"

"No."

"Katia has been shot. In her bedroom; on the wedding night. Her husband is in a police cell. They think it was an accident."

Out of the air, the face of his would-be killer, in Athens, in Santorini, reached out and tore at him. The signs he had ignored for so long came back, dark omens, like

Furies that spat and hissed. *"Blind, blind, blind."* But the more he pleaded, the more their hideous grimaces confronted him.

****

26th AUGUST   ATHENS

Inside Elena's house the huge sitting room looked empty since the betrothal guests had departed six days ago.

They kissed perfunctorily. "I'm sorry I had to break such news."

"I want to see her as soon as possible."

"I'll come with you." She called the chauffeur and they set off.

He knew instantly that he would remember that journey forever, its every corner and turn. The streets, bustling as usual, the frantic traffic, the sky grey like slate again.

Up the concrete stairs, along the trail of disinfectants fanned by the heat. In the ward, Katia's bed was at the far end, last in a row of about twelve.

She was covered by a single white sheet, face and arms showing, hair brushed and shining, breathing. There was nothing to show she had been hurt except a small plaster on her forehead to cover the bullet's entry. He lifted her hand and it rose limply. "Hullo, Katia; it's me, James." There was an imperceptible movement, as if his voice had reached the depths of her brain and she had mustered the effort to grasp at him. But nothing more. Inwardly startled, he stroked her fingers. "You are all right, Katia," he said again and again.

All around, the ward functioned routinely. The sister ushered herself in and rebuked them, for none of the girl's relations had visited. Nobody knew whether this patient would come out of her coma. She could not describe her condition. All they could do was wait. She was beyond medical help.

The bed-sheet had taken Katia's contour, like a cloak over a marble statuette. Everything about him, except Katia, lay strewn in tatters, small and trite, the whole pompous universe shrivelled to bits.

Elena had stood back, but now she ventured a little closer. "James, I'll have to go. I'm late and the office is panicking."

"What time is it?"

"Half past eleven. I have a midday meeting that can't be changed. Are you staying?"

"Only briefly. I want to talk to the police."

"Would you rather I sent a lawyer to meet you here?"

"Yes, please."

She nodded and hurried off.

He held Katia's fingers again. She breathed easily, without any machines attached to her, no tubes, no drip-feed. And no more signs of waking.

A young Greek doctor walked over to him. "You are English?" he smiled, the first sympathetic face to be seen.

"Yes."

"I'm going to England in January. To Middlesex." He regarded Katia. "Are you a friend of the family?"

"A friend of Katia's."

He signalled a vague acknowledgement. "Come to my office."

He sat at his desk and pinned some X-rays to the light-box. "The bullet entered the forehead here and travelled up, a short distance, otherwise she would have died instantly. As it is, we don't know what damage it's done except that it is considerable." His finger traced the path of the bullet and stopped where it had lodged itself, hideously distinguishable in perfect shape. "She must have been lying flat on her back with the gun somewhere above her feet." He looked up significantly. "Not my department."

"Is there just a chance of survival?"

"She wouldn't be the same again. She'll drift in and out for a few days but I doubt that she could talk, or even remember."

"You don't think she can hear me now when I talk to her?"

The doctor considered this a little longer. "It's very unlikely but possible. You can't know unless there's some response." He examined James's face candidly. "I would hate to raise hopes."

Elena's lawyer arrived not much later, looking suitably sombre. They went to a street cafe' full of dark-suited figures with briefcases, a lawyer's haunt. Two Greek coffees fell on the table in front of them.

"We'll see the officer in a minute. What is your interest in the case, Mr Cromwell?"

"I'd like to hear their version. It's possible I have some evidence."

"May I ask what?"

"An incident in Santorini." He signalled he would not say more.

The lawyer snapped his notebook shut. "Very well."

Then up some steps into a crowded police building. Two plain clothes men came out and showed them to an interview room with considerable deference - whether for the tragedy or for Elena's lawyer was not clear. Introductions were made in Greek, then repeated.

Both detectives seemed down to earth, almost gloomy. "We were called to the house, two in the morning, by the man himself," one started in English police-speak, "and found him in a very agitated state, as you would expect. He surrendered the fire-arm immediately and an ambulance took his wife away, seriously injured."

"How did it happen?" James asked.

"She was sitting in bed and he was demonstrating his collection of fire-arms. He had several. This one was old; he had kept it but never used it. Unknown to him, it was loaded."

"Had he ever shown this gun to someone else?" the lawyer prodded gently.

"We don't know. The thing went off and that was it."

"By itself or was it triggered - accidentally?"

"This isn't established yet. He cannot remember exactly what his hands were doing."

"And how are you treating the case?"

The policeman looked genuinely saddened. "As far as we can see it was a tragic accident. There might be some charge for possessing hand-guns; it won't be murder or anything like that." He was trying to reassure them.

"I am more concerned about the victim," James said. Both detectives now scrutinized his face closely. "I knew the man; had met him twice. Last Friday he assaulted me."

Their hush hardly disguised the scepticism. "Did you report this?"

"No."

Heads shook. "I don't see the relevance."

The lawyer interrupted in Greek and the detectives nodded agreement. At the street cafe' outside, he breathed deeply to indicate possible difficulties. "I asked them to ring me before the man was released."

"I don't think they believed me," James seethed.

"No. But it doesn't matter. What surprises me is how they fail to see the discrepancies. He told them that Katia was sitting in bed while he demonstrated this pistol. If that had been true, her head would have been in a raised position to see what he was doing. However, I saw the X-rays in the doctor's office and it's obvious that her head must have been flat on the bed. The angle of the bullet is very acute."

"Why didn't you tell them?"

"We have to be careful here. I don't want to see a killer released any more than you do, but your own relationship with the girl complicates things. Some people still see a woman's honour as a matter of life and death. Even the courts used to be sympathetic until recently. In fact there still is a gut feeling, an understanding, let's say. The problem now is as follows: In order to claim this was intentional, we have to suggest what the possible motive was. And this would be difficult, even though we damn well know. Let me make it clearer. My guess is that you had some relationship with the lady. It might not have been her only pre-marital relationship, I don't know. But he found out."

"We spent an evening together, that's all. No pre-marital relationship."

"Yes, but she was engaged already."

"I can't believe what you are telling me."

"It is my job to put the facts before you."

"This was an attempted murder and you tell me the court would be sympathetic to the criminal? The man knew about me and Katia before the marriage. Perhaps if he'd finished me off in Santorini he wouldn't have shot her. But now his pride hurt. The whole thing was premeditated. He went ahead with the marriage, perhaps to secure ownership in his own ego, or to show he suspected nothing. Just breaking off would not satisfy him.   He probably consummated the marriage and left her entirely unsuspecting. Then he got up and shot her from the foot of the bed while she slept."

"Possible. Now you try and tell your story in front of a jury. Will you confirm or deny that you had in fact a secret relationship with the lady? If you deny it then there is no motive, and the whole case against him is demolished. If you confirm it, he will deny he even knew, and leave you, the prosecution witness, guilty under the spotlight by your own admission. Do you follow me?"

"My only concern is that he doesn't get away."

"Leave this to me, Mr Cromwell. We have a few days. I'll look into it."   He offered a reserved handshake, professionally, and rushed off.

James Cromwell was left gloomy. He called Sonia at work. She told him to stay at the cafe' and hurried to meet him.

"Katia has been shot," he told her coldly as they met up. Even though she had not known the name, her knees buckled and she lurched back. For a moment he thought she might pass out. Cool, dauntless, indomitable, yet Sonia was not quite up to this. "Steady, Sonia. I'll get a glass of water. Hold on."

"I'm all right. That girl you had met? What happened?"

"Her husband shot her last night. After the wedding. And it looks like he's going to get away with it."

"Was it deliberate?"

He let off an angry breath.

"Stay out of this, James. They get very hot-blooded here about these things."

"All I can hope is that she wakes once. To speak to her."

"You want to apologize?"

He let his head drop as if Katia's body hang from his neck. "I wish I had been shot instead."

"Don't be stupid. You had nothing to do with it."

"You don't know."

"I can guess."

"This wouldn't have happened, except for me."

"Stay out of it. Just forget it." She finished her coffee and rushed off.

It was about four when he arrived at Elena's, just after she got back from work. In the bath her plants had grown and branches sprang up all over him. Elena pulled them apart to find him. "Sorry, James. Nobody's used this room since you left. I'll have to cut them all down when you finish. Have you been to the hospital again?"

"No."

"My men think another doctor ought to see Katia. It's been known for people to recover."

"I think if you asked her she wouldn't want to. She's spent too much time locked up in small dark rooms."

She shook her head in despair. "Do you remember that premonition we both had?"

"I don't believe in such things." He wrapped himself in a towel and went to the bedroom where he had last slept. In the drawer, under some clothes, that pistol waited undisturbed. He looked at it grimly. Too old to be trusted, probably never used.

Downstairs, Elena had spread paperwork over a table. She put her pen down as he approached and drew her feet onto the settee. "Sit down, I want to tell you something. I want you to forgive me, James, for everything I said - you know that nonsense about taking her away. I didn't know how cruel all this would turn out to be."

"God knows how many times I had said that to myself."

"You ought to be more of a fatalist. Like me. I don't believe you can change the future. See it, maybe, but not change it. Do you remember that night we sailed around Hydra? I more or less said it; when the gods decree something, you can't win."

"Don't blame the gods, Elena. The gods are innocent. We screw up each other and ourselves."

"I hate to see you tormenting yourself like this. It's like the Grudges drive you. You never rest."

"What drives me right now is very different."

"I hope you don't mind, but I've asked a friend of mine to come to the hospital with you. She's one of the best neuro-surgeons in Europe."

He hardly heard her. "All I want," he whispered, "is for Katia to die in peace."

Doctor Xenopoulou went with him to the hospital as a visitor that evening. She did not have to see much. Her face mellowed from professional detachment to gentleness, and James knew.

"I had hoped to stay here," he said. "How much longer do you think?"

"It's impossible to tell. There's no reason why you can't wait for a few hours."

"I've heard of people coming out of a coma, briefly."

Her smile stayed unchanged. "There is nothing you can tell her that she doesn't know already."

His hand abandoned the flowers on the bed. "I wish she could spend her last hours in a better place. Can you move her to another hospital or even a house, maybe?"

"Let me talk to the ward sister," and she strolled away purposefully.

He turned to find Katia's eyes had opened looking upwards, and he clasped her hand.

"Katia," he whispered. "Can you hear me? It's James."

She turned her gaze towards him, without expression. Her lips moved faintly. "My mind is gone."

"Katia, you are all right. You've just been sleeping, that's all."

"Who is in the house? Who are they?"

"You are in a hospital and you are safe. You'll be back home soon."

She closed her eyes again and he did not dare wake her. Doctor Xenopoulou returned. "She came round," he announced briefly.

Xenopoulou touched Katia's wrist and the eyes opened a little but shut again. "We'll have to remove the bullet," she declared.

"It'll kill her."

"Not of itself. I've seen the X-rays. Let's move her first."

"A large room, please. Quiet, plenty of light. You know where is best."

Katia's face remained tranquil. "Open your eyes," he called to her.

She blinked imperceptibly.

"I'll tell you a story and you mustn't stop me until I finish. Agreed?"

The same lethargic effort again.

"It's a funny story," he said and watched her eyes close in deep sleep and her breath soften.

He leaned back against his chair and let her hand fall on the sheet. In the distance, two nurses struggled with a cantankerous patient. The matron flicked a switch and yellow bulbs glowed from the ceiling. A young domestic took the bouquet to put away. She smiled coyly and whirled to the far end. The nurses cast half glances at him, whispering. Xenopoulou appeared in the distance talking to the young doctor and two policemen.

She came over to him. "We are ready to move. It will be a half-hour ride in the ambulance. I'll have to operate immediately." Her face had furrowed deeply in the last minutes. "She will be much better there," she said.

****

27ᵗʰ AUGUST   PSYCHIKO

Xenopoulou came out of the operating theatre and removed her surgical gown. "She might not live but we've done our best for her."

He had waited outside the whole night watching the city flicker beyond the foot of the hill. Psychiko lay at the outskirts of Athens, secluded on higher ground by poplar trees. Here the houses stood detached, in large gardens, a world apart from Plaka's narrow streets. At day-break it rose like a green island amidst the concrete and steel, and the endless traffic.

"She'll have to fight if she's to come through. Talk to her all day today, whether she's in a coma or not. If you get tired, play her some music. And tactile contact. Stroke her face now and then. More coffee?"

"No."

"We'll resuscitate you if you come to a halt. Just keep going."

"How much damage did you have to do?"

"A small piece of cranial bone was removed and replaced. The bullet was right underneath. Most damage had been done already."

"She is sleeping now, is she?"

"Yes. You look tired. Let's go in."

He sat on a chair at her bedside and watched a nurse take her blood pressure again and again. She breathed at the same rate as last night. Xenopoulou waved and left him. Then he was alone with her, a clock ticking, the cardiographic machine bleeping monotonously. He just watched.

A huge window took up most of the outside wall and through it one could see the mountains of Penteli and Parnitha. He wanted to sit her up and show her - then felt foolish and stroked her fingers instead.

And so the day drifted until his eyes could not keep open and tiredness put him to sleep.

She gave signs of consciousness some hours later. Her eyes squinted at the light - so much light, like streaks of paint - yellow, blue, brilliant white - the sun, the sea, and a tall sail slicing through. They were racing on squally waters, battling and driven forward by the wind. Nurses rushed in and out again, watched the machine, smiled and spoke between them.

"You'll make it Katia. You'll be all right," he said.

They disembarked and checked the landscape round them. The place was bleak. There was no welcoming party, no embraces, not even a hand waved a greeting. Looking back, the ocean stretched interminably. The ship that had brought them had disappeared. What a place! What a place, he said again and again.

In the afternoon Elena came with Xenopoulou to see him. "I'm flying to New York this evening for two weeks. Business trip." She took a long look at him. "I'll see you."

He stood up and they shook hands. Panos the chauffeur appeared at the door to show urgency. Then, before he knew it, the door shut behind her.

It had been quick, without ceremony. He crossed over to the window and watched the *Rolls-Royce* cruise through the leafy roads downhill. Hydra, Rhodes, even her house in Athens seemed such a very long time ago.

"There is a lady outside who wants to speak to you," the nurse pointed. "In the lounge."

A vanguard of perfume greeted him before he could turn the corner. The gaunt, wiry woman, about fifty, wore a dark grey suit and a black hat with two feathers. The blouse underneath heaved uneasy, her lean legs crossed at the ankles, and she looked at him with eyes he recognized instantly.

"I'm Katia's aunt. How is she?"

"Better than expected. But critical."

"Thank you, Mr Cromwell for doing this." She dabbed one dry tear with a lace handkerchief.

"I've done very little."

"I feel ashamed coming here. My whole family have betrayed her."

"I don't know what you mean."

She pulled off a glove, finger by finger. "Her own father and mother should pay for this. I wish he'd lived to see what he's done to his daughter."

"We'll have to be strong for Katia's sake, Mrs ..."

"Miss. Korilou." She waved his admonition dismissively. "You don't understand, Mr Cromwell. I used to tell my brother, 'Don't be so hard on her.'" She shook her head in despair. "They took no notice of me."

He pictured the mother, the crooked house, the room where she had lived.

"Take her away, Mr Cromwell." The day before she married she came and told me she did not want to go through with it. She wanted to run away but didn't know where. And I'm the guilty one. I should have stood up for her. But once again I failed her. Just when I shouldn't have. I ought to be shot instead." She squeezed her knuckles as if to pain herself. "That man... I don't know how this thing happened." She darkened again. "Let's not discuss *him*."

"He was a friend of her father's, she told me."

"It was his last punishment on her. They wanted to own her, control everything. In a tomb forever. Like an imbecile. The most cruel thing you can do to your child is to deny her who she is. I tried to be friends with her but it's not the same. Besides, I'm not educated. She was much cleverer than me." She put her hand on his knee and leaned forward. "The gift, Mr James," she whispered. "I've always believed in it. Katia had the gift," and she sobbed a little. It was some time before she recovered from her own narrative. "You think she'll live? And be normal, I mean."

He did not answer.

She understood and spat out a bitter sigh. "A girl like her. Being crushed, destroyed. God must be cruel."

"God didn't shoot her, Miss Korilou. Perhaps you and I did."

She bowed her head. "We did. We certainly did."

A nurse came. The patient had asked for him.

"Come with me."

She followed three steps behind him, trembling.

Katia's eyes remained closed.

"Your aunt has come to see you, Katia."

The woman began to talk in Greek. Something approaching a smile spread over Katia's face, a soothing, like a mist.

"Talk to her," the aunt pressed him before she dissolved in tears and staggered out again.

"How are you feeling Katia?" he whispered.

"O.K.. This beep - beep is irritating."

"They'll turn it off soon."

"I hope not." She blinked, her eyes half-opening with a hint of that mischief. "Where did you go?"

He did not know what she meant. "Nowhere special. I should have stayed."

She was a long time silent. "It doesn't matter."

"This time you're coming. Whether you like it or not."

It took such an effort for her to speak. "I don't think I'll make it."

He fought to keep his throat dry. "We'll go together. Rhodes, Corfu, Ithaca - wherever you want."

"Tell me... Rhodes. Did you go?"

"For one day. The town and the butterflies. Have you heard of them? Millions of butterflies in a ravine. Very beautiful. It made me think of you."

That faint smile again. "Silly... Those... not butterflies. They're only tiger moths."

****

28th AUGUST   PLAKA

In the early hours of the morning Katia suffered a massive brain haemorrhage and died while she slept.

They woke him up in the neighbouring room and told him. He sat alone for a few minutes, then went to see her, stayed briefly and withdrew. Aunt Korilou's perfume lingered in the lounge, but he found it comforting, almost as if Katia was there with him in another form.

The strangest feeling was a compulsion to do something, the mind constantly straying to the most trivial things. He looked at the hanging paintings, the vases, and had the urge to re-arrange them all.

He would not go into the room again. Wild imaginings prayed on him. How could they be sure, he wondered. It seemed unreal, *he* felt unreal, this place the strangest he had ever seen.

There would be the funeral to consider. And something dark to wear. The thought circled like a crow over his head. Still four in the morning. A long, long night to kill.

He heard Xenopoulou confer with other voices in the corridor. Finally she came in and sat in the chair opposite. "I'm deeply sorry, Mr Cromwell. We had a weak artery some-where. We ruled out emergency surgery; it was too late by then."

"I don't think she would have wanted to live."

The doctor gazed down. "We have sent someone to contact the family. And I telephoned your lawyer; gave him a medical report. Is there something else you would like us to do?"

"No. Thank you."

She stood up. "I'll be in the office for the rest of the night. Do come and talk."

He opened his briefcase, checking the contents, finding objects he had not seen before. A phone-call interrupted his fidgeting. The lawyer. There was no distinction between night and day here.

"Mr Cromwell," he said in a subdued voice. "I have good news."

"Good news?"

"I do apologize. Forgive me."

"The doctor says you have been told."

"Indeed. We acted without delay; placed great pressure on the authorities. He was re-arrested only minutes after the death. And I have just heard he has confessed to the killing. There will be a charge by the prosecutor in the morning. Murder."

For a moment he had to remind himself what all this was, who had been arrested, what the murder. "I won't be available for some time," he said.

"You won't be needed."

Strangely, he was disappointed. The morning streets would have been more bearable with a killer on the loose. At nine o'clock he took a taxi to a hotel and on to the shops in the city centre. It was a refreshing morning, the air yet cool, and it felt comforting to be amongst crowds again. Had anything really happened since he had crossed this street a month before?

"A suit in black. Certainly. Try this one, Sir."

His knees gave. Sheer tiredness. "I'm sorry, I must have tripped."

Yes, he would take the suit, slightly altered. He smiled a 'thank you' and strolled out, perfectly composed - stiff upper lip.

From there he headed for Katia's house, taking the same old route of cobbled streets. Aunt Korilou opened the door, her eyes swollen. The French shutters remained half-closed, the gloom was beyond belief.

In the front room the mother occupied an important chair like a tribal chief. All around, in lesser corners, silent figures sat brooding. The rites of sympathy. He went up to her and mumbled condolences which she made no effort to acknowledge. The aunt whispered a synoptic translation after him.

There was an unseen figure in the kitchen who prepared the coffee for aunt Korilou to serve. He drank his standing, for lack of seats. It was difficult to make out whether the awkwardness had been caused by his presence or if he had walked into it. He was intrigued by that mysterious person who floated about the house, now on the stairs, now in that tiny bedroom overhead. It was impossible to see her when she came down and, whoever she was, seemed to be making it a point to avoid him.

In the lounge, the mother dominated everything. She controlled the mournful proceedings speechlessly, while her fingers stayed crossed loosely over her chest. Her large body, her presence, remained visible no matter where he turned. It was as if everyone else had come to worship this tearless goddess, reluctantly, out of contingent necessity. To display sadness would have been beneath her; a mere inclination of the head to the side was her only concession to the death.

He felt grateful for the absence of open grief. And the silence continued interminably.

With the last bitter drops swallowed in concealed haste, he went over to murmur a few more words and bowed for his departure. This time she nodded she understood. The aunt followed him out to the yard, desperate for relief herself.

"You know about the funeral?" she said. "Tomorrow, four p.m.. At the church of Metamorphosis and then at Kolonus cemetery. Papa-Viron is doing the service. He did the wedding."

"I'll need directions."

"Come to my house later for a talk." She scribbled an address down. "Any time after seven. I'll be waiting."

He had so much to do. Call Maxine in London, confirm his ticket, order the flowers, collect from Elena's house, pick up the suit.

It was siesta time by now - everything shut except for the kiosks and the tourist-shops. Must pay the hospital and the lawyer, he remembered, and added them to his list. The waiter fetched a lukewarm soda which he rejected. Then he was looking at two lovers tempting the pigeons with a *souvlaki*, the pigeons laughing back at them.

He walked from Syntagma to the flea market, past Monastiri and round again. Back at the hotel he called London and listened to Maxine's voice seducing her boss to talk. His presence would be superfluous at the office from now on.

"Maxine. I'm calling from Athens."

"Oh, please! Isn't it time you came home? I need a break. I want to see my children a little more."

"I have to stay a little longer. What would you like me to bring you?"

"Don't know. What is Athens famous for?"

"Euripides, Aeschylus and Sophocles."

"Oh, fine. Any one will do."

It was difficult to tell which was real, her world in London or this one here - his office or the hospital the night before. Talking with aunt Korilou might solve the riddle, if it could be solved.

He got there in time for supper. Humbly served, on a humble table, in a spotlessly clean and ordered room. Inside, the same plethora of inconsequential ornaments, the brown photographs, a younger one of Katia amongst them. This also could have been Katia's house, cram-full but neat, the furnishings over-polished, old. He had never seen so much brown. It was like stepping into a sepia photograph - the lamp-shade on the table, the light it gave, everything the same muted tone.

And such informality. People - friends, neighbours - walked in every minute, said something quickly, were offered a morsel, refused and shut the door. The scene was repeated countless times and became part of the table proceedings, yet supper managed to continue unspoiled, even improved.

"You are very popular," he told her. "What do all these people have to say to you?"

"Bits of gossip. Have I seen so-and-so, do I know what the other did. Some simply want to take a look at you."

"Who was the mystery person making the coffee at Katia's house this morning?"

"What mystery person?"

"There was somebody who never came into the big room. Just wandered from kitchen to stairs, went up to the bedroom, came down again."

"My other niece; from my sister. Katia's paranymph." She cut a huge melon, appropriate to the meal. "Why do you think this happened, Mr James? I can't take it in."

He stayed silent. This house still haunted him, almost as if he could turn round and find himself seeing Katia, her mischievous smile and lips. Even Korilou looked so much like her, now. Her mannerisms and expressions, the fathomless eyes, the same detachment from her mundane world.

And the voice. That voice was the strangest thing. "I think there was something in her that did not want to live," she continued. "She must have longed to escape, fly a little higher, maybe."

He nodded but there was nothing for him to say, for all the words necessary had just been said.

It was well past ten o'clock now and no more melon to be served. The casual visitors had stopped coming, the minutes had slowed down - only this vague expectancy held out, making him reluctant to leave. Outside, the children played in the cobbled lane, just inches away from them.

She opened the shutters and let in the first cool breeze.

"There was one thing I wanted to ask you," she said in a low voice. "About Katia." Her eyes became troubled. "Perhaps she told you," she hesitated. "Do you think, she ever knew... love? That someone loved her? Someone she liked herself?" It had taken a huge effort to utter those broken sentences.

What could he possibly say without betraying Katia's memory. "She knew with all her heart." And he looked straight at her.

****

29th AUGUST   KOLONUS

Daybreak. In the distance, the all-night revelling of the tavernas was winding itself down. Plaka was hushed, the street beneath his hotel balcony abandoned.

Somebody burned endless cigarettes two floors overhead, the ashes parachuting slowly down. Far beyond - street after street - the ancient city still roosted, its people oblivious, tucked up in bed. He alone counted the minutes drifting, never quite reaching the earth. There was that expectation in him of something about to happen, the dread of a last wish. In the morning, he thought, but morning and evening mixed. This was that measurable gap of time before crucifixion was due.

Then the sun rose and it looked more like the joyous Sunday it should be. There was a rush of activity below, people and scooters making a mad dash for it. He checked the one-handed clock on the wall. Too early. There would be time to finalize arrangements and cross checklists: cars, flowers, church-hymns, her girl companions getting ready...

He had an impulse to visit the place early, get there before she did.

"Kolonus, garden of lovely white marble, a river, a thickly wooded hill."

Where in Athens could it be?

He left the balcony and circled the room once, like a prisoner in a death-cell. Stark, endless rooftops bricked up the window view. They piled up like steps on top of each other, leaving a narrow band of sky. To the left, the balcony door framed a street-side, one single interminable wall.

He opened the suitcase, took out the pistol and looked at the inscription carved on it.

Then the phone rang.

"Hullo, dear husband."

The voice was unmistakable. "Catherine."

"You remember!" She was in her enigmatic mood.

"How did you know I was here?"

"I always do."

He stood listening to her breathing, one step behind him ever since they had first met.

"Happy birthday, darling. Tomorrow, isn't it?"

"Catherine, you are calling at a difficult moment. What did you want to tell me?"

"I want to drive you mad for leaving me behind and going from place to place while I die for you."

Well, there had always been a certain drama about Catherine. "I'm sorry but I can't talk to you."

"Oh, I love you, darling. Do tell me, was it all my fault?"

"Nothing could possibly be your fault." He covered the mouth-piece so she would not hear him seething.

"I'm sorry, James."

"Catherine, where are you? I'll try to get back to you another day."

"Oh, don't worry. We'll speak sometime. I'll come and see you. Good bye." There was no sign that she had rung off, just a void at the other end of the line.

He hammered the door in anger, wanting to flee, not quite knowing where, away from that voice, from her.

Then someone came up to say his clothes had been delivered, and spread them flat on the bed. Shirt, suit, and a white carnation. It got screwed up and crumbled in his clenched fist.

He checked his face, pale against the black cloth. Must keep clear-minded, self-possessed. Then he did the buttons and glimpsed the mirror again.

Two more hours. He paced the room from door to balcony over and over. Then, at three thirty, he stepped out and pulled the door shut.

Aunt Korilou's directions proved just adequate, if vague. He followed her street-plan walking until the dome rose above the surrounding houses. This was the other church Katia had wanted to show him, with that priest who converted heathens over a coffee and a cake. And now, she would soon be there with him.

There was the crossing of an open space and in the distance two black limousines waited, like scarabs indolent in the summer heat. A notice board translated *Metamorphosis* to *Transfiguration* in English.

Outside the church of Metamorphosis a girl was pinning leaflets to the tree-trunks. That other niece? She saw him and burrowed into the dark safety inside. Black borders, a cross, the ink hardly dry on the Greek writing. He made out the names of Katia and Kolonus Cemetery. Then he stepped in and back to eleventh century Byzantine, just as he had done three weeks ago in another church, with her beside him.

This place was smaller but just as uplifting. It had the stability of permanence, such that had lasted for centuries, undiminished. Original medieval frescoes stared divinely from the dome down, loose chairs filled up the floor, possibly borrowed from the taverna next door, but hallowed and transformed in the subdued candlelight.

She, that other niece, had sat and chatted to her maiden friends quietly while the priest, unconcerned, patronized them humbly.

Overhead, the sky burst through stained-glass windows, scattered, and exited the other side. The priest bowed and strolled a few steps devoutly, rehearsing his fatherly smile. He was a shy old man scarred by the years of devotion, his face already beatified. From a pew at the back, James Cromwell watched him pace his sanctuary, absorbed in the smell of incense and burning candles.

Four exactly. They must start coming now. Suddenly doors slammed and there was noise from a crowd. People faltered in and lost themselves in the shadows. Aunt Korilou sat next to him and squeezed a gloved hand over his to greet him. She was suppressing quick half-breaths under an agitated blouse. He echoed her greeting in the same manner and stayed silent.

The niece approached from a side aisle and brushed past him. She stopped next to aunt Korilou, hardly seeing him, her deep gaze fixed forward as if he did not exist.

The mother was escorted to her seat by two young men who looked distinguished and dignified. Then they stepped forward, drew the curtains back and removed the cover. And there her face slept in a sea of flowers, under a sun-beam, the whole sky shrunken beneath the cupola in kaleidoscopic fragments. Suddenly he realized she must have been there all along and let a gasp out. Aunt Korilou swallowed hard and gazed down.

The two men returned either side of the mother. Calm, aristocratic-looking, there was a certain nobility about them. Almost too respectable for their middle twenties, they rescued the formal proceedings from sentimentality and bathos.

Now the priest's voice rose and Byzantine music floated gloriously upwards. His stature suddenly lifted too, from meekness to joy and benediction.

A gloved hand opened the Bible and traced a finger across the page. He must have heard those words in an English church many times.

> "...Though I speak with the tongues of men and of angels, and have not love, and though I have all faith and have no love, I am nothing..."

They brought her down the short aisle, past the congregation, to the festive brightness outside. The guests followed and scattered quietly about. James Cromwell waited until last, then stood at the door-step, half sun-drenched, half in shadow. In the open space the limousines gleamed, their drivers sitting on a stranded boulder, talking. Some children began to kick a ball noisily and were shouted down. An old woman swept the pavement into a cloud of dust. She too was bawled at.

A hand held him back, aunt Korilou nudging and guiding him through the formalities. They had been left behind quickly, alone except for the priest.

"Don't go," she whispered. "Not now."

He was watching the procession and hardly heard her.

The niece came up and looked at him like checking a curious passer-by. The two women communicated something and she left again in a hurry.

He stood transfixed, following her sprightly path mesmerised.

"They will drive to Kolonus slowly - get there in half an hour."

"Don't you think we ought to follow?"

"We'll get a taxi. It doesn't take a minute. Let's sit over here for awhile."

They moved inside the front door for coolness and shade.

"I don't think you should come to the house afterwards. There have been rumours."

"I wasn't planning to. What rumours?"

"About the hospital - what right you had to take her - you know how they talk. Stupid things."

"How many here knew that it was me?"

"They all did. It makes no difference. Things will turn ugly, with him and his trial. It's better you stayed out."

He turned away angrily.

"Can I write to you in London?"

"Yes," he blurted. He had wanted to see the funeral to the finish. What happened afterwards was a different matter.

Korilou watched him, then raised a desperate hand to her forehead. "Don't think so hard," she puffed out. And they stood up abruptly.

They formed a circle at the grave-side, with room for the cortege to come through.

"I am the resurrection and the life. He who believes in me, even if he dies, he will live."

It did not last long; ten minutes. Then he was climbing downhill, alone, in the opposite direction to the rest of the crowd. He waved a hand to Aunt Korilou, discreetly, and she returned a last greeting.

When the phone rang at the hotel the second time, he took much longer to answer it. First, he picked up the pistol, broke it and blew through the barrel. "Yes, Catherine."

"My deepest sympathies, darling." The line had a strange metallic sound. "Elena sends hers too. I just spoke to her in New York."

"Oh, Elena..." he echoed absently as if not remembering.

"Your *deus ex machina,* darling."

He could sense the sarcasm at the back of her throat but stayed silent.

"I knew about the girl," she continued. "And the fiance." There was a change of tone.

He pulled a small rag through the muzzle, still saying nothing, his silence forcing her hand.

"Remember our little trip underwater? The drowned fisherman? Remember the labyrinth?"

She obviously did not remember he probably had saved her life. He still said nothing.

Now she paused for a long time. "I am sorry for you, James."

And he hung up.

It was darkening when he found himself circling Kolonus hill for the second time with a small bunch of flowers. The grave-diggers were just finishing the ground. He watched from a distance as they gathered wearily and trudged under the fading sky. At first he followed them, tentative, then he cut through a direct line. From the shadows, that same fragile figure walked away from him. He had not expected to see her there and stood back gasping. Suddenly she turned up the slope, to the brow of the hill and over, rising and vanishing. There was a burst of traffic noise and his thoughts scattered after her: Who had he just seen? The other niece. Or was he just conjuring up Katia in his mind? It seemed inappropriate to leave flowers when he had just seen her alive. Bound to meet up again sometime.

Dusk, and the last rays shone on white marble as far as the eye could see. The darker it became, the more beautiful. He climbed and stood at the very top, a silhouette on Golgotha. The river looked back serene, the gods benevolent. "Ah, to be in her arms forever, rising and falling with each wave, moving from a shade of blue to one deeper and more mysterious."

Behind him only a large cloud, then a red strip. Some light still reached the city-scape, as if the sun had turned back and had began climbing.

"She's happy," he said, his eyes weary. "Now to the gentle sea, please, in its gentlest guise." His fingers tensed. "That's right. That's right."

Underneath, the city droned eerily a collective cry. There, to the south, the white Parthenon, Psychiko on the other side. It was the most beautiful, warm, lovely night. Just a few more hours and it would be bright again. On another island. And a last harbour.

****

"As for your home-coming,
I myself never was in any doubt."

30th AUGUST   ITHACA

A cloudy morning, the sunlight not strong enough to break through yet. Chilly. He put one shoulder to the window pane, sea-droplets clinging to the other side, the view blurred. It seemed like winter - the earth subdued, burdened with moisture, gleaming from its overnight birth.

The small room behind him nestled in wool rugs and fleeces, a haven from the mountains outside rising rock-like from the sea. Not here the back street of some downtown harbour, nor a hotel honeymoon suite. This was a spartan place with home-spun tapestries hanging, hand woven, the spindle and loom dismembered in the far corner, long disused. In the middle, the fireplace smoked feebly, struggling, on its last breath. The floor-boards, black and bare, smelled of old varnish, the cross-beams strained to his every move. There was a trunk for wardrobe, the scent of oak, steam from a copper cauldron on burning logs. There were curious objects crammed on wall-shelves, folk patterns crafted on the bed-sheets and pillow-tops.

And a sprung bed that creaked and rattled with every breath she took.

"Wake up," he whispered almost reluctant to be heard.

She wriggled on the soft mattress and he watched her unfold and loosen and stretch.

"Come and see."

She opened her eyes and squinted at the soft light – warm browns, pastel white, a cut-out frame of grey-blue. "What is it?"

It seemed a pity the calm was broken, that such tranquillity had to end. "I think the summer is over. Look."

She wrapped herself in a blanket and stumbled across to him. There was a squally sea outside and spray scattered on the wind. Last night a sail had come from the mainland looking for shelter and getting lost in the plunging cliffs. Once in the harbour, a couple had sat and talked until late in the halcyon heat. They had looked from place to place and had found the notary and the registrar. Then the moon had risen and it had become more like the wedding night it should have been. A thousand-odd jubilant bells had echoed, and an old house had been opened to put them up in.

But it was different today with the first drizzle being carried on a brisk breeze. Her eyes swept the scene quickly, for it was too cold and early, and she too sleepy for this. She shivered and stood in front of the fire, turning to catch its last gleam.

"I was telling you a story last night and you fell asleep."

She made a funny face, almost playful, with a quizzical grin. "Wasn't I supposed to?"

He watched the mischief in her eyes, the fickle yawn on her lips. "I'm not going to repeat it," he answered piqued.

"Oh, please. This evening. After I go to sleep."

He chuckled indifferently. "You were supposed to hang by your finger-nails, down to the last word."

"Tell me now," and she sat on the floor pulling her knees up expectantly.

He just grinned back. "Did you hear all the commotion in the middle of the night?" he changed the subject. "I think a ship came in."

"I heard them talking next door. The landlord is missing. They said he set off on a journey years ago, and was never heard from. The house has been empty since."

"Didn't the old woman say we could stay as long as we wanted?"

"Mmm. Something must have happened."

"Look at his clothes over there. He's not coming back, I don't think."

She studied the four walls as if for a hidden face, then gazed at him. This had been a vacant house from the first moment, unlived and unhaunted, with shutters stuck, withered window-boxes, its dusty doorstep unvisited. "Shall we take a look?"

They found a scuttle behind the cabinet in the corner. He hesitated, then pulled it open and bent low to get through.

Darkness. The light switch resounded in a tiny room. There was a single straw chair, a writing desk, a mirror on the wall. Then a school map of the world, books about ships, sea-crossings and charted routes. This had been his humble retreat before escaping, where he had sat to dream.

She crept up behind him and put her head through. "There's no window," she murmured, her voice freeze-dried in the damp chill. "Such a small room."

She backed out, dressed, and opened the bigger door to the stairs. Much more light here. Gaps showed between the stones on the outside wall. They took a step down slowly. Well-crafted in their young days, the balusters and hand-rail now tittered with age, the stairs shook. The house got bigger as it got lower. On the first landing they stopped and pondered whether to venture in.

More clothes hang from a bar in a curtained recess. He seemed to have dressed well, his suits from expensive cloth, hand-stitched. They had seen one or two like him debating with the priest and the mayor at a street-cafe'. A notable figure about town, probably, the house itself set separate from the hotchpotch sprouting in other streets.

A folk costume guarded a wooden post propping up the ceiling. Then a flag, wrapped round its staff, two gold tassels holding it knotted, and a school emblem. There were no pictures on the walls, no clues to his origins. He seemed to have had no roots, nothing to tie him to anybody. Even the icons of the Virgin had been dismantled, their frames hollow and toppled over.

Some keyboard instrument, home-made or knocked about beyond recognition, pretended to be a piano, unconvincingly. She struck a few keys - out of tune. There had been a double bed here, going by the chest and a bed-lamp on a night-table. Reed baskets provided storage space, all of them emptied and tidied, and hung from ropes.

The ground floor combined kitchen and living room, a vast sprawling space with no partitions. Here lay scattered the most signs of past activity, enough to keep a few people busy. There were barrels and kilo-measures, crocks, pitchers and demijohns. Some wine-casks showed signs of being full, others stood parched and uprighted, with hoops split and segments missing.

They did not open the back-yard door. A giant tin stood in front of it, once converted to a flower pot, now dead with earth, a dead geranium stalk, dead weight. In the laundry area at the far end, they put more firewood under the cauldron. The gentle steam rose softly and filled the stair-well.

He dipped a half finger at the misting edge. "It's not too hot," he said breaking the stillness. "Let's get in."

"It will tip over."

"We'll keep still."

She dropped her clothes to the floor and sank in, then he joined her.

"Sit low, down to the bottom."

The water surged and spilled over. Underneath, sparks flew in a muted protest. She let her head back against the rim and breathed deeply. It was the most lovely moment.

"What would they have used this thing for?"

She closed her eyes. "Washing the linen, probably. Or to baptise heathens like you."

And there they sat unspeaking, nothing but the hissing logs to count the passing minutes. Footsteps and conversations hovered beyond the wall, hands scraped against the stone, inches from them but remote, the parish and its parishioners disembodied.

Then the clouds broke and a sun-beam shone on them, and everything lifted up and floated.

They dried and tip-toed back to the top floor, stocked up the fireplace with logs, and listened to the sap spitting. Outside, a tired sun had struggled to the mid-skies dispersing some of the dew.

"And now just to convince you, let me show you Ithaca, the scene, the harbour."

She lifted the lace curtain to clear the panoramic view. Not much in the port as yet, no tall masts or passing travellers to speak of - the sea transparent and lucid. Out in the open the last caiques headed home. A blue and white spinnaker pushed northwards disappearing downwind.

"What is this?" He held out a garland of withered flowers dried to a straw wreath.

"It's the wreath of May; for door-posts on May Day - the rites of Spring to you. Where did you find it?"

"In a corner." He looked it over and put it with the fire-wood. "Have I not seen these at Greek weddings?"

"Never. They might use them at funerals," she blurted as he joined her looking out, and their two faces gazed back half-reflected on the window pane.

Two figures approached in a small boat, with oars splashing towards the shore. They disembarked and checked the landscape round them. The place was empty. There was no welcoming party, no-one to embrace, not even a hand waved a greeting at them. Looking back, the ocean stretched interminably. The ship that had brought them had disappeared. "What a place. What a place," he said again and again.

"I'll get some of that wine," she whispered.

He nodded watching the rippling sand, calmer as the day drew longer. You could see far off when the air was stiller. The bay, the meadowlands, the cliffs on the other side. There were ever-rolling pastures on top of hill-sides, turquoise sea-scapes, vineyards and olive groves. Then wild, untrodden mountains, rugged and bleak.

She brought enough for a wedding feast, a jug in each hand and a pitcher.

Inches away, the logs snapped and writhed, fresh sap and wine mingling, the whole heady mixture intoxicating. It was so lovely to be cocooned in this room, with just a window to the world, where no earthly distraction could reach them. And the room glowed in a soft light, and flames jumped and flickered deliciously.

"We could stay through autumn." He went over and held her face, pulling her gently so he could reach her lips.

"Mmmm... Maybe."

It was an erotic kiss, mellow and knowing, her delicate features like touches of pure ecstasy. He spread more rugs and covered the floor corner to corner, then laid her down naked.

"First time I'm looking forward to a winter," she breathed. "I wish we'll never have to leave."

"What would you be doing in Athens now?" he whispered, letting go gently.

"Working. And you?"

"I might have gone back to London. There seemed nothing more to do in Greece."

She brushed a lone finger through his hair. "Why did you come after me at the last minute?"

"I wanted to marry you."

She pressed her body to him. "Crazy."

And he just watched her, spellbound that she should be there with him. Would not shut his eyes in case she vanished into a mist.

"What if I'd slammed the door to your face?"

"I would have slammed it back at you."

She laughed and pretended to push him, then shrugged her shoulders. "What if... What if I hadn't come with you?"

He shook his head absently. "You nearly didn't."

"And what if not?" she persisted.

He put a hand to her lips to silence her and dismissed the thought. "Who knows what would have happened then."

****

42162519R00190

Printed in Poland
by Amazon Fulfillment
Poland Sp. z o.o., Wrocław